What people are saying about

The Malaise

David Turton has entered the realm of post-apocalyptic horror in a big way with *The Malaise*. Technology has been engineered to give us what is believed to be nearly a perfect society. Only, not everyone agrees it is perfect, and mistakes bring it all crashing down around us in a tale that could easily fall into the wide net of near-future horror in works such as Netflix's *Black Mirror*. A thrilling and gripping mix of science fiction and horror which will have your eyes glued to the page from start to finish!
Stuart Conover, HorrorTree.Com

The Malaise is a cautionary tale with all of the shocking and chilling moments you expect from a proper horror story. Fiction with a futuristic bent, it provides a "what if" that is both fascinating and disturbing. It will have you gripping your chair as you read and provides an ending that leaves you wanting more.
Chantal Boudreau, author, the *Fervor* series

David Turton's *The Malaise* is a smoothly flowing, well thought out dystopian novel that kept me engaged throughout.
Ed Ahern, author of *The Witch Made Me Do It*

David Turton has proved again and again that he is not only one of the most riveting new voices working today, but that his work bears a unique quality that is seldom seen. His ability to transform his style of writing, work within varying genres, be it Lovecraftian fiction or literary horror, separates T
C.P. Dunphey, Gehenna and Hinno

The Malais   ik we might

be heading to. A techno class that knows how our world should work, and is determined to give us exactly what they think we want. Only, like with all false gods, mistakes are made … and death ensues.

Turton shows a world destroyed, but encapsulates the human spirit in the tiny group that bands together. He writes vivid horror scenes, and touching moments of humanity at its best. *The Malaise* will keep you turning page after page, racing to get to the ending, and all the while hoping the technology giants of today don't throw us into his horror of tomorrow.

David Beers, Best selling author

One day the world falls apart. That's the set-up for David Turton's thrill-ride post-apocalyptic novel *The Malaise*, but also a reoccurring theme behind each event in the story. All the glittering promise of our bleeding-edge present disintegrates in a single day of terror and blood. *The Malaise* pulls the reader in from the first signs of onrushing disaster to the somber but still dangerous aftermath. In terms of genre, Turton flows smoothly through a variety of styles, mixing zombie horror, near-future technological speculation, to a coming-of-age story set in a haunted landscape of Britain shorn of most of its population. While evoking the pleasantly meandering digressions of *Earth Abides* and the gruesome terror of *World War Z*, Turton finds his own solemn, ruminative voice for this story. Recommended for fans of near-future dystopia literature and zombie survival novels.

Morgan Crooks, author of *Speculative Fiction*

The Malaise

The Malaise

David Turton

COSMIC
EGG
BOOKS

Winchester, UK
Washington, USA

First published by Cosmic Egg Books, 2018
Cosmic Egg Books is an imprint of John Hunt Publishing Ltd., 3 East St., Alresford,
Hampshire SO24 9EE, UK
office1@jhpbooks.net
www.johnhuntpublishing.com

For distributor details and how to order please visit the 'Ordering' section on our website.

ISBN: 978 1 78535 902 6
978 1 78535 903 3 (ebook)
Library of Congress Control Number: 2017962227

A CIP catalogue record for this book is available from the British Library.

Design: Stuart Davies

Printed and bound by CPI Group (UK) Ltd, Croydon, CR0 4YY, UK

We operate a distinctive and ethical publishing philosophy in
all areas of our business, from our global network of authors to
production and worldwide distribution.

For Vanessa,

Because sometimes horror is shared with love.

Acknowledgments

Thanks to the support of the following amazing people, without whom this novel would not have seen the light of day.

My wife, Vanessa, for being patient while I tapped away on the laptop for hours, weeks and months, and for always believing I could do it.

Liam and Olivia for support and motivation. Your achievements help spur me on to chase my own success.

Mum and Dad, not just for your proofreading, but for the encouragement and motivation to read and write, going back to my early days reading Noddy and Tintin, and writing various stories as a child. Your proofreading was also much appreciated.

Claire, my sister, for not only encouraging me and proofing an early draft of this novel, but doing it all the way from Adelaide. I hope to visit soon, and maybe squeeze in a book tour while I'm at it…

Luise Ruddick, for enduring the warts-and-all first draft and highlighting elements that didn't quite work. And for accompanying Vanessa and me to the cinema to enjoy countless horror films. One of these days I'll stop being the jumpiest person in the cinema.

The Sunderland author community, particularly Iain Rowan, Amy McLean and Tony Kerr, for all the advice and encouragement. Although each of these authors have different genres, I implore you, the reader, to check out their novels.

The writing networks I've joined, both in person and online, including the excellent Holmeside Writers in Sunderland. I now know that writing isn't purely a solitary, lonesome journey.

All the publishers who enjoyed my writing enough to publish my work. Particularly the brilliant C.P. Dunphey, who saw fit to publish three of my short stories in 2017 alone, and continues to be a source of encouragement and inspiration.

All at John Hunt publishing and Cosmic Egg Books, who took a chance on a first-time author writing a story about the end of the world. I hope that, together, we can do the story justice and reach as wide an audience as possible.

Finally, to all friends, colleagues and family who said anything nice to me about my writing. You might not have realized it, but your small comments made a big difference.

David Turton

Prologue

Razor Interview #1
Technology Magazine, Man of the Year 2035.
By Paul Miller

It's not often you find yourself in the presence of the man who changed the world.

I look out of the window down from the lavish top-floor office of RazorTower. The people walking at ground level could be ants dressed in tiny suits, circling, bustling their way through their busy lives. Nothing overlooks RazorTower. The glass structure overtook the Shard as the tallest building in Europe when it was built in 2033. It towers over London, jutting over the skyline with its impressive crown, a giant red "R" nestled on a huge diamond-shape which imposes itself on the city below, a magnificent symbol of power. Much the same could be said of its creator and namesake, Rick Razor, Technology Magazine Man of the Year 2035.

Everyone has heard the Razor story. Just when a select few technology giants looked like they were running the show, Razor came along and blew them all out of the way. Razor cut them down, if you will excuse the pun. While they were competing on social platforms and the World Wide Web, Razor came from a different angle and connected everything together. The social network they created was only a small part of their plan. Soon your fridge was connected to your online shopping. Your bed talked to you about your sleep quality and the position of your body. Your chair told you about pressure on your spine. And your car began driving itself with only the most basic instruction from you. RazorVision even introduced the ability to create messages and emails using the user's thoughts. In short, Razor changed the world, almost overnight.

I take my seat and look at Rick Razor. He's not what you might expect. Rick is modest and shy. *No wonder he doesn't give many interviews,* I think to myself. He almost seems embarrassed by his success. He is a striking, handsome man, with slick, black hair combed into a neat side parting. He has an endearing habit of running his fingers through it when answering my questions, a nervous tic that highlights his modest approach. He's dressed sharply in a designer suit and a white collarless shirt.

"It was simple, really." He smiles from across the desk. "I wanted to connect the world. It sounds ambitious, egotistical even. It had already been achieved with Bluetooth speakers and cars connecting with phones. But I wanted this connectivity to tell a story to the user. I put myself in their shoes. Tell me about my health. Tell me if I'm stressed. Save me time. Save me money. Add up the stats and tell me the best way to live my life. Join up the devices around me so they all dance to the same tune. *Read my mind* and tell me what I need. And that was my plan, really."

He makes it sound so simple. Technology that literally changed the world and Rick Razor says that it was just telling people a story about themselves. I decide to ask him about his pricing strategy.

"Yeah, it was a risk, making all the products free to consumers," he replies. "But I didn't want it to be an elitist thing. For this to work, as many people as possible should use this technology. So, all of our revenue comes from advertising and donations."

Ah the advertising. It's the one sticking point that comes up when Razor technology is part of the conversation. The invasion of privacy that enraged people in the 2010s, with the big social networks and search engines mining personal data, was an even bigger issue when every aspect of people's daily lives could be made available to advertisers via Razor's technology. Got back problems? Change your mattress! Dehydrated? Come to the store on your way to work and buy our spring water! Need to relax? Book a night away in our five-star spa hotel this weekend!

"Privacy is a fluid concept," Razor replies. His smile is still there, but it's slightly wilted at the edges with this line of questioning. "Advertisers see data that helps them sell to people. The advertisers solve the problem around the same time that the consumer realizes they have one. Remember, people can block advertising they don't want at any time. And one other thing. How do you define "privacy"? Are these things really private? Is your face private? If so then why do you go outside and show it to hundreds, thousands of people every time you walk down the street?" Razor gestures outside the window at the tiny ant-size specks in dark suits. "We know the data. We sell your stats. The *feelings* you have? The reasons you have the emotions you do? Your raison d'etre? They're all yours to keep and we have no interest or no reason to see them. Your device might be able to read your thoughts when you send messages, but we can't unlock your innermost feelings. Now *that's* privacy."

His smile broadens as he finishes his point. It's a convincing argument and one he makes well. This is not his first rodeo when it comes to this subject, I realize.

I decide to get personal and ask about his relationship status. As we know, outside his work, Razor is a mystery. In this day and age of 24/7 news content that pries into the most dark and secretive parts of anyone in the public eye, Razor's history is a blank slate. Given his views on privacy, maybe this shouldn't be a surprise. He has lived out his own philosophy. If he can keep himself to himself, maybe we can trust our private details with him.

"I'm not in a relationship at the moment," he laughs. "I had a couple of girlfriends a few years back and I've been on a couple of dates recently, but nothing's on the cards."

He really is an enigma. At 27, most billionaires would throw themselves at the latest Miss World or glamorous Hollywood actresses. Razor is good looking in a classic way, like a young Sean Connery; his face full of intensity but also humor and a not-so-insignificant touch of mischief. This is underlined by his smile, which turns up comically at either side of his mouth.

I decide not to press him. If the day comes when he falls out of a nightclub or rocks up to an LA premiere with a girl on his arm, this reporter will write an article on it. But that's not for today. Today I congratulate him on his achievement as Technology Magazine Man of the Year. He is visibly elated by the accolade, the mischievous smile broadening into a bright, wide grin when I mention it.

On my way out of the door I turn and ask him, "What's next then, Rick?" He flashes that trademark wry smile and replies.

"Oh, Paul, I could never tell you that, could I? But I will say this. I've got a few irons in the fire."

I turn and take a look out of the window. From this position I can no longer see down onto the street, but I gaze over at the sky. On the top floor I can't see any other building – it's like looking out of an airplane window as it soars a mile in the sky. I smile back at Razor. He's soaring indeed. The question is, how much higher can he go?

Part I

The Time Before
14 April 2038

1

Professor Mike Pilkington stepped into the RazorShower unit and allowed the water, specially mixed with all the vitamins and minerals suited to his skin type, to wash his body. It was a good job the washing and drying process only took fifteen seconds. Mike was running late.

Clean and refreshed, he dressed himself and grabbed his packed lunch from the kitchen bench. As he opened the front door he heard a loud and throaty "Ah-hem" from behind him.

"You forgetting something, Professor P?" It was Charlotte, holding their baby, Zara. They were both peering at him, two sets of large and lovely brown eyes. Mike grinned, walked over to his wife and child and gave them big, exaggerated kisses on the lips.

"My two favorite girls," he said. "Of course I didn't forget. I'll see you tonight, Charlie."

"Don't stay too late," she called after him, but Mike had left the cottage and was heading down the path, expanding his RazorBike and setting off on his three-mile trip to work.

Cycling was a refreshing way to dust off the haze after a sleep interrupted by a baby's cries, and the off-road route to Windermere University was a scenic one, untroubled by the noise and smog that used to plague his London commute. *London*, Mike's mind considered the word as he gazed across Lake Windermere, whose ripples were glimmering with the light of the morning sun. The shades of blue and green from the water moved delicately against the green and grey backdrops of the hills and mountains, giving the impression of a deliberate work of art. *No, I don't miss London at all.*

As part of his daily routine, Mike used the morning commute to organize his thoughts and prepare for the coming day. Today, he had three lectures and a seminar to deliver. The first lecture was to a group of around 200 undergraduates, studying various courses relating to digital technology, marketing and media.

His calves throbbed as he pushed his way up a steep hill. The first time he cycled the route from his house to the campus, he had to dismount halfway up, covered in sweat with burning legs, and push the bike the rest of the way. He saw two versions of his adult self. The first, the fun-loving and hard drinking London scholar who pioneered several studies and had ground-breaking papers published, receiving praise and building a brilliant reputation. He viewed this version, in his early 20s, as a romantic version, leading a life-style that could not be sustained. The first version was extremely unhealthy; with bad skin, the beginnings of a paunch and the inability to carry out even the most basic physical exercise, Mike 1.0 was a flawed genius.

The new Mike, the one who found himself effortlessly pedaling across the rolling green hills of the Lake District on a sunny day in May, was version two. At 32 he was older but healthier, with a flat stomach and muscular arms. He had a fulfilling job, a beautiful wife and a baby daughter, the most precious thing that had ever entered his life. But deep down he knew there was a payoff. He had dulled his genius. Although he was still seen as a leader in his field, his choice of a quieter life had slowed down his output. His role was now purely in the teaching of others and the occasional opportunity to give his opinion via national news broadcasts. Maybe he could have been Rick Razor, an ultra-rich entrepreneur using his talents to push the boundaries of digital technology. *Maybe a family life and a dynamic career are mutually exclusive,* he wondered. With another breezy blast that blew his hair right back against the top of his head, he shook away the thought. His life in the Lake District had delivered his daughter to him and this was a better reward than any work could have given him. And as he looked to his right at the shimmering lake and then to his left at the distant snow-topped peaks, he confirmed to himself that he certainly didn't miss London. He breathed in deeply; the air was cool and fragrant with nature. He could feel the moisture of the lake, the crisp and sharp oxygen-rich output of the luscious green trees and plants.

He arrived at the campus and his RazorVision glasses flashed a big 'thumbs up" in the right-hand corner of his vision. He'd beaten his average speed by 47 seconds and it was his fastest time of the month. He'd burned 278 calories in the process, too.

The campus buildings were all made of reflective glass, which gave a strange watery quality to the area, with Lake Windermere's ripples visible on some of the walls when viewed from the campus entrance. The buildings were not tall, but they had a curved appearance, looking like space-age igloos. The paths around each building were beautifully landscaped with borders of shrubs and trees. Several benches dotted the path, with students reading and using RazorVision before their classes.

He gazed at the campus with pride. Windermere University would never be Oxford or Cambridge. Most of its courses were vocational in nature and the University was outside the top 50 in the UK in all the respectable league tables. But it would be bottom of the league tables if Mike wasn't there. His presence ensured that Digital Technology Studies was the best course of its kind in the United Kingdom, something he was immensely proud of.

He pushed the "fold" button on his bike and it reduced to a carry-case for him to take into the University. Walking through the door he was greeted by the RazorCom in its mellow, female tone.

"Welcome Professor Pilkington. Please enjoy your day. Your lecture room is ready."

"Thank you," he told the invisible voice and headed to the theatre, his RazorVision reminding him that it was 8.25 a.m., 35 minutes before his lecture was due to start.

"Where would we be without technology?" he thought to himself and grinned.

2

Mike found his lecture room and walked in. It was a large, circular room, the biggest lecture hall in the university. All seats were made from translucent glass, making the room feel even bigger than it was. The automatic lights illuminated the room and he was welcomed by the RazorCom voice once more.

"Project file please. Digital Sociology 117 – the History of Social Media," he told the system.

"Presentation loaded, Professor Pilkington," replied the voice.

Mike stood in the center of the room and looked at the shimmer of the holographic projection. He recalled his own University experience and the days of whiteboards, chalkboards and slide-based presentations. He had to pinch himself at times at the progression of technology. He still appreciated it. Not like many of his students who would barely remember the days without Razor's magical touch on the world. For that reason, this was a lecture Mike most enjoyed delivering. Students were wowed about the early versions of social media and the various stages of internet communications. The disparate, disconnected technologies seemed more laughable the more time passed on.

Mike looked up to see the first few dozen of his students streaming in to the seats, each one engrossed in their RazorVision glasses. This was going to be a receptive audience indeed. As the auditorium filled and his own RazorVision told him the time had passed 9.00 a.m., he looked to the back to see Simon Churchill closing the door and taking his seat.

Simon was Mike's best student. Not just out of the current crop but over his entire academic career. Although Simon's quiet, unconfident manner gave him an unassuming presence, his passion, enthusiasm and drive were awe-inspiring but even more impressive was the genuine decency and belief that his talents would make the world a better place. Simon was a year into his PhD, studying how the effect of the Western advances in technology could have an impact on aid work, charity donations and healthcare provision, and could eventually benefit the Third World. With the average life expectancy in the West over 100, the life expectancy in the Third World could be as low as 40 and was worsening. The question of how to push the wealth to the Third World had been a topic for many years. Maybe Simon, Mike's very own protégé, would be the one to crack it. Certainly, Rick Razor himself had publicly declared his intentions to fix this particular issue, although things had gone quiet on that front in the last few months.

The lecture began with rudimentary social media experiments in the 1980s: instant messaging, discussion forums and message boards. The explosion of dating sites and how they actually progressed social networking sites in the early 2000s. The use of social media by world leaders to influence public opinion and wield more power.

"*Power.* Power is an operative word when we talk about this form of communication. Barack Obama realized that when he became president. The power of social media can make someone a king amongst men. It can help groups of people rise. It can make institutions fall. It can bring down governments and destroy individuals. And it has. History shows us that the *media* aspect of social media is transient. It can change. Platforms can come and go in a short space of time. Some can dominate, plateau, change or disappear. But *social?* Social never changes. Social is society. A society of human beings who have been communicating since man learned to make fire and draw paintings on cavern walls."

Mike went on to discuss the Internet of Things. He enjoyed the laughter that burst across the room like a wave. *The Internet of Things.* That rudimentary phrase that was coined in the 2010s to describe the connectivity that was possible across devices and appliances. What began with simple exercising wristbands developed at breakneck speed to include self-ordering fridges, self-driving cars and devices that measured every element of body health to the point that an "obesity crisis" in Western countries was effectively flattened within a year. The fact that the audience found the phrase hilarious was symptomatic of how much the students took this technology for granted. They had no word for it because it existed beyond their knowledge. Much how an unscientific mind can process the logistics of a simple telephone call or the chain of events that led to television being broadcast across homes in the 20th century. You don't question how; you just know it works.

Then Mike came to the final third of his lecture, the part that the students had been waiting for. The rise of Razor Incorporated and the enigmatic founder, Rick Razor. The company that took the Internet of Things to the next level. The pioneer of the first mass market driverless car. The first company to make wearable technology a practical, useful and now essential element of daily life with RazorVision. The revelation by the company that, due to an amazing and ground-breaking deal with advertising companies who bought the resulting customer data, the technology was completely free to users. Soon all major buildings and streets were fitted with RazorCom technology, an artificial intelligence solution that interacted with people's own Razor Technologies. It could immediately identify someone within its walls and know their health, history, purpose and needs.

"And where can we go now?" he asked his awe-struck audience. "What possibly could be invented that could be useful now? What new strides could we make in technology that haven't yet been made? Well – I'll leave you with this quote that will make you think about the exponential progression of technology."

The quote, projected in the center of the room in a heavy, dramatic 3D font simply read: "Everything that can be invented has been invented."

"Ladies and gentleman, that quote is from the year 1899." The audience gasped and then giggled as Mike let it sink in. As always, Mike finished by asking for questions.

There were a few standard questions from the students that Mike expected. But then he spotted Simon Churchill's name flashing on his RazorVision. He enabled Simon's microphone via RazorCom.

"Dr. Pilkington, I was wondering what you thought of the anti-movement to Razor Incorporated. Those who think that the technology has led to a huge decrease in privacy. That the "Big Brother Nanny State" fears have steadily increased since social technology and huge corporations got their hands on it. The fact that RazorVision is capable of reading the very thoughts of users. The underground group who refuse to use the technology, as the price paid is too high. Those who recognize that the power, a word you yourself use throughout this lecture, and quite rightly, is something so dangerous in the wrong hands that they don't trust any one corporation with it. And what does anyone really know about Rick Razor? What are his intentions?"

You bastard, thought Mike. He had blindsided him in his own lecture, after everything Mike had done to help him. Simon's research must have taken a new turn.

"Well..." said Mike, unsteadily. "That's quite a set of questions, Simon." There was more laughter and Mike sensed a small element of disdain in the room towards Simon, which pleased him. This was Mike's stage, not Simon's. He could have any manner of heated discussions in seminars or small groups but there were a lot of people here, including several academic colleagues and even some students from other Universities. This had put Mike under pressure that he could have done without.

"There are measures that Razor is under. Strict measures employed by the government. Measures that I personally sat on an advisory committee to pass. And in that respect, I can whole-heartedly say that there is nothing untoward. Advertisers get data to advertise to exactly the right people and people get exactly the right adverts. No one uses their data for anything but advertising and research. There are strict protocols in place to ensure that personal data can never get in the wrong hands. It is completely impossible. These rebel groups would rise up against oppression on a desert island if they could!"

Mike's earlier feeling that the room was in his favor was correct. The whole auditorium stood and applauded. They whooped and they grinned. He could see several live reactions on his RazorVision, with dozens of people posting on their public network how it was the best lecture they'd seen.

He looked at the back of the room and Simon's seat was empty.

3

Wrapping up the lecture, Mike spotted a group of excited Malaysian students heading towards him. Feeling buoyed by his handling of Simon's questions, if slightly disturbed by the way his protégé had tried to trip him up, Mike welcomed the opportunity to bask in his popularity.

"Hello. Hope you enjoyed the lecture. What w—," he was cut short by the group all trying to talk at once.

"Have you seen it, Professor? Have you watched it yet? What do you think, Dr. P? What does it mean?"

"One at a time, please!" Mike pleaded. "What on earth are you talking about?"

He had, as he always did, turned off all notifications on RazorVision that didn't concern his lecture. He switched them on and saw that several people had shared the same video to his network.

"Okay, I think I've got it," he told the excited students and turned away to watch it without distraction.

It was the strangest thing Mike had ever seen, and in all the years of analyzing content shared over digital platforms, he had seen plenty of unfathomable, strange stuff, ranging from the downright weird to the truly sickening.

But something about this was different. The video was 94 seconds long. It started with a black screen and had a strange humming sound. The humming sounded like nothing he'd heard before. It sounded *alive,* like a throbbing that had begun as a hum on the video and then reverberated around his head, in his body, even through his own bloodstream.

But that wasn't even the strangest thing, and it wasn't the most disturbing thing. The visuals seemed to match what he was hearing, what he was feeling. Patterns swirled in front of his eyes. Flowers morphed into buildings, buildings morphed into cats, cats morphed into birds, birds morphed into knives, knives into eyeballs and it went on seemingly forever. The colors morphed from green and purple to yellow and red to deep red to bright pink. The screen seemed to pulse and swell as the changes occurred. The changes themselves were like liquid. Just as Mike's brain was trying to process the visual and auditory experience of the video, a high-pitched scream entered his head. He felt the scream at the base of his spine as a tingle which built and progressed up his backbone towards his head. The scream seemed to whoosh past both his ears, like a train rushing past a platform. Then it reached its peak around his brain before he felt it leaving his body with a sharp, sickening pain. Darkness followed, which made Mike feel like he was staring into an horrific abyss, a void of unlimited nothingness. The video ended.

Mike put his hand on his forehead. It was cold and clammy. His temples were throbbing. He removed his RazorVision and looked up at the ceiling. He was thankful it was over. But what was it? What had he just experienced? He'd had the displeasure of watching all sorts online in the past and RazorVision certainly made it an immersive experience, whether it was pornographic, violent or emotional, you felt like you were there. But this experience seemed to overwhelm his entire body. His entire nervous system was shaken.

Mike turned back to the students, who were still excited. It felt like hours since he'd turned away from them rather than the two minutes it had actually been. When they saw Mike's face their expressions changed.

"Professor. You don't look well, dude. It get to you? I got such a buzz!" said Liam Chen, Mike's 2nd year BA Social Technology student.

"A buzz?" replied Mike. "Wow. Yeah it got me. It got me good."

"Whoah, I never saw anyone go bad off it, Prof! Most people

get a buzz off it, like a line of coke!" Liam put his hand to his mouth, embarrassed. "Not that I'd know about that," he added.

"That was like no line of coke I ever heard of," Mike replied. "Not that I'd know that either," he added and winked. His down-to-earth nature and good humor was one of the reasons the students liked Mike and he knew it. He tried to talk to them on the same level as much as he could.

The students all laughed with him. "So, what do you think it is?" asked Susie Kam, Liam Chen's girlfriend and a second-year psychology student. Not one of Mike's students but then his lectures did tend to attract a wide range of people.

Mike placed his RazorVision back on and, ensuring he avoided re-watching the video itself, searched around the Razor network. It had been viewed 13.7 million times and the first instance of the video was only at 9 a.m. from what looked like a normal account.

He turned to the group. "I really have no idea. You see a clever thing like this from time-to-time, using age-old hypnotic techniques but taking advantage of newer technology to exacerbate its effects. A great prank and if people get a buzz out of it, then, why not? But take my word for it, I wouldn't watch it again if I were you."

"Why not, Prof?" asked Liam. "I've seen it about six times and get the same buzz every time. Amazing!" He high-fived his friend.

"Well it's up to you. Let me know if you find out any more. Drop me an email if you like. It's an interesting piece of content, but by this time next week we'll have moved on to something new no doubt."

He bid his goodbyes to the group and headed to his next seminar feeling hazy and unable to shake off a nagging feeling of uncertainty and confusion. As he walked he put his hand to his head. It felt cool and damp. His throat was dry and prickly, like he'd swallowed a rotten cactus. But much worse than that, a feeling of foreboding and dread hung over him, like something dark on the horizon that he just couldn't shake off.

Rick Razor Interview #2
Rick Razor Official Network Channel
Video – posted 23 June 2035. Views 1.3 billion.

[Rick Razor, wearing a polo shirt, sits in his office on the top floor of RazorTower in Canary Wharf, London. He faces the camera. He has sunglasses on top of his head and has five o'clock shadow.]

"Hi guys. Rick here. Okay then, this is a new thing for me. As some of you know and some of you have commented, I don't do many interviews. And I definitely don't do stuff about my private life. Well, lots of you have commented and I get a mad amount of journos asking me what I do in my own time, what makes Razor tick," *[Razor counts the questions off on his fingers]* "who am I seeing, am I gay, will I ever have kids, what's my favorite color, all sorts. I can't believe what people are interested in. Now, let me make this clear. I'm not a celebrity. You won't catch me acting like one and you'll never see me trying to use my fame *[Razor uses his fingers to display air quotes]* to get me anywhere faster. But at the same time, I don't want to shut you guys out. I suppose you guys that love the products, especially you guys that bought into our stuff in the early days. I guess I owe you one. And as much as I can't understand why you wanna know all this crap about me, why you should care, I want you to be happy. Just 'cause I don't understand *why* doesn't mean I can't help you out. Now, I'm not comparing myself for one second to him, but when I was little I wrote to Daniel Radcliffe asking him about what it was like to act in the Harry Potter films, 'cause he was my age when he filmed the first one. Jeeeee-sus I loved Harry Potter. The magic of those films, man. They blew my mind. I think I've watched the Harry Potter films about twelve times over. Now there's a snippet of myself I've given you there by accident, without even planning to. Anyway, I'm getting away from my point. In fact, no, that is part of my point. I've told you about something I love. Now I'm gonna go in the other direction. Do you know what I really don't like? It's when people treat other people bad. Bullying. I was bullied at school, you know? Bullies are weak. They prey on people they think are weak 'cause it makes them feel stronger. But no one is weaker than a bully. Here's some advice. If you're a kid at school or an adult at work being bullied – don't stand for it. Push it back. Someone told me that there has been a rise in bullying after Razor Technology was launched. Now I can't have that. I refuse to use my technology for that. So, here's a little announcement for you. I've worked with my tech team and my HR team and we've created a new role here at Razor. I've got someone working with me now who's the head of anti-bullying. We've got a team scouring the network for any sign of bullying. And I can tell you, if we find someone who's been bullying someone over the Razor Network, they will be officially shut down. No Razor tech that you own will work anymore. We can do that, you know? No bullies will prosper out of my technology. I hope you'll all be happy with that news. And at the same time, you've learned something about me. Everyone's happy, eh?" [*Razor raises both thumbs and grins cheekily into the camera*].

"Rick Razor Over and Out." [*Rick Razor leans forward and switches off the camera*].

4

Mike's next two lectures and seminars passed without incident but he approached them as if in a dream where he was an independent observer, without too much control or involvement. His students were disengaged too. The seminar, usually a highly-charged debate across various viewpoints, was actually quite mundane. The topic, online consumer behavior, was an interesting one, but his digital marketing students' minds were elsewhere, and so was Mike's.

Between all his thoughts was the video. The humming, throbbing, morphing and screaming video. The fucking video. The video that had made his body feel like it had run a marathon only to be beaten to a pulp at the finish line. What was it? And how could a video have such a physical effect on him? The unanswered questions circled around his mind like a tornado, jumbling up his other thoughts and distancing him from any tasks in front of him.

Any normal day at work and a colleague or a student would have asked him, "Mike, what's the matter? Why the long face?"

But today was different. Today a malaise had taken over everyone around him. Everyone seemed like they were on autopilot, their thoughts elsewhere. And not just elsewhere but somewhere dark. Somewhere positivity had no place.

Mike signed off from his final lecture and headed for the exit. On a normal day, he would stay behind in his office and watch videos, catch up on the day's technological news. It was important to keep up-to-date with trends.

Recently he'd been following Rick Razor's strange activity. Razor was unusual in that, as a successful global entrepreneur, the most successful that had ever lived to be more accurate, he didn't seek out publicity. Where in the past Bill Gates and Steve Jobs had been in the public eye, Razor actively stayed away. Of course, this ultimately had the effect of making the media want more and more. In a move of genius, Razor had used his own network to show videos of intimate interviews, inspirational talks and various monologues where he shared his philosophies. The views of these videos were in the billions. And they were good. He came across as a down-to-earth man whose genius had happened to make him successful. He didn't seek fame and in Mike's book that made him a good guy. Paradoxically, it also meant that Mike was less likely to meet him; maybe a more fame-hungry entrepreneur would have come and delivered a guest lecture at the country's top digital technology course, as other leading figures had done at Windermere. But not Razor, Mike had never even spoken to the man, despite his headquarters only being in London. And recently Razor had stopped doing his videos. The top of his RazorTower headquarters in Canary Wharf had been sealed off even to its own staff. Razor had been planning something huge, some sources speculated. A new product? Something that would push the boundaries of technology even further? Or maybe Simon Churchill's dream would be realized and Razor's next move would be an anthropological, philanthropic act? The thought of Churchill brought Mike back to the present and his current problems. Simon Churchill, his protégé. His friend? Mike had thought so but now, after his disruptive questions at the end of the lecture, he wasn't so sure.

Mike considered the eerie video again and his mind cast back to his early 20s, full of carefree abandon, when he experienced his first, and last, LSD trip. It had been the best and the worst thing he had ever done. It was everything he had expected and anticipated: colors floating, the very fabric of his vision and his understanding of the world around him challenged in a way that he could not explain nor even recall now, 15 years later. Visual tricks such as trees bending, grass changing color like a kaleidoscope, had been mixed with physical hallucinations. At one point, he lost all feeling below his neck, like his head had been placed on someone else's body. The emotions and thoughts he had experienced that day were wonderful. Some of the most unique feelings he had ever known. But some had been truly terrible: thoughts, worries and a feeling of utter vulnerability which had almost crippled him. The next day was one of the worst in Mike's life. All feelings of wonder and enlightenment had been replaced by a bleak depression. A dark cloud of fear held above his head until the moment he drifted off to sleep at the end of that horrid day. A day spent in confusion and apathy of the entire life that lay ahead of him; a malaise that would not lift until he woke up the following morning wondering why he had previously felt so inconsolable about all aspects of his miserable life. A feeling almost exactly the same as he'd felt since viewing the video.

Had the video roused some dormant effect that the LSD had left in his body? Had it triggered a switch of depression in his psyche that would never be turned off? Is that why he didn't feel the "buzz" that others did on seeing the video? Or would he wake up tomorrow wondering why he had been so stupid as to feel the way he had before, just like the morning after the hazy day he'd spent coming down off hallucinogenic drugs?

These thoughts were swirling around Mike's head and he almost passed by the Malaysian group of students without noticing. He looked up to see Liam, Susie and their two friends just as he was passing them. They, too, had vacant expressions, and just waved in his direction.

"Goodnight, Professor," Susie said in a soft, expressionless voice that was uncharacteristic for a girl known for vivacity and her outgoing personality.

"Guys. How are you feeling? Do you feel a little... odd?" he asked, gingerly.

Liam and Susie looked at each other and then back at their group of friends. "Not really, Mike. Why is there something wrong? Did we do anything we shouldn't?"

Mike looked at them, confused. They seemed genuine. Did no one feel like this, other than him? Maybe it was the decade-and-a-half acid coming back on him. A flashback? Possibly.

"Never mind, it's been a long day. Get yourselves home. I'll see you on Thursday for Data Ethics."

The group turned away, muttering to each other. Probably thinking their esteemed professor had gone a little crazy, Mike guessed.

He pressed his thumb on his folded-up bike. It recognized his thumbprint and sprang out into its 16-inch frame. He started out on his journey, hoping the windy evening and the breeze through his hair would go some way to brushing away the darkness that had set into his thoughts.

5

The journey did make him feel a little better. The cycle ride to and from campus was often the highlight of his day. The view of the majestic lake, with its hypnotic shades of greens and blues, could make him feel upbeat about any given situation. His mood improved slightly, but even the therapeutic benefits of Lake Windermere could not completely blow away the dark, threatening clouds that had begun to gather in his mind.

He used his RazorVision thought activation to call Simon. It was 4.25 p.m. and Simon was undoubtedly in the library, researching for his PhD. Had he found something which brought him in line with the thinking of the anti-Razor heathens? The fear-filled Luddites that would have stayed adamant the world was flat even when it was proved otherwise. Some of the anti-Razor arguments were made on a sound basis but fell apart under any scrutiny. The data laws in place prevented any misuse. Advertisers used behavioral data, key words and messages across the Razor network, but this just ensured that the right people got the right messages. The widening gap between rich and poor was a harder one to explain. The UK had benefited exponentially from the emergence of a company from its own shores growing to be the biggest on the planet. The success attracted huge investment, London had grown richer and even the most northerly parts of Scotland and parts of Wales and the North East, which had previously seen high levels of deprivation, experienced a huge upturn in fortunes. Even the wider reaches of Europe had benefitted. But it had not spread to Africa. Parts of Asia and the Middle East had suffered. The Third World had never seemed further away. *Yes*, thought Mike, *that one is harder to explain.*

But he knew there was a turning point about to come. Charitable donations were higher than they had ever been, in line with record levels of UK employment and income. Technology was becoming more affordable, free Razor products in the UK could be sent over to poorer countries to enable them to take advantage of new technology and build better infrastructures, improve awareness of health, education. The world was in the hands of Razor Incorporated and they had a track record of delivering. The Third World was not a new problem created by technology. But the fact that technology could potentially solve it was an exciting prospect. It was a debate that had been had over the years in a dozen seminars that Mike had led and no one had ever convinced him otherwise. Even Rick Razor himself had made it a personal mission to solve the issue.

Simon answered after three rings.

"Hi, Mike. You look like you're on your way home. Not like you to have an early finish, everything okay?" He sounded relaxed, blasé even.

"Yeah felt a bit iffy so thought I'd blast away the cobwebs and head home. How'd you think this morning's lecture went?" he asked, tentatively.

"Great. As you know I've seen that one a few times. Always a favorite." Simon's answer gave no indication that he had rattled his mentor.

Mike paused for a few seconds and contemplated this. Was he overreacting? Had his protégé genuinely been interested in his opinion? He decided to go straight to the point.

"About that question you asked at the end. It was a bit... provocative. I think I answered it pretty well but in the future, I'd really appreciate it if you asked me that in a smaller session. I'll be honest with you, Si, I know your intentions were probably—"

Simon cut him off mid-sentence. "Yep. I'd just come off the back of two hours of research. Mike, that gap between rich and poor has been getting worse, you know? Life expectancy, income, disease. While we get healthier and richer, other parts of the world are dying in agony. In poverty. And there's a journalist in London who has proof that data from Razor gets used for prosecuting people. People in politics. There's even some links to arms deals, although I've not seen the—"

This time it was Mike's turn to cut his student off. "Bullshit. Conspiracy theories like this have been thrown around for years, Simon. I'm surprised you're taken in by it. You don't think I've studied this? Researched it? I thought you had more sense." Mike spat the words out in between heavy breaths as he pedaled the bike up a steep hill.

"Mike you're taken in by the glamor. You love the tech. It blinds us all. We fall in love with it. We use it. They even give it away for free, for fuck's sake! What does that tell you? Nothing in this life is free that is that good? So, what's the catch? We're all in the pocket of an evil organization."

"Oh, spare me the hyperbole! I'm going to talk to you about this tomorrow, Simon. Let's have a seminar debate about it. Trust me, I know where you're coming from but you're wrong."

"Well guess what? I've got a call with him tonight. That's right, Rick Razor himself! I finally got hold of him and I'm gonna lay all this in front of him. I can't wait to see what he says. He'll probably tell me to shove it up my ass but whatever he says is going in my report. I bet he'll never have had a call like this before. He thinks he's gonna save the world but he's well on his way to destroying it. I'll make the bastard squirm. And if you can't see what's going on, fuck you, too." Simon hung up.

Mike, confused, rattled and angry, pedaled on. He admired Simon researching this so deeply but he was worried his protégé was lost, caught up in the mindless conspiracy theories; the exciting idea that such a large organization could be the evil that is wrong with the world. The conversation had been so angry and argumentative that Mike didn't have a chance to ask Simon about the strange video. He must have seen it, surely. Mike was in half a mind to call Simon back but given the abrupt ending and the heated nature of the call he thought better of it. They would make up. There was nothing wrong with a bit of passionate, healthy, academic debate between two scholars. Mike made a mental note to congratulate Simon on pinning down Rick Razor to an interview, although this thought came with a pang of jealousy. Mike himself had never come close to interviewing him, despite numerous attempts. He just hoped Simon wouldn't make a fool of himself with his 'evidence' and his conspiracy theory.

Half a mile from home, Mike freewheeled down a hill with the lake on his right, still shimmering and beautiful, reflecting the orange sheen of the setting sun. He saw the familiar sight of the Windermere Inn, a mock Tudor pub that he and Charlotte used to visit frequently before she fell pregnant with Zara. Without thinking, Mike pulled up, zapped his bike so it folded back into its tiny form and walked through the pub doors.

6

The pub was quaint. When was the last time Mike had actually been in here? It must have been at least 18 months, maybe a couple of years. He looked around. It was a real snapshot in time.

Mike walked up to the bar. Glancing at the beams above, he noticed a Manchester City football shirt. He gazed at the shirt, recalling the time he'd acted as a consultant on City's marketing technology strategy. City were trailblazers in digital technologies, being the first football club to install RazorVision links in their changing rooms, not only allowing fans to hear and see the team talks but for them to add their own motivational messages to the players, which were beamed in all their holographic glory into the changing room. City, with a forward-thinking player development strategy that saw them invest in young players from as far south as Birmingham to as far north as Windermere, had improved every year. They were now considered the best football club in the world, dominating the Worldwide Champions League and winning the English Premier League for the past seven consecutive seasons.

The player's name on the back of the shirt was one that Mike didn't recognize. *Goater*. The shirt did look old, possibly from the 1990s. Steve, the landlord of the Windermere, walked over to Mike and followed his gaze to the shirt.

"Shaun Goater. My favorite player as a boy. Long, long time ago. We were in the old League One back then, two divisions off the Premier League. Couldn't imagine it now. Best time of my life as a City fan, back then. Goater was a legend. "Feed the Goat and He Will Score" we used to say."

Mike burst out laughing at the ridiculous pun but also at the fact that the landlord felt City were actually *better* two divisions below the top league. In a lesser, lower quality league, they were somehow better? What was happening to the world? First

Simon's anti-Razor vitriol and now his local pub landlord was harping back to the good old days, which were quite obviously the bad old days? People were never happy with their lot and these two conversations in the space of less than five minutes had proved this beyond doubt to Mike.

"I'm sure he was a superstar. I'll have a pint of Lakeside please, Steve."

Steve obliged. The pint was crisp and strong. After the bike ride, Mike felt that each sip of this drink would help him revert to his mental state before he watched the video.

The video. He pulled on his RazorVision glasses to see if there had been any news or developments since he'd last looked in the lecture room.

Steve noticed the glasses. "Ah yes, I didn't think it would take you long, Professor. My pub not entertaining enough for you, is it? Or is this purely for research purposes?" Steve had a smile on his face but there was a steel in his voice that made Mike think he was pretty serious.

"You're joking? You never pull these on to catch up with news? To search for anything? To make your orders for your pub or promote your quiz nights?"

"Nope. Don't believe in it." He grinned warmly. "I'm what they call a traditionalist, Professor. I don't need to strap a pair of glasses on to connect to the world. My world is that big beautiful lake out there, this grand old pub, my wife, my kids and my best mates. I don't need no fancy specs to tell me what's going on in the world. With all respect, of course."

"No disrespect taken. But don't you think you'd get more business if you just went with the flow? Promoted yourself across the Razor network?"

Steve frowned, but even in doing so he still managed to look positive. "My business is word of mouth, mate. The day people stop telling each other about my pub, by the lake in the most beautiful town in the country, I may as well pack my bags and do something else. I don't need any Razor man telling me how to sell my wares thanks very much."

Mike's eyes brightened. He knew when he had someone cornered in an argument, a situation he loved. "Ah. But there you have it. What is word of mouth exactly, Steve?"

Steve rolled his eyes. "Come on, man, it's when people tell each other about how great it is here and they want to come see for themselves. Best recommendation you can get is one from your mate, who you trust."

"Yes!" exclaimed Mike, probably a little too loudly, as the young couple turned around to look before returning to their call. "That's it. That's exactly it, Steve! That's what makes technology so great. It's not new. The social interaction side of social media is stuff that has been taking place since the cavemen days. Seriously. Technology just makes it happen better. Faster. It supercharges word of mouth. Gives it power. You should come along to one of my lectures someday."

Steve looked at him blankly. "Okay," said Mike, turning his RazorVision to projector mode and pointing it at the pub's interior wall. "Let's see what people have been saying about this place."

The wall became alive with videos, comments, star ratings and reviews. Some of the images were of the lakeside view, some were of the food and the specialty ales. The average RazorReview score was 4.9 out of 5. There was even an image or two with Steve in the background.

"Steve," Mike said, in a serious tone. "These reviews are amazing. People love this place. And yes, word of mouth has obviously had a huge part to play. But don't think for one minute that, just because you don't use the tech yourself or you're not hooked up to the Razor network, it doesn't have an impact on your business. How many customers do you think these reviews have sent your way? And you think Razor's technologies are a negative thing?"

Mike sat back triumphantly and assessed Steve's face. Steve, though, was nonplussed.

"Hey, that's what they pay you for, Professor. I get it, I really do. No wonder you're the hotshot. The day I'm struggling to pull the punters through the door, I'll come and ask your advice. But in the meantime, I'm doing okay, Razor or no Razor. You enjoy your toys and your 'tech'. But also, enjoy your pint. My great-great-grandad brewed that first with the original recipe. Now that's something Razor can't improve."

It was hard to dislike Steve, the big, rugged, man's man with his checked shirt, his expansive beer gut hanging over his well-worn jeans. He knew Steve was traditional, in fact he thought they'd had a similar conversation about two or three years ago. He raised his glass.

"I tell you what, Steve, I think we might have to agree to disagree on this. But if anyone's gonna convince me to ditch the tech, it might well be a man like you, with a Man City shirt on his wall and a pint as good as this to hand over."

Steve threw his head back and released a booming laugh that made all the pub's other customers turn and look. "I tell you something else Razor's tech can't touch, Professor. Come behind the bar and look at this."

Mike obliged and walked behind the bar, where Steve led him to a large trapdoor. Mike looked at Steve with a touch of unease in his expression. Steve, sensing this, released his great big booming laugh once more.

"Don't worry, Professor, I'm not going to do away with you! This is the entrance to my man cave. It goes back to 1940, an old air raid shelter."

He lifted the door and Mike peered in. It looked cozy. There was a bed, a sink, a fridge and a cupboard. He could see a window that looked over the lake.

"That's where I go when I want to get away from it all. Sit and have some time by myself. If it was good enough to avoid

German bombs in the 1940s, it's good enough for an old bugger like me to sit with my own thoughts and relax."

"I can't disagree with you there, Steve," Mike said as he slapped Steve on the back. "Looks like you're planning for the end of the world, but it definitely looks cozy."

Rick Razor Interview #3

Broadcast TV Interview. The Carl Carruthers Show, London. November 2036.

[Rick Razor sits on a sofa with two other famous figures. The interviewer is Dave Carruthers.]

DAVE: I'd like to welcome our final guest. He needs no introduction. And we're privileged to be the first show to interview him outside of his own channels. Ladies and gentlemen, the most successful entrepreneur in the history of the world, Mr. Rick Razor.

The audience applauds heartily.

DAVE: So, Rick. You're famous for keeping yourself to yourself. *[audience laughs. Razor shifts in his chair uncomfortably].* That's a touch of irony, isn't it? I mean, you're famous for connecting the whole world. For allowing people to see directly into others' lives. Yet you are a deeply private person yourself?

RICK: It's been well documented, Dave. I use my technology like anyone else. You wanna see my sleeping stats? My health? You can see it. But I don't ask to see anyone else's private life and you shouldn't ask about mine.

DAVE: *[Addressing the audience]* Well that's me told! *[Audience laughs].* In all seriousness, Rick, you've been hammered recently by several left-wing groups that claim human rights don't exist anymore and you're the reason why. Also, even those who think you're a good man are worried that the information may get into the wrong hands and worse men could use it for bad.

RICK: We have things in place. I can assure you that couldn't happen. It's impossible. I made sure of that personally.

DAVE: But what about the dissenters? They get by without using your technology. They claim it's evil work.

RICK: Oh, I admire them. The world needs people like that. They're not sheep, they see something they don't like and they fight against it. Without people like that, the world would not have made the strides it did. The Martin Luther Kings of this world are important and I admire them with all my heart.

DAVE: Even if the evil they are pushing against is your good self? Even though, to use your example of Martin Luther King, the problem in this instance is your business, your technology? The modern day societal problem they're fighting is something you've introduced.

RICK: Look, Dave, the reason I came on this show is because you push harder than anyone else and I wanted to come on here and prove that Razor Inc. is a good organization. We've contributed to 360 percent improvement in living standards in the UK and enhanced the lives of thousands of people. We have helped detect illnesses, improve diets and the well-being of countless individuals. As I said before, I admire these people who fight against the system. But I will say this to them [*Razor looks directly into the camera*]. Your concerns are misplaced. I commend you for your attitude and your strength. But you are wrong on this one. Put your efforts to the things that make a difference to the world. Because my technology has made the world a better place.

[The audience applauds. The applause gets louder and louder and becomes a standing ovation.]

DAVE: Okay, Rick. One last question. What are you doing to spread the wealth to the poorer states of the world? While we've got healthier, happier and richer, people in the Third World are dying earlier than ever before. Disease has worsened. Poverty is rife. What's the answer, Rick?

RICK: Look, Dave I'm five years into this. We've changed the face of the western world unrecognizably. All my efforts are going to be focused on making the whole world a better place. My next step is to dedicate myself to this, to find a solution. And if anyone knows anything about me, it's that I always get my way. I'll stop at nothing to save the world. I've started at home, in the UK and success and happiness has spread outwards, like you said. I'm working on it, Dave. But Rome wasn't built in a day. Watch this space.

DAVE: Watch this space, indeed. Well, what did you think? Beam us your thoughts via the Razor Network, ladies and gentleman. No matter what your thoughts are on this man sitting before me, one thing you could never say is that he's lazy. Watch this space indeed. Thank you. Ladies and gentlemen, Rick Razor.

[*Another standing ovation from the audience*].

7

Mike sat in the Windermere Inn and drank a further three pints of beer. Guzzling half of his last pint in a couple of swigs, he felt a slight thrumming at the top of his head and an almost silly feeling of contentedness wash across his body. He felt a bit drunk. He chuckled at this realization. How long had it been since he had felt drunk? At least a year. Possibly longer.

He sat and looked around the inn with a childish grin on his face. The couple had finished their RazorVision call and were now watching a TV program that they had projected onto a wall. A couple of other customers sat alone, gazing into their glasses.

As he turned, his seat wobbled under the movement. Mike yelped and then steadied himself, before laughing out loud at his own clumsiness. Yes, he was certainly feeling the effects of Steve Smith's great-great-grandfather's beers.

"Here's to you, old Mr. Smith," he muttered to himself and drained the rest of his glass. The feeling and the taste jolted his mind back 15 years to his university days. His memories of university were bittersweet, full of the hedonistic glee that he never experienced now.

There had been the brilliant nights. Nights when he'd danced until daylight with the best friends he ever had, gone for an English breakfast and then started all over again. There had been the women. Never one who had confidence with the opposite sex, something had clicked for Mike at university.

He looked at his empty glass and felt a tinge of pride that he had burned the candle at both ends with such a degree of success. Winning the "Student of the Year" prize at his University and going on to complete his PhD, all while having the time of his life, bedding women he would never have imagined would even have looked at him before, and partying until the sun came up.

He could handle the booze. But it took him several years

to realize that the booze had the last laugh. Mike often took to drinking alone while working. Drinking before friends came around. Drinking before going on dates to calm his nerves. Drinking to celebrate a success as small as finishing a passage of his thesis or a win for a friend's rugby team. Then came the drugs. Cocaine to keep him going on the nights out. Speed to help him work through the night. Weed to relax. Ecstasy when going out and having high-energy sex with beautiful women was on the agenda. And that one experience of an LSD trip.

Yet his work still didn't suffer. Even as the drinking sessions increased in intensity and duration and the drugs and drink combined to make the nights more raucous, tearing up his memories. It was during one of these coke-and-booze-fueled benders that he met Charlotte.

Charlotte was a good-looking girl but not Mike's usual type. The well-endowed blondes that had been stacked up like trophies in a compartment within Mike's frazzled brain had started to morph into each other after a few years. It was early evening in London on the South Bank of the River Thames and large groups of people had gathered to enjoy the Indian Summer heat that had blessed the capital in late September. Term was still only a few weeks old and both the undergraduate and postgraduate students had the fresh enthusiasm and excitement that a new year at university brings.

Mike sat with friends, wearing a white Ralph Lauren shirt while sipping out of a bottle of lager. He spotted Charlotte, sitting three tables away, drinking a margarita. The sun's red rays bounced off the Thames and illuminated her face. The small, soft hairs on her cheek glowed and reminded Mike of a perfect peach, soft and lovely. She had a habit of linking her fingers and fidgeting with a ring on her little finger, swiveling it on and off. It immediately endeared her to Mike. Such a small gesture but it spoke to him of modesty and thoughtfulness.

Mike, his head buzzing with the effect of three beers and two lines of highly concentrated cocaine, thought she looked like the most perfect girl he had ever seen. He had made his way over and asked if she'd like another drink and everything had progressed from there.

They had spent the whole night out together. Mike, although drunk, didn't end up as wasted as he normally did. She had asked him back to her student house and they made drunken but passionate love for three straight hours. They had only fallen to sleep when the milky shards of daylight burst through the gaps in Charlotte's blinds over the east facing window.

It was Charlotte who had persuaded him to tone down his self-destruction and he obliged. He had a respect for Charlotte that he had never found possible in any woman before. Mike was in love for the first time in his life. He'd had experiences before that he had called love, as much as one labels something when others tell them what it is. If someone gave you food and told you it tasted good, why would you not believe it was what they said it was? But this *was* love. He would do anything for Charlotte.

He cut down on drinking and cut out drugs. It had been a lot easier than he thought. He finally had a reason to live other than work. He had someone who relied on him and he was beginning to rely on her. Even with London's compelling and wonderful party scene, he found he could find something else to do. Mike found himself drifting away from his friends who were the ones who partied the hardest or the most regularly. A lifestyle which came so easily and suited him so well had been discarded with the minimum of trouble.

Mike returned to the present with a bang as Steve grabbed his empty beer glass, clashing it next to one he already held in his hand. "Want another?"

"Yeah. One for the road if you will, my good man," Mike slurred. "But make it a bourbon this time. Just a single, on the rocks." *Why not,* he thought. *Not like I'm going to jump straight back into it.*

Steve nodded and poured the measure of bourbon out of his ancient optics behind the bar before scooping a small amount of ice and dispensing it into the glass. He handed it to Mike.

"To old times, mistakes… and love conquering all," Mike announced, raising his glass to Steve.

"Jesus, Professor. Maybe that should be your last, mate. Your Razor doodah will be having your life with that alcohol intake."

"You're a good one, Steve. Cheers!" Mike drained the glass and stifled a burp.

Steve was right, of course. Since RazorVision included a module that had tiny inserts onto the skin, it could measure all the body's intake and its current status: body fat, blood-sugar level, water percentage, calorific intake, heartbeat and, of course, alcoholic units. It would certainly tell him he'd had too much to drink and that it was having an effect on his heart rate and his motor functions. *Fuck it,* he thought. He held out his hand for Steve to shake. "Good day, Steve, it's been a pleasure."

"See you around, Professor. It's been too long. Come back again sometime. And you have a safe trip back home."

"Cheers, Steve. And I'll persuade you on the Razor gear at some point. I can promise you that. If there's anything I'm good at, it's getting people to embrace the future, Steve. What is it you said? Feed the Goat and he will score?"

Steve nodded.

"I'm the fuckin' Goat, Steve. I'll score on this one, I tell you."

Steve broke out in a smile. "You tell yourself that, Professor. Watch what you're doing, son."

Mike put on his RazorVision glasses as he walked out the pub. As predicted, a large warning flashed up in front of his eyes.

WARNING> BLOOD ALCOHOL RATE 0.5g/100ml.
RECOMMENDATION > DRINK WATER AND REST.

Mike chuckled. "Turn off alcohol warning," he instructed using his thoughts, and the warning disappeared.

He expanded his bike, mounted it and, after a wobbly start, rode the half-mile back home.

8

The Pilkington's house was small and quaint, but also luxurious. As Mike pulled up on his bike and zapped it to its micro size, he stopped for a couple of seconds on the walk up to the house and admired his family home. The birth of his daughter Zara, just two months ago, had thrown him into a new stage of his life. Their yellow cottage, set aside from any other houses within a quarter of a mile, was somewhere he would remember forever. His daughter was a home birth, her beautiful entrance to the world made in this very cottage, aided by the brand new RazorBirth home system that made safely delivering a baby possible without the physical presence of a midwife. The walls of the house were full of love. Happy memories pulsed through the beams, the bricks and the pipes like living matter, creating an energy of tranquility. It was fitting that it had a view of one of the most beautiful lakes in England. The yellow cottage was unique. The winding stone path that led to the white oak front door was like something out of a postcard from the old English countryside. Charlotte had joked about their "fairy-tale cottage" when they bought it. They had both fallen in love with it on first sight. It was deceptively big inside, sitting on two floors, with large, breezy living spaces.

As could be expected for the leading academic expert on digital technology, Mike had the house fully kitted out with RazorCom technology, which greeted him as he entered.

"Good evening, Mike," said the softly synthetic female tone. "I detect dehydration due to a high blood alcohol level. Please drink water to hydrate."

As he walked through the hall and into the kitchen, his refrigerator pushed an iced glass of water out of its door. Obediently, he grabbed the glass and drank.

As he turned, he was startled to see Charlotte stood in the

doorway, holding Zara. Charlotte was without make-up and wore a dressing gown. She managed to look tired, disheveled and utterly sublime all at once.

"Hi, love," Mike said and kissed his wife on the lips before planting a delicate kiss on Zara's tiny, clammy forehead. "How's it going?"

"Fine," she said and turned away.

"Hey, whassup?" he asked. "You seem annoyed?"

"I heard the RazorCom say about alcohol? You had a drink?"

"Yeah. Sorry. I just had a hell of a day. Just had a few beers in the Windermere."

"And you couldn't let me know? Do you think I've just been sitting about back here, relaxing?" She was angry. Livid, in fact.

"Hey, it's not like I'm wasted."

"That's not the point!" Charlotte screamed. "This is the kind of shit you used to pull before. Well I tell you what, pal – you've got responsibilities now. Look at her. You think getting pissed up because you've have a shitty day is fair on her? You'd rather sit in the pub feeling sorry for yourself instead of coming home and looking after your fucking daughter and your fucking wife."

Mike sighed. Charlotte only swore when she was really angry. She was right, of course. Why had he felt the need to go and have a drink? And why did he stay so long? *It worked, didn't it?* said a voice distantly in his head. And it had, yes. It had made him feel a hell of a lot better.

"I'm sorry. Truly. I'm really, really sorry. I was feeling really odd and I just went into the pub without thinking. I just... lost a little track of time..."

"You lost track of time?" she shouted but the tone had been turned down a notch. Her iron wall of anger had started to soften. "Mike, come on. I thought we were in this together. I was expecting you home earlier."

Mike walked over and kissed her gently on the cheek, carefully putting his arms around his wife and daughter. "We are a team. We're *the* team. And I am sorry. I'll make it up to you. Starting by cooking you a lovely meal." He smothered them both in exaggerated, cartoon-style kisses. It was their little thing, the shared joke. Part of the secret language that made them laugh.

Charlotte, against her own will, broke out into a smile. The smile became a grin. Mike looked into her big brown eyes, feeling relieved that he'd got out of jail after the argument. The cross words from his wife had also sobered him up. He matched her grin and laughed. He was utterly in love. Sometimes Mike felt that arguments like this were worth it, if only just to remember what he had in front of him. His baby daughter and his beautiful wife. Life really could not be better.

How could I have been so stupid? he thought to himself. His wife and child were his entire life. He would crawl on his hands and knees back to them if he needed to. Mike made a mental note to never take them for granted again. No more impromptu pub visits in the future.

They put Zara in her cot and both stood over her tiny sleeping body. They had tried for a year to conceive and almost gave up at one point. The pregnancy had been smooth, although they both worried each other sick to make sure nothing went wrong. They watched every video guide to pregnancy and bought all the Razor applications to monitor Charlotte's health. The first two months of Zara's life had been amazing, an adventure for the three of them. *The Team.* No matter what would happen, no matter what the world could throw at them, they were The Team and nothing would ever come between them.

After they ate, Mike and Charlotte projected a film onto the wall, one of the classics, *Love Actually*. They loved the classics. The new films had all the 3D computer graphics and Mike felt that something had been lost with the technology. The old films were more honest, more real.

As the credits rolled and Charlotte yawned, Mike remembered the video he had seen. The one that had disturbed him so much and made him feel so strange afterwards. So strange that he had gone to the pub like a rotten old dad that neglects his family. A rotten old dad that Mike was not and never would be. How had he forgotten?

"Did you see that video that's been doing the rounds on the network?" he asked, cautiously. "It's a bit mad."

"No, Mike, I've not looked... I've been a bit busy today." She glanced at him, the embers of the earlier argument still not fully extinguished, it seemed. "What was so mad about it?"

"It's the craziest thing I've ever seen," he replied. "Seriously. Made me feel a bit iffy afterwards. I think that's why I went to the pub without really thinking it through."

Charlotte looked at him through squinted eyes. "Show me."

Mike mulled this over for a second. Did he really want to watch it again? Was it safe for his wife to see it? He wasn't so sure. "Look, Charlie, it's getting late. I'll show you tomorrow. It just made me feel strange. Felt wrong."

"If it's doing the rounds, I'll find it." Without further consultation, she flicked her RazorVision to the network and there it was, at the top of her feed.

Mike sat forward at the projection, astounded. 2.1 billion views. That was 98 percent of the network's users. It was record-breaking. This bizarre piece of content was going to be the most accessed article ever seen on planet earth.

Charlotte played the video. The black screen and the strange humming sound signaled its beginning, and Mike remembered why he was so reluctant initially to let her watch it.

"Charlie, love, I think—" His wife held up a hand to silence him. She was engrossed.

The throbbing he had experienced before returned. Mike put his hand on his head and rubbed vigorously. He didn't wait to see the morphing visuals and he certainly didn't want that high-pitched scream running through his spine again. He walked back to the kitchen to get a glass of water. Charlotte didn't even notice him leave the room.

He heard the scream two rooms away but it was muffled by the distance and by the rhythmic buzzing sound of a helicopter flying over the cottage. The video did not have the same effect on him as it had previously, although Mike assumed this was because he had not watched its full length this time.

Charlotte walked in. Her big brown eyes were alive and sparkling. "Well that was wild!" she said, excited. "That was absolutely and utterly MAD!"

Mike looked at her suspiciously and then remembered Liam Chen's comment about the cocaine-style effect the video had on most people.

"You happy now you've seen it then?" he asked. "It freaked me out."

"Ah it was just a daft video someone's made but it doesn't half draw you in. It's funny more than scary really."

"Come on then, we might have to agree to disagree on that one," Mike said and thought of his technology discussion with Steve the landlord.

They went to bed. Charlotte, wired on the cocaine-style buzz from the video, demanded that her husband make love to her. It was frenetic and full of energy. They both fell fast asleep just after ten o'clock.

9

Mike dreamed a strange and disturbing dream. He was in the middle of a desert, all alone. The heat was sweltering and he was naked apart from an old pair of white shorts. He had scrapes and cuts and was bleeding from various places.

He looked up to the sun, covering the top of his eyes with his hand to shield them from the harsh brightness. The sun was red, burning down and amplifying the pain from the cuts, which were still oozing bright red blood.

As he walked, he passed dead bodies. He recognized these as his students at Windermere University.

After passing over a dozen bodies, he stopped over one, knelt and looked at it closely. It was a female he recognized as Mel Westmorland, from his digital marketing class. Her skin was dried up so much it hung off her naked body. It made her look like a woman in her 90s rather than the handsome 20-year-old she really was. Her hair was thin and allowed glimpses of her sore scalp, which had been burned by the intensity of the red sun. Her mouth was gaping open as if in awe of something truly amazing – or something truly terrifying. The open mouth revealed a set of black and rotten teeth, with a thin, purple and black tongue poking across the cracked lips.

But the true terror was in the eyes. Both sockets were sunk into the skull. They weren't empty. Eyeballs sat deep in the well of the sockets, but they were like no eyeballs Mike had ever seen before. They were small and red with white patches and a large black circle in the middle, which Mike guessed was the pupil. He looked closer and recoiled. One of the eyeballs was moving.

It moved further upwards against the well of the socket, further towards the surface of Mel's face. Mike tried to scream but no sound came out of his dry throat. It felt like it had been burned from the inside.

Mel's eyeball popped out of the socket, limply rolling down the side of her leathery face like a red-and-white lump of frogspawn. Mike, sweating profusely, looked down the empty eye socket. It wasn't empty. A finger was pushing its way out of the space the eyeball had vacated. Mike froze. He could do nothing else but peer down, closer and closer into this blood-curdling scene.

The finger doubled, there were now two fingers. Now three. Mike looked at Mel's face. Her skull was expanding and he could hear a crunch and a crack. Mel's face broke in two, her skull a dusty mess, and the skin tearing like wet paper. A large fist slowly emerged from her face, a diamond-encrusted RazorWatch gleaming on the gore-covered wrist.

Mike awoke with a flash of terror. He gathered his thoughts long enough to realize the terrible experience he'd just lived through was a dream. It wasn't real. His breathing slowed and he regained his calm. Swinging his legs out of bed, Mike grabbed a glass of tepid water and glugged it noisily.

He looked at his watch. It was a minute past midnight. He hoped he hadn't disturbed Charlotte. But Charlotte wasn't in the bed.

Mike got up and walked out the bedroom towards the small room where Zara slept. Charlotte was probably just seeing to the baby, who no doubt had been crying. He walked into Zara's room and sure enough, Charlotte was hunched over Zara's cot.

"Hey, Charlie, how is she? I had a bad—"

But Mike had been stopped dead in his tracks. His mind, still hazy from the nightmare he'd woken up from barely a minute previously, couldn't process what his eyes were seeing.

Charlotte was holding a pillow over their baby girl's face.

10

Mike rushed forward and grabbed his wife.

"What are you doing? What the f—"

There was no recognition in his wife's eyes. Not only that, but they didn't look like her eyes anymore. They were red, bloodshot. No, more than bloodshot; the big brown eyes that he had stared into only hours earlier had been transformed into vacant chasms of blood. Her head was twitching violently and foaming, chalky-white drool poured from her mouth.

Her hands went to his throat and clasped around his neck, her thumbs pushing hard on his Adam's Apple, which made Mike's throat gurgle in reflex. A huge twitch pushed the thumbs against his throat even harder.

With considerable effort, he grabbed Charlotte's hands and forced them away. He pushed past her and looked at Zara. She was breathing. He picked her up into his arms and she began to cry. The cry became a high-pitched wail.

Mike then felt Charlotte's hands around his neck, pushing hard against the side of his throat once more. He wriggled free.

"What the hell, Charlie. What's happening to you? Wake up!"

Wake up? he asked himself. *Is she sleepwalking? Am I still dreaming?* He couldn't take any chances and ran from Zara's room, onto the landing.

Charlotte, still twitching, white slobber dripping from her jaw, jumped and flung herself at Mike and Zara. Mike moved to the side, making his body as thin as possible to keep Zara from harm and avoid his wife's dive.

Charlotte missed her intended victims and tripped on her own feet. Her ankle went over at a right angle with a loud cracking sound. She released an inhuman scream, something that sounded like the wail of a rabid animal rather than a woman, and fell down the full flight of stairs.

A series of crunches, cracks and pops sounded up the hall into Mike's ears. He watched uselessly as he saw the woman he loved tumble down the hard, wooden stairs and land at the bottom with her head at a right angle to her neck. Her body was still twitching.

"Charlotte Pilkington, injury detected. Charlotte Pilkington, multiple injuries detected," said the RazorCom synthetic voice. "Attempting to call ambulance. Attempt failed. Attempting to call ambulance. Attempt failed."

Mike froze at the top of the stairs, his head racing, trying to process what had happened. Zara wailed as his wife's broken body twitched at the bottom of the stairs for the final time.

"Charlotte Pilkington, no heartbeat detected, emergency situation. Use CPR machine. Use CPR machine," the synthetic voice repeated.

Mike overcame his temporary paralysis and ran down the stairs, still clutching his baby daughter. He placed her in the downstairs cot and grabbed the CPR machine from the cupboard. He was moving so fast when he returned to his wife's body that his bare feet slipped on the wooden floor and his whole body slid down next to her.

He pulled open her nightshirt and pressed the CPR machine against her. "Activate CPR," he instructed. It whizzed into life.

"Activating CPR," said the synthetic voice. "Failed. Failed. Failed. Failed," the voice became slower and faded. "Malfunction. RazorCom shutting down."

Everything in the cottage, Mike Pilkington's house of utopia, the birth place of his daughter and the headquarters of *The Team*, went pitch black.

11

Tears ran down Mike's face in the darkness, tickling his cheeks and dropping in tiny pools onto the wooden floor.

The love of his life, the mother of his child, was dead. Mike could not comprehend what had happened to his wife. He had made love to her just over two hours ago. She had tried to kill their baby. She had tried to kill him. The woman he loved more than anything.

His eyes adjusted to the darkness and he could make out Charlie's shape in the moonlight that cascaded through the window. He moved over and kissed her on her cheek.

"I love you, Charlie," he said aloud through tears. "I'll always love you. Always have, always will." He hugged her broken body and felt his heart beat against her like it was trying to break out of his body.

His concentration was broken by his daughter's cries. He looked over, still desperately clutching his wife's corpse. Mike made a decision. He had to get out of the house. He had to leave this madness, to make sense of this situation. He stumbled across the hall, using the moonlight as a guide. He grabbed Zara roughly and bundled her into his arms. He walked back through the hall, glancing briefly and solemnly at his wife's dead body.

Holding his baby in one arm, Mike opened the cottage's front door and burst into the darkness outside.

12

Mike shambled down the path that led out of his home, dressed only in boxer shorts and a plain white t-shirt with nothing on his feet, the crying Zara clutched to his chest. The lake, which by day had been gleaming and beautiful, now twinkled reflected moonlight back at him in a way Mike felt sinister and malevolent.

He stopped by the lake and looked back at the yellow cottage. Breathing short breaths, tears and saliva began to spit from his nose and mouth, an ugly outpouring of grief for his lost wife. Mike's thoughts became gluey and uncontrollable. One sentence in his head would be interrupted by another as his brain tried to make some kind of sense of the situation. The cottage held so many memories for him. The place he had been the happiest. Now, like the lake, the cottage had a darkness to its appearance, like a malignant sheen of despair that would never be lifted. Mike looked at the cottage and realized that he would never live there again.

"Why?" He asked the darkness. "Why? Why? Why? Why?"

He sank to his knees, still clutching the baby and let out an agonized scream that came up with a retch. It came again and Mike vomited onto the grass in front of his family home.

His head ached with the stress, the confusion and the agony of his grief. He had to get away. He had to get some kind of help.

"They'll think it was me," he muttered to himself. "They'll think I killed my own wife." The thought brought with it a fresh batch of tears. He walked away, following the moonlight which reflected eerily from the lake. Zara was wailing even louder now and every cry felt like a dagger into his heart.

He held his daughter in his outstretched arms and looked at her face. She had the same large brown eyes as her mother. The same eyes he had fallen in love with all those years ago: eyes that had somehow turned glazed and bloodshot without an ounce of recognition. Eyes that would never open of their own accord ever again.

His daughter's wails stopped as Mike and Zara's eyes connected. It was just the two of them now, *The Team* stripped brutally of one of its members. The trio had become a duo. They were all each other had. Zara would rely on her father for the rest of her life and he would need her support equally. His wife was dead. *Dead*, he repeated in his own mind. Such a cruel and abrupt word. One awful syllable that summed up so much melancholic meaning. The end of his wife's life. His Charlie would never make any more imprint on the world.

It was too much to take in. He pushed his head back so he was looking up at the night sky and let out a desperate cry. This sparked his daughter back to her own wailing.

He walked across the same path that he had cycled home from work. He wasn't walking with any purpose other than to get away and to find another human being who he could somehow attempt to converse with, to tell his story... or some version he could make sense of. His own gasps of tearful grief merged with Zara's wails to create a cacophony of overwhelming misery. The cool breeze that had refreshed Mike during his morning bike ride was now an icy chill that rippled the sparkling waters of Lake Windermere, which still seemed to keep its newly sinister edge.

Not even a hundred yards into his journey, Mike looked up to see the shadowed outline of a person standing on the path in the distance. There was a body lying at their feet. The silhouetted figure was twitching in the moonlight.

13

Mike froze on the spot. The figure slowly edged towards him. It twitched in a harsh way, not unlike the throes of an epileptic seizure. Mike grimaced. It was the same twitching movement his wife had displayed in her murderous rage.

The figure's face became illuminated by a beam of moonlight and Mike had a fierce realization. The narrowed Asian eyes and the black hair. This bumbling, twitching figure was Liam Chen, the very student who showed him the horrendous video. Liam's face was strained. Even from a distance Mike could see the same chalky drool cascading from his mouth. The same white saliva that was pouring out of Charlotte before she fell to her tragic death. He was moving closer now and Mike was still frozen. His face still visible from the flow of the moonbeam, Liam's eyes had the same vacant, bloodshot look as Charlotte's had and his jaw gaped open as if dislocated. Mike's terror doubled when he saw a gleam of light in Liam's hand. He was carrying a large kitchen knife.

Mike, forced into action by a surge of fresh fear, turned and ran. He felt like he was running in treacle, before he felt the weight completely disappear from his feet. Mike's foot had struck a log, invisible in the darkness, and he was heading for the ground, still clutching his baby daughter. With an instinctive move of protection for Zara, Mike shifted his entire body sideways to take the full impact of the fall. He hit the ground with a sickening crack as he felt at least two of his ribs fracture with a sharp bolt of searing hot agony in his side. But broken ribs were the least of Mike's problems. Liam Chen, still twitching, was standing over him, the moonlight reflecting sharply from the blade of the kitchen knife in his hand. The knife was covered with dark lumps of blood which dripped from the tip of the blade and landed in thick drops next to Mike's legs.

Liam lowered his body slowly, his head jerking intermittently to its right-hand side. Mike pushed his daughter, who was now screaming, to the soft grass verge on the side of the footpath to remove her from immediate danger. Liam's knife-wielding arm came down towards Mike's body. With a surge of adrenaline, Mike kicked out his leg, his bare foot connecting firmly with Liam's wrist. The knife flew from his grip, somersaulted in the cold night air and landed with a loud clang behind Liam on the footpath. The effort shot more hot pain into Mike's side and he cried out in agony. Liam, surprised by the loss of the knife in his hand, turned to look behind at where it had landed. In spite of his aching body, Mike landed another well-struck kick, this time aimed squarely at the Malaysian student's testicles. His aim was good. Liam howled and fell backward onto the path, the back of his head connecting with the concrete with a heavy smack. He lay still on the ground.

Groaning with the pain, Mike leaned over to take his daughter back in his arms. First his wife and then Liam Chen. It was like something from a George A. Romero film. "Zombies," he muttered to himself over his daughter's cries. If it wasn't so terrible it would have been laughable. Was it a disease they had caught? A virus? Two people he had spoken to the previous day. Two people he knew had never acted violently before, one of whom he loved with all of his heart. Both physically changed and both tried to kill him. And now both were dead.

Mike staggered on and looked down at Liam's body. His face looked different. Although his eyes were now closed they still looked changed. Colder, somehow, the swollen and pale eyelids reminded Mike of aliens in crappy old sci-fi movies. His clothes had bloodstains all over them. Mike remembered what he had seen when he first noticed Liam's silhouetted shape. Liam had attacked someone else and their body was further down the path. They might still be alive. They might need his help. He looked over and saw the heaped shape fifty yards away and began to walk towards it.

He felt a tight grip on his ankle that abruptly stopped his progress, fingernails digging into the thin flesh. He tried to pull free but couldn't. He looked down. Liam's eyes were open and his fingers were curled around Mike's ankle in a vice-like grip. Liam began to twitch again. With surprising dexterity, he pulled himself to his feet and pushed Mike backwards. Mike fell and hit the soft verge, a small mercy from his previous landing on the hard concrete. Again, he shielded Zara from the fall and then pushed her aside onto the grass. He hoped to God he hadn't caused her any injuries. Liam bore down on him, his hands aiming for Mike's throat in an eerie echo of his wife's attempt to kill him earlier in the night. Some of Liam's chalky white drool dropped on Mike's t-shirt, the wetness making it cling to his chest. A gleam of moonlight caught the corner of Mike's eye. It was the kitchen knife, which now lay half a meter away from his own body. He moved to his side, more white-hot pain in his ribs, and grasped it. He upturned it as Liam descended on him and felt the blade sink into his attacker's chest. Warm blood leaked out of the wound and covered Mike's face. It flowed onto his eyes and into his mouth, with a strong taste of copper. An earthy smell engulfed his senses and Liam's heavy body flopped onto him. With a burst of effort, Mike shoved Liam off and to the side. No doubt about it, he was dead this time.

Once more, Mike picked up his daughter and stood up over Liam's body.

"Why?" he asked the dead man. "Liam... what the fuck? Why?" And then, with another surge of energy he shouted up to the sky. "What the fuck is happening? Someone fucking tell me what the fuck is fucking going on!" The burst of expletives felt like a relief. He started again for the body that was lying further down the path.

He recognized it immediately, despite the horrific injuries that Liam had inflicted on it. The body was Susie Kam's. Liam

Chen had brutally murdered his own girlfriend. Her face was a mess and there were large patches of blood all over her torso. He could see a stringy segment of brain through a hole in her skull and blood had streamed out of her nose and mouth. She had died a terrible, violent death at the hands of her usually placid boyfriend.

Zara's cries grew louder, piercing the night. Small waves lapped on Lake Windermere as Mike stood looking over the third dead body he had seen in a little over twenty minutes. He breathed in deeply and held his breath, in an attempt to pump energy into his flagging body. He turned to look at the lake, the night's darkness making the water appear like black silk, and walked on further down the path.

14

Mike staggered, walking on instinct, without direction or intended destination, his side aching and tight. Still he held his baby daughter close. Her cries and screams continued but Mike had tuned in to them now. And maybe, he considered, silence would be worse. This awful night deserved to be played out with the soundtrack of wails, cries and screams. Mike was shocked, frightened and alone. His thoughts alternated between outright grief, the pain of loss, anger and finally confusion about what had happened to turn his world upside down in such a short passage of time.

A light further down the path caught Mike's eye. He looked over and saw the Windermere Inn. Had he walked that far already? The lights were on. It was well after midnight now, past the pub's usual closing time. Maybe this could be a safe house, somewhere Mike could go and call the police. Maybe Steve would be there to talk it through and together they could make some sense of what was happening. Maybe he could use RazorVision to see if there was some kind of virus or a terrorist attack using some kind of gas. Maybe the water had been poisoned in the town. Maybe, in minutes or hours, Mike himself would begin to twitch and drool, develop large pupils and bloodshot eyes and a craving for murder. He made his way up to the inn's front door and pushed it open.

Even the night's earlier scenes of horror could not have prepared him for what he saw in the Windermere Inn. He counted six dead bodies strewn across the tables. Each had died a violent death. Some had bled, others looked like they'd had the life strangled out of them. One person's neck had been squeezed so hard that it was a combination of black and red, and their eyeballs were protruding from the sockets in an almost cartoon fashion. Another had a knife planted in their forehead, slimy chunks of brain slipping out of the wound, white shards of the victim's skull visible through the gash around the edges of the blade.

He turned to the bar and saw Steve. He was holding a cricket bat. A twitching, shambling figure was reaching over the bar. Steve swung his bat, connecting with the figure's hands. He spotted Mike at the door.

"Professor! Holy fuck, Professor," he shouted. "Your daughter. Jesus Christ your daughter. You've got to keep her safe. Come over here, quick."

"What's happening? My wife…" Mike replied.

"Not a clue. Not a bloody clue. Come over, now!"

Mike rushed over to the bar. The twitching figure was starting towards him. Placing his daughter on the top of the bar, Mike pulled one leg on top and, with a grimace of agony, he swung his other leg over and landed at the other side. Steve slapped him on the back.

"Good to see you made it, pal," Steve said. "Quick, you'll be safe in my cellar. Get down there now. Another two figures, both twitching, appeared at the door of the pub. The man whose fingers had been smacked by Steve's bat, was trying to reach over the bar again, his fingers visibly broken from the impact. His chin was a waterfall of white saliva.

Mike turned and lifted the heavy trapdoor, shifting his daughter to the injured side of his body with a wince. He pulled her onto his shoulder and descended the ladder. Once down, he placed his now screaming baby daughter on the small bed at the back of the room and then climbed back up the ladder.

"Steve!" Mike shouted, his head just protruding from the trap door. "Steve! Come down here. Stay safe." Steve didn't reply but Mike could hear commotion, tables moving and glasses smashing. He pulled himself up out of the trapdoor in time to see Steve killing one of the twitching attackers with the cricket bat. He had used it to cave half his assailant's head inwards. Another of the attackers was lying half-on half-off the bar in a similar state, a mixture of blood, skull splinters and brain oozing out of the crater in his head. Mike slowly made his way back down the ladder, leaving the trapdoor open so Steve could slide down but then he saw something which made him realize that Steve would not be joining Mike and Zara in the old bomb shelter under the pub. Steve wouldn't be joining anyone in this world. The third and final assailant had skewered him with a pool cue which had been snapped off into a sharp, deadly weapon in the melee. The cue had entered Steve's body through his mouth and the force had been applied upwards, directly into his brain. Steve's large body flopped forward. He was dead before his face slapped onto the stone pub floor.

Mike's eyes widened, his heart galloping. He fumbled with the trapdoor, eventually pulling it shut from inside and bolting it tight. Breathing in short, shallow bursts, he lay on the bed and hugged his daughter. Tears fell heavily from his eyes and his throat felt choked. His side ached and his head throbbed. Over the high-pitched wails of his baby daughter, he heard a heavy banging on the trapdoor.

15

Mike jumped to his feet, grabbed a broom and reciprocated the action, banging the trapdoor from the inside. The banging from above stopped. He looked around the room. Although it was dark, a small, square window at ground level let in some moonlight allowing him to see the layout of the room, some of which he remembered from Steve's tour the previous day.

There was a cupboard without a door that held several dozen tins of beans, tuna, spaghetti and various meats. A hotplate stood on a worktop in the corner of the room. Several tools hung on the wall including a spade, a rake and a long-handled axe. The bed which Zara lay on was a small one. The floors and the walls were stone. It was cold. The window itself gave a strange view, with the ground being level with the bottom of the window, giving Mike the impression of the porthole of a ship.

The banging began once more from above. Mike felt a flash of anger. "Haven't you done enough?" he yelled at the closed trapdoor. "Leave us alone. You've all taken enough."

He started for the stairs. *Fuck it*, he thought to himself. Sick of the death, sick of the horror and sick of this dark, terrible night. He would go and fight. If it meant his death, then at least he would have tried. The banging stopped and Zara's cries jolted Mike from his mission. "Zara," he said to himself. He couldn't leave. If he died what would happen to her? He had to stay alive for his child. He had to keep her safe and safe meant sensible actions.

All thoughts of safety were shattered with a smashing sound coming from the window. Mike looked over. A hand was poking through the small window trying to grasp, grab anything in its wake. The hand was twitching and jerking. Mike went over to the tools and took the axe off its hanger. He walked over to the window, raised the axe high over his head, clipping the stone ceiling. Mike's ribs flashed with pain at the unexpected jolt to his body but he held the axe firmly over his head. He looked at the grasping arm, its ropey muscles flexing, and brought the axe down with as much force as he could muster. There was a scream of agony from the unseen face behind the window. A yell so primal and so full of pain that even Zara stopped crying and turned her large brown eyes to see what was happening. When Mike thought about the incident later, he only hoped that his baby's underdeveloped brain could not comprehend nor process the images that the eyes were transmitting back to it.

What Zara saw was an arm, not quite severed, hanging by a series of thick veins. It was leaking blood at a fast rate, viscous, red matter pouring on to the stone floor with a damp slapping sound. The hand was still moving, twitching. Baby Zara watched her father raise the axe over his head a second time. This time the blow separated the arm from its owner, who produced another blood-curdling howl of fresh agony. Mike grabbed the severed hand. To his amazement and terror, it was still twitching. Squirming at the warm, still-living feel of the arm, he threw it out of the window. Moving quickly, he used the axe to tear down some shelving at the far side of the room. Gathering the wood and a handful of nails, he hammered the planks across the square window, covering it completely and plunging the room into total blackness.

Mike staggered across to the bed and lay on it with his daughter, who had stopped crying. His earlier thoughts had been accurate. The silence was worse. He filled it with his own cries, short, sharp gasps as he considered what he had been through. The horrors of the last hour had changed his world forever. He raised his arm to look at his RazorWatch for the first time since he had awoken from that terrible dream an hour earlier. It was blank.

* * *

Mike shut his eyes tight, still breathing and crying at the same time. He didn't recall how he fell to sleep that night or if he even considered it sleep. Maybe he had passed out from the shock of the evening's events, seeing so much death and gory violence.

It would be eight weeks before he left the safety of the pub basement and faced the fresh horrors of the new world outside.

Rick Razor Interview #4

Internal Message to Razor Inc. Employees 13 January 2038

[Razor sits in a dark suit with a white shirt and bright orange tie. He is in his office, clean shaven. His face is serious and formal.]

"Hi, everyone. First of all, I'd like to thank you for all the hard work you've put in over the last few years. We really created something, didn't we? Don't worry, I've got no major announcement here, I'd just like to reassure everyone that we're still working hard on new developments. I know there's been some speculation about what I've been up to over the last few months, with me sectioning off the top of the Tower, but we're just so close to a breakthrough. A group of us on the top few floors have been working night and day on our new product. It's top secret but you'll all know soon. I'll tell you this, though, it's gonna be pretty amazing. Everyone always tells me I changed the world but they've not seen anything yet. Seriously, this is an absolute humdinger. I'm talking about bringing equality to everyone. I'm talking about everyone not just being connected but an atmosphere of love across the world. A work ethic where we're all in it together. I realize I probably sound like a madman! *[Razor laughs]*. But don't worry. You're all going to be a big part of it. I'm just sorry I haven't been able to tell you anything. But all will be revealed. In fact, I can tell you I'm a little nervous. I've worked so bloody hard on this; I really want it to work. And believe me, no one will be happier than me. Some of those who criticize me, criticize the company. Well, I can tell you this. They will be eating their words. Or maybe they won't *[Razor laughs again]*. Sorry. I know this is a bit cryptic, but I just wanted to thank you all for your patience while I've worked on this. It's my masterpiece and you'll see soon enough. You're gonna love it, I just know it. You're all so important to me, you're like family.

You've made all my dreams come true. But now it's time for the second wave of Razor Incorporated. I can't wait for you to see it. It's been one hell of a ride and it's about to get so good!

[Razor straightens his tie and gulps audibly.]

Rick Razor, over and out. See you on the other side. *[He reaches over and turns off the camera.]*

16

A sliver of sunlight pierced through the tiny gap between two boards which covered the square window in the basement. It was enough to wake Mike from his heavy sleep. He glanced down at his sleeping daughter, next to his chest. Her sleep had worsened over the last couple of weeks, so it was with some satisfaction that he saw her tiny chest moving up and down next to him, eyes closed in the midst of a deep sleep. Mike wondered if she was dreaming. And what kind of dreams could a baby have? The thought made Mike shudder. His daughter's eyes had seen sights that would send any adult straight to a psychiatrist. If Zara remembered even a tiny split second of this experience, she was in for some pretty awful night terrors in the future.

But any worries about Zara's future psychological damage could wait. He was more worried about her physical health. The basement was equipped with enough food to last two people a few months, so stocked was the cupboard with tins and processed food. But feeding a baby, not yet three months old, mushed-up beans and peas washed down with water and small doses of UHT milk was not going to meet its nutritional demands.

It was eight weeks since Mike had seen his wife, the mother of his baby and the love of his life, fall to her death. But the time that passed had not allowed him to make more sense of it. If anything, the events were less clear in his head. He went through what he knew for what felt like the thousandth time. Everything seemed to start when he saw the strange, hypnotic video, shown to him by Liam Chen and Susie Kam after his lecture.

What else did he know? The power was out. All the Razor technology had turned itself off. The people outside had stopped banging on the window the day after he boarded it up. His terror had calmed somewhat, turning into a feeling of almost acceptance at the diabolical situation he found himself in.

Mike stroked his beard. He had been clean shaven when he came into the basement on that terrible night in April. He felt dirty. He had not had any form of wash for the duration of his stay. Mike's thoughts were broken by a loud cry. Zara was awake. Mike picked her up and looked into her eyes with a pang of hurt. It took Mike a couple of seconds to realize why. Zara's eyes were identical to his dead wife's. Mike looked away and a grisly thought arose. Charlotte's broken, twisted body would still be at the bottom of the stairs, in their quaint, yellow cottage by Lake Windermere.

He looked up at the trapdoor and sighed. He had to make a move. If not now, then when? He had to get out. And it had to be today, in the daylight.

17

Mike grabbed a rucksack from the cupboard in the corner and stuffed a few essentials into it. Tins of beans, UHT milk, six bottles of mineral water and a sharp kitchen knife. After some consideration, he strapped the long-handled axe to the back of the rucksack.

As he picked up Zara and headed towards the ladder, he took one last look at the place which had been his home for the last eight weeks. Cold and uncomfortable, the basement had been his savior. His eyes made their way to the boarded-up window. A smattering of dried crimson blood was still visible on the section of stone wall underneath the window.

He made his way up, undoing the bolt and pushing the trapdoor upwards with one hand while he cradled Zara with the other arm. It was heavier than it should have been. Mike had to exert double the effort he'd anticipated, his muscles burning. He heard something tumble from above, and the load became lighter. After another push, it swung upwards.

Poking his head out to look over the floor behind the bar area, Mike realized what the weight had been. Steve's head, covered in blood so dry it appeared to be a brown color, lay on the floor an inch away from him. The parts of flesh Mike could see on the dead man's face were white, with blue veins branching out like the roots on a stubborn weed. Mike closed his eyes for a few seconds to compose himself. He had to be strong.

He pulled himself and Zara upwards, clear of the basement. There were eight other dead bodies, all in a state of decomposition. He breathed in and nearly vomited. The smell was horrible. It hit the back of Mike's throat hard and he felt that he could actually taste death, a rancid mixture of copper and earthy decay. Flies buzzed around the dead bodies and on one of them, slumped against a table, he saw maggots burrowing into the loose skin. A rat scuttled across the room and disappeared underneath a table with something pink and fleshy in its jaws.

Holding his breath, Mike hurried past the bar, carefully stepping over the bodies so he didn't have to touch any of them. Pools of partially dried blood lay across the floor and smashed glass littered the room. It looked like a bar fight had gone wrong. Mike made his way to the front door, which was slightly ajar, and made his way outside.

He staggered out of the pub and headed towards the university, not wanting to see the cottage where his wife still lay. Not yet.

He hadn't walked thirty yards when he saw another body. This one was missing an arm. The arm that Mike had liberated with two downward strokes of a long-handled axe lay a few yards away from him. Dried drool covered the man's chin and neck.

Mike walked on. The sun was now blazing down on him and he used his free hand to shield his eyes. He looked in the distance to the vast lake but saw nothing but a couple of seabirds gracefully gliding over the water.

He turned back and flinched. In the distance, a tall man was walking towards him.

18

Mike raised his hand again to shield his eyes from the midday sun. He squinted to take in what he was seeing. After seeing so much death, so much terror, his defenses were stronger than they'd ever been. The approaching man was less than fifty yards away but he didn't seem to be twitching or drooling.

"Hey!" shouted the approaching man. "Hey, how are you? You okay?"

Mike sank to his knees and wept uncontrollably. He never thought he'd be so happy to see another human being. The man came closer. He was wearing a baseball cap, shielding his own eyes from the sunlight. He was an older man, Mike guessed around mid-fifties by his weather-beaten face. His grey hair was thick and untamed, falling out from under the cap in silver clumps. Although his face was old, with cracked lips and a large, red nose, there was a friendly quality to his features, something trustworthy.

The man smiled warmly at Mike's reaction to his greeting. He understood. As he came closer, Mike regained his composure and stood up again. The stranger offered his hand.

"Hey. I'm Matty. Matty West. Shit, am I glad to see you. And look at this gorgeous girl."

Mike, overcome with emotion once more, pulled West's hand to him and gave him a firm hug, engulfing Zara within the embrace at the same time, and adding fresh pain to his sore ribs. His tears came again, harder than before, and he blubbed on this stranger's shoulder.

When Mike's tears had stopped, West grabbed him by both shoulders and looked him in the eyes. "You're the first living person I've seen for two months now, apart from my wife. By Jesus I've seen some things," West said.

"Shit," replied Mike. "Haven't we all?"

West walked Mike and Zara back to where he lived. It was a motorhome, West told him, a 2016 model that still ran on old fuel. It was a thirty-minute walk back to where West had parked, and Mike used the time to find out his new friend's take on what had happened eight weeks ago.

"I can tell you right now I've got absolutely no idea," he replied. "Some kind of new virus I reckon. Probably terrorists. I haven't ever seen anything like that before. It'll be a radioactive man-made virus, I'm telling you. I drove across here from Newcastle to get away from what was happening there. Safety in the countryside, if you know what I mean."

Mike gulped and looked back at West. "What happened in Newcastle? What was it like?" West looked at Mike out of the corner of his eye.

"You seen one of 'em? The twitchers?" Mike nodded in confirmation. He wasn't ready to tell this man about his wife yet.

"Me and Trish had been out for the night, we were in the taxi queue to get back to the caravan park when something just seemed to snap. At first, we just thought it was kicking off in the taxi queue. I mean, this is Newcastle on a Saturday night, it wouldn't be the first time scuffles broke out. It took us a while to realize that this was different. People were choking each other. Then someone smashed a beer bottle and put it right into someone's heart. That's when we knew something really bad was happening. And the twitching! Never seen anything like it. Then we see everyone dribbling thick white foam. Like the rabies. That's what it was like! Like they had rabies. Then when they turned on us, I grabbed a loose plank of wood from a fence next to me and managed to fend them off. Then we walked seven miles to the caravan park. Some of the things we seen on the way…" West shook his head and looked at Mike intensely. It needed no explanation. "After that we just drove until we ran out of fuel. Of course, we couldn't get any more, all the petrol's been locked down when all the Razor technology's gone off. Got none left, ran out just at the side of the road, another mile from here. Worse places we could've landed I suppose. Drove past a fair few cars, just abandoned along the A66. People lying on the road. Some people we saw looked like they'd died on top of each other. Some of 'em looked like they'd topped themselves."

"Topped themselves?" Mike asked, eyebrows raised.

"Yeah. See, I got a theory. This virus, this thing that makes someone do this. It makes them wanna murder whoever's nearby. Gives them a whole load of anger. Like some kind of hunger that they just can't shake. Then after a few hours of finding no one to murder, they turn on themselves. Cut their own throats. Throw themselves off a bridge. I saw one of 'em who looked like he'd just bashed his own head off a rock at the side of the road." West looked back at Mike. "So, what's your story? You're alive. You must've seen some shit? I got to say, Mike," he said, looking at Mike's visibly uncomfortable gait, "you don't look so hot. And by the look of that axe strapped to your back, I'd say you fought your way out of somewhere and took no prisoners."

Mike felt trust in this man immediately. He'd liked Matty West right from the first moment they met, when Mike broke down and cried like a baby on his shoulder. He recounted his story, leaving nothing out. Mike had to take a deep breath when he told him about Charlie.

When he had finished, he exhaled in a long, unsteady breath and choked back tears. It felt so strange to tell this story out loud. Hearing it in his own voice gave it a sheen of realism.

West patted him on the back. "I thought I'd been through some shit, mate. Jesus, I'm so sorry. That's awful. I knew you were in a state when I first saw you and I did think that having a young baby... I thought something must've happened to the mother but, fuck me. That's hard. I don't know what to say."

"Nothing you can say," Mike replied, staring straight ahead. "I'm still trying to make sense out of it. Can't get my head round it. Why are you and I okay? What happened? And what now?"

"Slow down. We aren't gonna solve this here and now." West pointed ahead. "There she is."

Mike squinted his eyes against the sun and saw a large white motorhome in the distance. It was parked at the side of the road, dusty and dirty but not unwelcoming. "That's my baby," West said, smiling. Mike was relieved. His legs ached from the long walk and his shoulder was screaming in agony from carrying Zara. His ribs, barely healed, creaked with sharp pain. He was exhausted.

Mike, Zara and Matty West climbed into the motorhome to join Trish. Like her husband, Trish had a friendly nature. She dressed very much like a grandmother, wearing an apron stained with the day's cooking tasks, along with what seemed like a permanent smile, even at this darkest of times. They enjoyed a dinner of hotdogs and baked beans and discussed what the new world would hold for them. Matty West had been a plumber and owned his own company but retired five years ago when Razor Technology provided the ability for modern homes to diagnose and fix their own problems. They had a son based in Buckinghamshire who was married and had a five-year-old daughter called Evie, their granddaughter. A hard-copy photo of Evie sat above the dining table in the motorhome.

The Wests were impressed that Mike was head of a university department, although they confessed they didn't exactly understand the subject he taught. Mike asked them about the video. They hadn't seen it, in fact they hadn't used any Razor Technology, mainly as a protest at the fast-changing nature of the world. With a touch of cynicism, Mike also conjectured to himself that there was an element of bitterness about Matty losing his career. He enjoyed the West's company and realized that it had been the longest his daughter had gone without crying since the horrible night that the madness had begun. Matty was engaging, with a sense of humor that comforted Mike, even in this bleak and uncertain time. Trish was motherly, a lovely woman who liked to fuss around her guests and ensure everyone was comfortable. After they ate, Matty opened a bottle of whisky and they all had a plastic tumbler with a couple of fingers of the lovely, smooth liquid. Even Zara was fed a small drop to help her sleep. This was something that would have mortified Mike a few weeks ago but his outlook had hardened now. To Mike, who had survived on basic rations for eight weeks, the whisky tasted like drops of heaven. He savored every sip and his head began to spin.

As the sun began to set in the late evening, Trish looked after Zara to allow Mike to rest his tired body. He placed his head on the pillow and slept a long, dreamless sleep.

19

The clean-up operation was as arduous and as upsetting as Mike had expected. After spending a pleasant week at the Wests' motorhome, the exploring began. Trish looked after Zara and was delighted to do so if it meant missing out on the grim task that lay ahead.

Windermere was strewn with dead bodies. The main street, the bars, restaurants and the tourist hotspots held the highest number. The dead children were the worst. The first one that Mike came across, a girl of no more than six, made him vomit. He had come across the girl on the ground outside a high building. Looking up at the smashed window four stories above, it was obvious where she had come from. Although there were no obvious wounds, her body was bent in an unnatural "S" shape on the concrete. God knew how many sights there were behind closed doors. And Mike had no appetite to poke his nose anywhere he didn't need to.

His thoughts were never far away from his cottage by the lake. He needed to build himself up for a visit back there. He needed a project – something to distract him until he was ready to face his wife's decomposing, twisted body.

Mike and Matty had a good system in place. They worked through the main areas of Windermere and collected all the bodies in piles. It was heavy, gruesome work. After several attempts at pulling bodies along by the arms and feeling the shoulders of two bodies pop right out of their sockets, Mike realized that it was easier to pull them along by the legs. He did this facing away from the bodies, like a Husky pulling a macabre sled. They both used makeshift masks from Matty's wool jumpers and elastic from his underpants, to save their noses from the stench of the dead.

The plan was simple: to find as many bodies as they could

and spend a couple of days digging out a nearby field. They would use the wheelbarrows from a local barn to take all the bodies to the mass grave and then cover them with the loose dirt. They decided to leave the houses, apartments and homes and only concentrate on public areas, shops, restaurants and anywhere they felt was useful to them in their new lives.

The whole operation took three weeks of grueling, back-breaking labor. Mike was almost glad of the exertion. The task, no matter how morbid, made him think less about his loss and gave him a purpose, even if it was temporary. Mike only knew the names of a few of the dead, people he recognized as local shopkeepers, well-known characters like the local MP and a few of his students, including Mel Westmorland, causing Mike to recall the harrowing dream he'd had about her just before he saw his wife die. Instead of graves, they broke in to the Windermere Garden Center, their RazorCom alarms asleep, like all technology, and planted a tree for every person in the ground below. Altogether they buried 82 people in the field.

Mike regarded the upturned soil and the infant trees, his muscles burning. His ribs ached with the effort.

"We did it!" Matty said.

"Not quite, Matty. There's something else."

"The people in the houses?" Matty asked.

"One person. One house." Mike said and looked down at the ground, his spade resting against his leg.

"Okay, I get it. I see. Maybe that's something I should take care of."

"No," Mike replied. "This is something I need to do. I can't explain. I just…"

Matty put his hand on Mike's shoulder. "You don't need to say. I know what you mean."

Mike didn't waste any time. He didn't want his wife to be buried in a mass grave. She deserved her own special place. He knew a body was just a shell but he didn't want Matty, someone he admired, to see his wife in that state. Maybe in the future he would be able to tell Matty about his previous life, about all the good times. And when that time came he wanted Matty to picture his wife as she was, the beautiful, wonderful woman he fell in love with.

He walked the four miles back to the cottage and came across Susie and Liam's bodies. He still had a couple of hours of daylight left so he took care of his two former students, digging a deep hole a few meters from the side of the lake and burying them together in the dirt. He had saved an apple tree, which he planted in the soil where the students now lay, and looked out to the cottage for the first time since his world evaporated. In the light, it still held its quaint charm but he knew what lay waiting for him inside.

He made his way up the path to the cottage and stopped in front of the door, clenching his fists. Shaking his head, he walked away and picked up the spade he'd left lying at the foot of the path. He found the place he was looking for, under a large weeping willow tree where they had made love on the first night they had moved to Windermere. With no one around on the hazy, summer night they had sat outside until the early hours of the morning, laughing and cuddling until things had taken a more passionate turn under the stars. Mike stared at the spot for a few seconds and let the memories engulf him. Then he began to dig.

The mask stopped Mike from inhaling most of the rotten stench that came from his wife's body, but not all of it. Tears spilled down his cheeks and on to the woolen mask as he saw Charlotte's body, in the same misshapen bundle in which he had left it. Bruise-like discoloration was blotted around her legs and arms and they had a bloated look, as if she had been pumped full of water. Her face was drawn and pale, the skin hanging off her skull. Her hair had thinned and was falling out. Charlotte's lips, fingernails and toenails were dark blue.

Mike propped the door open and dragged his dead wife by the legs to the spot under the tree where she would rest for eternity. He resisted the urge to look back at her body as it dragged along the ground, but he could hear the scraping and a couple of times he worried that she had been caught on part of the fence or a rock. Once she was by the tree he pushed her in the hole. It seemed ungainly and unceremonious but what else could he do? He couldn't kiss her and lower her down as may have happened in a movie; her corpse was far too rotten for that, and her head rolled loosely on its broken neck. As she dropped into her grave, Mike winced at the sound of part of Charlotte's body snapping. An arm? A finger? He didn't want to know. He grabbed his spade and began to cover his wife with the soil under the weeping willow. He looked down with a lump in his throat as every spade full of soil covered his wife up gradually until she was visible no more.

Mike flattened the soil and took a knife out of his pocket, carving *Charlotte Pilkington 2006 – 2038* into the bark of the tree. He knelt in front of his wife's grave.

"I'll find out, Charlie. I'll find out who did this to us. And I'll fucking kill them. I'll fucking kill them for you." He bent down and kissed the soil above her, leaving a few granules of dirt on his lips and chin and an earthy taste in his mouth. "I love you, Charlie."

Part II

The New World
18 August 2054

Report by Professor Michael Pilkington PhD, MA, BSc, PGCE. Published 9th October 2047.

1. Introduction and background

In the early hours of 15 April 2038, several events took place that led to the death of the majority of the known population.

While it cannot be ascertained exactly what led to this disaster, a mass changing of behavior was evident in the majority of human beings. It is widely agreed that the behavior changes took place in the majority of sufferers shortly after midnight, leading to murder and ultimately, suicide of those same people. The combination of the high volume of the individuals who were affected by this and the killing of ones who weren't, led to the deaths of nearly every person in the known world.

This report aims to collate anecdotal evidence in an attempt to:

a) Determine the cause of the disaster.

b) Document the current "known world" and the effects of the tragedy on society.

In total, since April 2038 to the time of writing this report, 4,229 bodies have been buried in various mass graves across the town. Most of these people were found in their homes.

1. Method of Research

At time of writing there are eighteen survivors known, all living in "New Windermere", a place in Cumbria, in the North West of England. Eleven of these survivors are adults, with seven children. Only one of the children, Zara Pilkington, was alive before the disaster, but at only six weeks old she has no recollection of the events.

Interviews with all eleven adults were undertaken, with a mixture of qualitative and quantitative questions. Each interviewee was asked the same eight questions in order to produce the most consistent answers. They were interviewed alone to minimize the possibility of prejudice, bias or outside influence. All respondents were warned about the potentially upsetting nature of the questions. The interviewer, Mike Pilkington, was also asked the same questions by another resident, Matthew West.

The average age of the survivors (including Zara Pilkington) who were alive after the disaster was 40 (based on age on April 15 2038).

2. Answers to Questions

1. At what time did you first see that anything had changed?

Of the 11 people surveyed, 9 (82%) said midnight, or ten minutes after midnight. Two people said that they only noticed that something was different after this time – one at 3.30 a.m. and one approximately around 6 a.m.

2. Who did you first notice was affected by this change?

Just over half said their spouse or partner had been affected, with six providing that answer. Two people said their children had been affected while the final three said that passers-by showed signs of change.

3. What symptoms and behaviors did the affected changed people display?

Every single respondent was unanimous in their response to this question. Each one noticed the following symptoms and behaviors:

- Twitching of the entire body. This was mostly evident with the head twitching to one side.
- Drooling. The saliva was a white color with a thick con-

sistency.

- Bloodshot eyes and dilated pupils.
- Lack of speech. None of the respondents heard any of the affected people talk or communicate in any way.
- Violent intentions. All respondents stated that the affected individuals acted violently, looking to cause death to everyone nearby. This does not seem to exclude each other – there were several sightings of the affected trying to kill each other. The object of the murderous tendencies seemed to be indiscriminate by age, gender or any physical appearance. The targets for this behavior seemed to be based on proximity; the affected people tried to kill others who were in the closest location to them.

Although not unanimous, some respondents noted the following behaviors:

- Lack of recognition. The respondents who knew the affected people said that they didn't seem to recognize them in their altered state.
- Suicidal actions. Two respondents noticed that, after a period where there were no targets for their murderous activity, the affected turned on themselves and ended their own lives.

4. Did you notice anything strange before the incident?

Views differed here. Of the eleven respondents, seven did not notice anything strange.

Two respondents said that they saw suspicious people in the area in the week before the disaster. However, both were in different places at the time, one in Newcastle and one in Carlisle.

Finally, two people cited a video that was launched on the Razor network the day before the disaster took place. The video was reported to be disturbing and hypnotic and had received

2.1 billion views the last time any of the respondents checked. Anecdotally, several viewers of the video received a rush of adrenaline after watching it, although the two respondents who saw the video both had the opposite feeling, one of sudden depression. When reminded, six others recalled seeing the video, although they were unsure about how it could be linked to the events.

5. How many people did you see in the changed state?

The average number seen was six. The highest was eighteen while the lowest was two. In total, there were sixty-six affected people seen.

6. How did you personally survive the disaster? Did you have to injure anybody?

The below are a collection of comments from all respondents (As Matty and Trish West were together, their account has been merged into one):

- I killed my husband with a knife and then hid in my bathroom for two weeks.
- I didn't kill anyone. I heard a banging on my front door and the person came at me when I opened it. But I got away, locked the door and then no one came in. I stayed in my house for six days.
- I killed two people including my wife. I then hid in a pub basement. I stayed in there with my daughter for eight weeks.
- I killed eight people, all with a shotgun out of my window. I stayed in my house for eight days.
- I killed no one but hid in my university bedroom with the door locked. I stayed there for two days.
- I killed six people. Two with a knife and then four with a brick. I ran home and locked myself in for six days.

- I killed two with a plank of wood and injured a few more. I then ran four down with my motorhome. I just drove and then stayed in the motorhome for three days until I was sure I was okay to leave.
- I didn't kill anyone but I held five of them off with a table that I picked up in the café I was in. Then I ran into the café's kitchen. I locked myself in for four weeks.
- I was walking my dog in the middle of the night and it kept them away, killing one of them by biting their throat. From there I went back home and shut myself in for three months until all my food and water ran out.
- I had to kill my three sons and my wife. I did it with an antique clock, by smashing it across their heads, trying to get them off me. I ran to my brother's house and had to kill him as well. He came at me with a knife and I had to turn it on him. Then I stayed in his garage for three months.

7. When was the last time you saw an affected person alive?

Out of the eleven respondents, eight people only saw the affected people on 15 April, 2038, with the last sighting that day being sometime after eight o'clock.

Two people saw affected people on April 16 although they displayed suicidal behavior at that point.

One person saw someone affected on April 18, but they were injured and lying prone on a road.

8. In your opinion, what caused the disaster?

Opinions were mixed about this, but each person offered some speculation:

- Five people stated that it was some form of chemical weapon, used by terrorists to destroy the country (several variations of this were mentioned).
- Two people said it was spread via RazorVision, with some

clues hidden in the video that was published.

- Three people thought it was a disease spread by immigrants to the country.
- One person felt it was punishment from God for the sins of the modern age – sex, technology and general modern living.

3. Conclusion

There are few conclusions we can draw from this research into the events of April 15, 2038.

However, we can draw these assumptions based on the testimony of the survivors:

- The first known incident occurred just after midnight. The last affected person was seen two days later although mostly it seemed affected people were around for less than one day.
- The affected people twitched, drooled, had bloodshot eyes and dilated pupils and had murderous, violent tendencies, before becoming suicidal. They no longer recognized people they had previously known.
- Every survivor either had to kill an affected person or fight them off somehow. Some had to kill members of their own family.
- The cause of the disaster is unknown, although common belief is that it was an illness, either manmade as an act of terrorism or some virus spread accidentally from an unknown source.

4. Recommendations

Survivors need to remain vigilant although it is unlikely any affected people will return. However, due to the trauma of the disaster, the community formed by survivors needs to be supportive, close-knit and self-sufficient.

The survivors should look to test the bodies of the affected to determine the possible cause of any virus. Currently, at the time of writing, there is no expertise amongst the survivors or the necessary equipment to carry out this research.

Reconnaissance activity should take place to find other survivors in the local area. Some kind of marker should be placed to attract the attention of anyone in the vicinity, including airplanes – although nothing has been spotted in the sky, at the time of writing, since the disaster. Establishing the community should be the highest priority. Food production, healthcare and education should come before everything else.

New Windermere Survivors Board.
Terms of Reference.
Drafted by Matthew West.
Version 4. Originally drafted May 2040.

1. New Windermere Survivors Party

The "New Windermere Survivors Party" was officially formed on 3 May 2040.

The party renamed the old "Bowness-on-Windermere" town as "New Windermere" to reflect the changes in the known world since the events of 15 April 2038.

The New Windermere Founders are the eleven adults who came together to form a community in an attempt to rebuild civilized life following the disaster in 2038.

2. New Windermere Residents

The New Windermere residents are listed below. Ages are correct as of May 2040.

Adults

Matthew Robert West
Age: 58
Place of Birth: Leeds.
Previous Occupation: Plumber, Business Owner

Patricia Colleen West
Age: 56
Place of Birth: Huddersfield.
Previous Occupation: Hairdresser

Michael James Pilkington
Age: 34
Place of Birth: London
Previous Occupation: University Lecturer

Robert Bowskill
Age: 24
Place of Birth: Penrith
Previous Occupation: Builder

John Jameson
Age: 28
Place of Birth: Morecambe
Previous Occupation: Salesman

Nancy Longstaff
Age: 23
Place of Birth: Carlisle
Previous Occupation: Primary School Teacher

Cassie Cuthbert
Age: 31
Place of Birth: Sunderland
Previous Occupation: Personal Trainer

Andy Pratt
Age: 20
Place of Birth: Southampton
Previous Occupation: Media Student

Iain Thomas
Age: 28
Place of Birth: Leicester
Previous Occupation: Caretaker

Samir Parshad
Age: 37
Place of birth: Leeds
Previous Occupation: Taxi driver

Penny Alabaster
Age: 81
Place of Birth: Scarborough
Previous Occupation: Retired Tax Officer

Children

Zara Alice Pilkington
Age: 2
Born 28 February 2038
Parent: Michael Pilkington

James Charles Jameson
Age: 2 months
Born: 19 February 2039
Parents: John Jameson and Cassie Cuthbert

Animals

"Roxy", Staffordshire Bull Terrier age – 2.
Toby, Mongrel age – 4.
39 sheep.
42 cows. Two bulls.
Six horses.
14 chickens.
8 goats.
7 domestic cats.
5 pigs.

3. Village roles

Mayor: Matthew West
Head of Education: Michael Pilkington
Head of Healthcare: Cassie Cuthbert
Head of Food Production: Patricia West
Head of Maintenance: Robert Bowskill
Head of Reconnaissance and Village Development: John Jameson

Please note that all village members over the age of nine are required to work on farm and food production tasks, working to a regular rota.

4. Rules and Regulations

The following actions are prohibited and are punishable:

- Violence towards other village members and animals
- Destruction of food or property
- Theft from others
- Skipping work duty without prior authorization or reasonable cause

5. Punishments for Rule Breaking

Punishments for rule breaches will be decided by the Founders. They include but are not limited to:

- Detention – either in groups or isolation.
- Hard labor on the farm.
- Jail – locked up for an appropriate amount of time.
- Banished from the village.

6. New Members

Any newcomers can be welcomed to the village, but this is subject to a vote amongst the Founding Committee.

7. Amendments

The following amendments have been made:

- Birth of new child – **Lorraine Jameson** (parents John Jameson and Cassie Cuthbert), 25 December 2039
- Birth of new child – **Olivia Jameson** (parents John Jameson and Cassie Cuthbert), 19 November 2040
- Birth of new child – **Louie Jameson** (parents John Jameson and Cassie Cuthbert), 19 November 2040
- Birth of new child – **Bobby Bowskill** (parents Robbie Bowskill and Nancy Longstaff), 31 December 2044
- Birth of new child – **Peter Bowskill** (parents Robbie Bowskill and Nancy Longstaff), 19 June 2050
- Birth of dogs – **Jess, Sammie and Silver** – 14 December, 2045
- Birth of dog – **Dave** – 23 April, 2050

1

Zara Pilkington dove into Lake Windermere head first, the cool water exhilarating her from head to toe. There was no better way to start the day. She used a bar of soap to wash her armpits, her breasts, her stomach, between her legs and her feet.

She swam out further from the shore and looked across to the far side of the lake. The red glow from the rising sun glimmered across the silky water. The morning swim had become a routine for Zara over the last two years, something that boosted her energy. Her days were filled with mental and physical work, both equally draining. As a teaching assistant to her father in the New Windermere School she needed to keep her wits, both to control the children and to keep up with her father's demanding academic program. As a member of the community, she also had to do her bit on the farm, digging crops and tending the animals.

Zara looked around, treading water to stay afloat, her eyes focused on the land. There wasn't a soul around. It was bliss. She wondered why nobody else came and appreciated the beauty of the lake at this time of the morning. It was always her favorite moment of the day, a time when she really felt alive.

She swam back and pulled herself up to the shore. Her stomach muscles rippled with the exertion. Pulling her clothes back on, she started back for the village.

As she always did each morning, another part of her daily ritual, Zara stopped by the weeping willow and paid her respects. She knew her mother had died during the terrible events that had changed the world. Zara's heart was always heavy with the loss of her mother and it was a void that had never been filled. She had no recollection of the first few weeks of her life and she was conflicted about this. If she did recall it, she would have a memory of her mother to cling on to. Something to remember, to grieve. But she would also have remembered something so dark, so horrible, that her father has only spoken about it to her once. She had read his report and she had spoken to some others about it. Uncle Matty, who was more like a grandfather than an uncle, had been more forthcoming with details. But both men had a haunted, distant look whenever the subject arose.

Zara reached out and touched the tree in front of her. To her, this tree *was* her mother. She had never seen any image of her. The elders in the village had told her about the Time Before. Moving images beamed on walls and inside special glasses. Things inside houses that spoke your name and knew things about you before you knew them yourself. It sounded fantastical, like something out of a dream.

The library at the school had been filled with books that her dad had found at one of the local houses, and there were science fiction novels from half a century ago that she loved. The irony wasn't lost on Zara. The books that spoke of the future were ones that reminded her of stories of the past. It was enough to make her head hurt. There was something else that confused her about the past. Was it a better time? Most people had died when things changed. Zara knew that could never be a good thing. But she'd heard some people say that life had never been as precious as it was now. She felt loved and she loved others. The thought of the world of "tech", as the elders called it, scared and overwhelmed her. She could stomach it in a novel but could she live it? She wasn't sure. Maybe she was just biased; this was her time and she was enjoying it. Zara Pilkington wasn't going to let anyone tell her that things were better in the old days.

She looked up at the sun and realized she was running late. She leaned forward and kissed the tree, whispering, "Love you, Mum," before heading back to the village.

2

When Zara returned to the village, the shift she had expected to take on at the farm had been cancelled. She walked through the metal gates that Bow had erected at the entrance to the community to see her father standing on the main path, looking solemnly and seriously towards her.

He looked disheveled. Zara guessed he hadn't slept. He had been with Uncle Matty and Auntie Trish at the bedside of Penny all night. She had not been well at all of late. At ninety-five years old, she was the oldest person in New Windermere. And that made her the oldest person Zara had ever met, by a long, long way.

No one was sure what was wrong with Nana Penny. Maybe it was old age, maybe it was cancer. Three months ago, she couldn't get out of bed and her breathing had become more and more difficult as time passed. The last time Zara had been to see her, Nana Penny's chest rattled, reminding Zara of the sound the Lake made as it displaced the loose pebbles on the shoreline. Everyone in the village knew she wasn't going to last long, but at the same time they hoped she would make a miraculous recovery.

They all knew the story about Nana Penny. She had been in a café at midnight when the affected turned. Suffering from insomnia, she had embarked on a late-night walk across town and ordered a hot milk to help her sleep. She was seventy-nine years old but when the attackers came, she picked up a table and thrust it towards them. The table was a solid oak one; it was one of those fancy coffee shops that sold macchiato espressos. A 79-year-old woman, not solid or unnaturally strong by any means, had no right to be able to pick up that oak table. She not only lifted it over her head, but she brought it down with some force against the affected people who were surrounding her.

They say that human beings are capable of immense, inhuman strength in times of dire need. Nana Penny must have had a surge of this power as she lifted it back over her head and fought them off again, before running into the café kitchen, where she stayed and survived by eating biscuits and drinking milk and coffee for a whole month.

She had wandered all over Windermere after she built up enough courage to walk out of the café, and had come across the village by accident. Unable to live with the idea of this empty post-apocalyptic world, she decided to end her life by filling her pockets with rocks and plunging into Lake Bow. Mike, Zara's dad, heard the splash as the old woman landed in the water and began to sink. He jumped in and hauled her back to the shore. Nana Penny had been fond of Mike ever since, calling him her "guardian angel" and Mike was equally fond of Nana Penny.

Everyone had respect for Penny Alabaster, but none more than Zara. She was in awe of her and would listen with her mouth gaping at the stories of old. Penny was quite the raconteur and would often tell tales of 1980s romance, stories of discotheques, video games and shoulder pads. The other adults used to laugh at her stories, saying that it sounded primitive, but Zara loved them, picturing herself in the same clothes, dancing to the same music, which Nana Penny sang to her. She was happy that she could speak to someone whose time went back so far, to a time that she didn't understand but could picture through the eyes of this wonderful woman. Penny was old but not haggard; glamorous in a timeless way. Her hands, although wrinkled and papery with several liver spots, still hinted at delicateness and artistry. Her features were well-defined and handsome in an English Rose way.

Nana Penny was the one she always talked to if she had any worries, or any questions about the Time Before. Of course, she could talk to her father, Uncle Matty and Auntie Trish, but there was something about Nana Penny that she really connected with. Once, aged twelve and in a pre-teenage panic about her future after reading a book about a "happily ever after" marriage between a prince and a princess, Zara confided in Nana Penny that she feared she would never get married. The next eldest adult male was 31 while the next youngest was 10, only two years younger than her, but still much younger a child in comparison to the more mature Zara.

"Married? Pah! You'll have your pick," she replied. "You are the closest thing to a princess this place has got, my little angel. It shouldn't be you worrying about who's going to marry you, young girl. It should be the lads worrying that you'll not want to take them to the dance!"

This made Zara giggle until her sides hurt. The idea of going to a "dance" with a boy sounded frankly ridiculous. She had only heard of dancing from Nana Penny, it wasn't something that she had experienced herself. It only existed in her imagination, fueled by Nana Penny's stories of the 1980s discotheques and all the young men who wanted to buy her a drink and drag her onto the dance floor. If Zara had needed to dance with a boy she wouldn't know what to do. After some consideration, she admitted these fears to Penny. "Don't be daft, lass," Penny had replied. They spent the next four hours dancing to Penny's vocal versions of old dance songs that made Zara scream with laughter, especially when Penny made the musical sounds that accompanied the sparse lyrics.

Zara idolized Penny. She was a surrogate grandmother, a figure of respect, and, most importantly, a good friend she could giggle with and learn from. She was strong, funny and wise. Zara was hit hard when Penny first fell ill. The hope she would get better was something to cling on to, but deep down Zara knew that it was an unrealistic wish. Zara was no doctor, hell, she had never met a doctor as far as she could remember and there certainly weren't any in their ranks in New Windermere. But someone who couldn't breathe in and out without sounding like a handful of stones rattling together was always going to struggle to make a full recovery.

So, as she approached her father, with his solemn look in his eyes, Zara knew that the news would be bad. Mike put his arm around his daughter as she came to meet him on the path to the village. Zara started to cry. Mike reached over and wiped his daughter's eyes with a tissue. He had come prepared.

"You'd better come and say goodbye. She doesn't have long."

Zara didn't answer, but walked with her father towards Nana Penny's death bed.

3

Penny Alabaster's living quarters were on the ground floor of the lakeside student accommodation block which now housed all the survivors. The rooms were simple and compact with a bed, a desk and an ensuite toilet in each room. The large wooden doors had students' initials thinly scratched on, a faint echo of the Time Before. Mike and Zara walked through the door to see Robbie "Bow" Bowskill sitting beside Penny's bed. Penny was lying on her back, her chest heaving with long intermissions in-between.

On hearing Mike and Zara approach, Bow stood up and nodded, his eyes tired and bloodshot. A solitary tear remained on his cheek. Zara wiped it away with her hand tenderly and hugged him.

"Oh, Uncle Bow," she said. No other words seemed to fit the occasion. Bow understood, hugging her in return, fresh tears flowing down his face, wetting his thick beard. Zara felt his large arms wrap around her. Bow's frame was huge, earned from pure hard work building, lifting, carrying, rather than any deliberate exercise. His size was matched by his personality, one of the more dominant members of the community.

They turned and faced Penny. The smell of death hung in the air. Zara sat on the stool next to her bed. Penny's skin was deep with wrinkles, saggy and loose. It was a grey color, and she had a large, bleeding sore on her forehead. Her hair was thin in large patches, showing her leathery scalp.

Through her rattling, tinny breath, Penny began to speak.

"Zara. You. You are. The one." Penny grabbed Zara's wrist with a sudden jolt of energy. "The one that made. Made me the happ—" her speech was cut off by her own dry, hacking cough which lasted several seconds. "The one that made me happiest. My granddaughter. This has been the best. The best part of my long, old life. Don't change. Don't go back. You will want to but don't go. Stop them—"

Penny was incapacitated with coughing, she sat upwards in bed to spit out the last of her coughs and lay on her back. Zara looked into her ancient blue eyes. They filled with water and her pupils rolled upwards before returning to the center. Penny had breathed her last rattling breath. Her Nana was dead.

Mike and Zara walked out of Penny's living quarters and sat on the bench looking over the lake. Zara focused silently on the distant mountains. Nana Penny had been family. She may not have been bonded by blood but they had shared so many special times together. How they had danced and laughed. Penny would not be around to tell her stories but they would live on. Part of Nana Penny would always be alive as long as Zara was around.

Zara's concentration was broken by the voice of her father. "She meant a lot to you, I know. She meant a lot to all of us. But if I could go like that, in my own bed at the age of ninety-five, I think I'd be happy. She had a good life."

"I know." Zara sighed. "It's just... I didn't want her to go, Dad. I didn't want to lose her." She buried her face against Mike's shoulder and wept.

"You know, you might not want to hear this, but part of me is feeling kind of happy right now. Thinking of Penny makes me smile. That day I dove into the water I really didn't know who or what she was. Trying to take her own life, that was a trait of... well, you know."

Zara nodded. Although she had no memory of ever seeing a twitcher, she knew the details. She had read her father's academic report. She felt it was important to know where they came from, their history.

"So, when I dragged her to shore I didn't know if she'd attack me, if she'd be angry that I stopped her, or what. She hadn't wanted to live in an empty world so seeing me had made her so happy. She later told me that it was the single happiest moment in her life. And you know what her life was like. All those stories of the 80s in London."

Zara smiled. She sure did. She'd been there herself, walked in Penny's Prada shoes, kissed the slick city traders and danced to New Romantic music, all through Penny's stories.

"And in return I told her that it was the second most important thing I'd ever done. She went on to love you. She loved all of us. After seeing so much death, so much horror in that night in '38, saving her was wonderful. And seeing her pass away, happy and peaceful, back there. Well, it's made me happy to see someone go out like that. She could be the first person to die peacefully since that night, you know that? The first person in the world, for all we know."

"What was the most important thing you did? If saving Nana was the second," Zara asked.

"Saving you that night. I know I've not spoken much about this before, but something just clicked inside me. Some primal, instinctive purpose washed over me to keep you safe at any cost. It even cost me three broken ribs, which still hurt now in bad weather," he said, drawing a smile from his daughter. "I really can't tell you how awful it was. I spent the first few years of your life worrying that you would be damaged in some way by it. I'm pleased you're not. It was the worst night of my life. The worst night in the history of the human race, I've no doubt. And I don't know why we're still here, our little family, in New Windermere, why we weren't affected in the way others were. I don't hold out much hope I'll find out now, either, or what the hell caused it. Not after sixteen years. But when I look at you everything just makes sense. And Penny thought the same. Light from the darkness, that's what she used to call you."

Using the past tense made Mike feel sad and he sensed the same in Zara's eyes, which began to fill with tears once more. "You know, she used to thank me for saving you. For saving my own daughter! If someone else had said it, I'd have thought it was patronizing. But from her – she meant it. You were my gift to her and she loved you more than she'd ever loved anyone, even in her long life."

Zara smiled. "Yeah, she told me that the last few years had been the best of her life." She looked down at her hands, which were quivering. "I loved her so much, Dad."

"Of course you did. She was family. We're all family. Do you know what your mum and me used to call us when you'd been born? *The Team*. We were in it together, everything was a joint effort. We used to support each other and we loved each other so much." Mike tried to talk about Charlotte as much as he could. His mind tried to put a wall up against the memory of her twitching and drooling, with her hands around his throat and the pillow on baby Zara's face. He wasn't just talking about her to ensure Zara built up a picture of the real Charlotte, he was doing it to reinforce his own memories of his wife. "That's what it feels like here. We're a big team, all eighteen of us in New Windermere. And it's all built on love."

Zara laughed at this. "You're so cheesy, Dad." But she gripped his hand in empathy and understanding.

"You're so much like her," Mike continued. "Your big brown eyes are just the same. Every time I look at you it helps me remember her. You would have loved her, Zara. You would have loved her so much." Emotion engulfed him and this time it was his turn to cry into his daughter's shoulder. "Before it all happened, she had a go at me for going to the pub after work when she was at home looking after you. I always think back to that. Thank God we made up before... you know."

Zara pushed her dad playfully. "Dad! You went to the pub! That's so bad! No wonder Mum was angry with you."

Mike remembered that there were some hazy circumstances linked to the terrible night but his brain failed to connect any dots and he had no inclination to force it. "I told you... you're just like her. Like my own little carbon copy. I love you very much, Zara. Fathering you is the best thing I ever did and the best thing I ever will do. And that's saying something, for a regular superhero like me."

Zara punched him playfully again. She had loved the superhero comic books when she was younger and she had been convinced that her dad had powers similar to Superman, something he loved to embellish.

"I love you, too, Dad. Thanks for making me feel better about Nana Penny."

He took her hand and gazed to the mountainous horizon.

"Dad?" Zara asked. Mike turned to face his daughter. "Before she died, Nana Penny said something strange to me.

"What was that?"

"She told me not to go back. She said that I'd want to but not to go and to stop them. What did she mean by that, do you think? Go back where? I've only ever been here."

Mike's eyes went away from his daughter and focused back towards the mountains. The tops of the peaks were invisible, shrouded by the cold, grey clouds hundreds of meters in the sky.

"I think I know," he said.

4

Penny Alabaster's funeral was held on the same day as her death. It was the first time a member of the New Windermere community had passed away, so it took a few discussions between the founders regarding the place and format of her burial. Mike had been prepared. Having buried his own wife under a weeping willow, he felt that it gave his wife a presence even in death – it could be admired, hugged, kissed and marked with the name of the person it was commemorating. It seemed apt for Nana Penny to be remembered in a similar way.

They dug a hole underneath a large oak tree. It was the obvious choice, a place where Penny used to sit and sketch pictures of Lake Windermere. Her frail body was wrapped in her favorite blanket, a faded tartan one that she used to wrap over her shoulders in cold weather. Her body was lowered into the hole and her name, *"Nana" Penny Alabaster* was carved into the large trunk of the great oak along with *1959 - 2054*.

Bow and Johnny filled the hole with soil. The memory of burying his own wife sixteen years ago forced Mike to look away as the soil made Nana Penny's body slowly disappear under the brown earth. When the hole was filled and the earth raked, the seventeen remaining residents of New Windermere held hands in a semicircle around the trunk. As Mayor, Matty said a few words.

"We all loved Penny. She was the beating heart of our community. She was a friend, a grandmother and a mother to many. She was the person to go to if you had a problem or needed advice. She loved to draw. I think we've all got a couple of Nana P originals in our quarters." The group murmured agreement. "She was our world and always will be. She was this community's rock. And this oak tree will stand in her memory. We will come and visit you here, Penny Alabaster, and remember your wonderful life as it was – brilliant and full of love."

The last line drew thick gasps of tears from several of the gathered community. The children were the worst affected. They had grown up with their Nana Penny and now she had been taken away forever. In this new world that had been born out of murder, death and chaos, this was the first time they had experienced life passing on.

The only sound was muffled cries and sniffling grief. Zara, without planning, broke out into song, singing *Let it Be*. It was Nana's favorite, one she had sung to Zara on a night-time to get her to sleep. It was by a band called the Beatles, who Nana Penny said had been the best and biggest music group in the world and they were just from a few miles down the road, in Liverpool. Zara's voice was soft and melodic and pierced the crisp afternoon air like a spear through thin ice.

Everyone joined in to sing the chorus. It felt magical. Nana Penny must have sung this beautiful song to all of them. It felt so right. As Zara continued to sing, tears dripped from her eyes. They were tears of sadness and loss but also of happiness. Nana Penny was loved by all seventeen members of their wonderful family and she was being remembered in a way that she would have loved. It was as if the song had been written about this wonderful woman whose body lay before them, under the great oak on the edge of the lake.

The group broke hands at the end of the song and one-by-one took turns to kiss the tree. Zara was last. She put her arms around the wide trunk and pressed her face into the bark.

"I love you, Nana. Whatever you meant, I'll do it for you. I'll never go back. For you, Nana." She turned to face the tree and kissed it.

Bow, always at the forefront of any revelry, organized the wake at the village hall. The hall had been a gym in the Time Before. The large, open space that had been used for people to jump, dance and run on the spot was now used for large gatherings for the New Windermere survivors.

They had a dinner of lamb and fresh vegetables from the allotment. The allotment was Trish West's pride and joy. And the result was delicious. Mashed potato, zucchini, sprouts, carrots and turnip. Of course, the children weren't always keen but they saw the importance of eating well.

Matty broke out the whisky. They still had over thirty bottles left. He had carefully rationed the good stuff over the years after one of Johnny's reconnaissance missions had resulted in a raid on a huge supermarket thirteen years ago. They had cleared it out over the years, although several tins and bottles remained in the storehouse that Bow had built in New Windermere.

Despite the loss of one of their beloved, the atmosphere at the wake was upbeat. It was a mood of celebration rather than grief. Nana Penny had lived a long life that was full of joy. Who could feel sad about that?

Johnny Jameson came and sat next to Zara. Johnny, although not drunk, looked like he was feeling some effects of the whisky. Johnny was tough, like Bow, his body was covered with hunks of muscle, although Johnny carried more weight. Strangely, the most noticeable part of Johnny's appearance were his hands. They were huge, like something that should have belonged to a mountain gorilla rather than a human being. Like everyone in the village, Johnny was kind and gentle, but Zara felt that if he wanted to, he could be pretty tough.

"How you doing, honey?" he asked. He always called her honey, and she liked it. Johnny was the adventurer of the community. He always wanted to push further, to find out more about the village's surroundings. While some were happy to stay where they were, Johnny was always planning the next trip. And he had delivered. Zara didn't know where their community would be without him, he had brought back so many vital things on his trips out of the village including food, building materials, books, clothes, cooking equipment, knives and tools. Zara wanted to see what he saw. He was always gone for a few days, with his camping equipment on his back and his group following behind him. There were usually three of them: Johnny, Andy and Iain, along with the dog, Dave. Johnny's son, Jimmy, would eventually be trained and primed in his father's reconnaissance activity but at fourteen, the founders felt he was too young to go. Sometimes they were gone for as long as five days and the trips were not without danger. Once they had to fight off a pack of wild dogs, Andy had a bite on his hand that needed treating and Dave, the dog, suffered scratches on his face. Another time, Iain had fallen down a large bank near the lower slopes of Scafell Pike. He had broken his foot, an injury which made them abort the trip and carry him home. It had taken over six months to heal. This danger, along with the heaped corpses in more populated areas, meant that no one had ventured further than the edges of the Cumbrian county borders since the world turned upside down. Maybe other communities of survivors would have been more adventurous, seeking out further places, but the founders always made it clear that the New Windermere community was the highest priority and with such a small population, they couldn't afford to take any risks.

"We're heading out in two days," he told her. He knew how much Zara liked to hear his adventure stories and his plans for the next trip. "There's a patch of land we've not been to yet, but it's a good 50 miles. We'll go on bikes."

Ah, the bikes, thought Zara. It was a great memory for the community. In the Time Before, all the bikes had been fitted with Razor technology. But all this technology had switched off for good in this new time, 'the Time After', as some of the adults called it, so no bikes could be used, and all the early reconnaissance trips had been made on foot. But one day, just under a year ago, the village awoke to whooping and yelling early in the morning. Johnny, Iain and Andy had returned from their trip, each on an old-style push bike. Even in the pre-2038 technologically-driven world, some people had enjoyed the beauty of the old mechanical vehicles. The bikes were rusty and missing some parts, but Bow soon worked his magic on them and even built a trailer for each bike to tow. Each person in the village had a go on them, the smallest children sitting up front on the adults' knees. Zara had been brave enough to try it herself and, after a few falls, she found she was a natural. It had been a wonderful day, full of fun and laughter. Matty had broken out the whisky that night, too. The bikes meant they could travel further and it reaped rewards, allowing them to explore more places. They had gathered many items from new towns and villages, but with every new place the group visited, they had to see more dead bodies. The bigger the place, the greater the number of corpses littering the streets. Sixteen years after the residents had met their violent deaths, they were little more than skeletons. The number of bodies and scattered bones in Carlisle had been particularly awful. Although it was a veritable goldmine for tools, tins of food and materials, it contained so much death that it hung over the place like a rotten, evil cloud. It was one of the reasons most people chose to stay in the serene, nature-rich community by the lake.

"The place is called Whitehaven. Lovely little place by the sea. Might do a bit of fishing when we're out there. It'll be a three-day round trip, maybe two if we make good time. Should be a fair bit of salmon in those waters and a few prawns. Bring back summat for us to cook. I was thinking of getting some sports stuff for the school, too. Your old dad's been on at me for a while."

"Yeah, I'd love that. He said he wanted to show me how to play football."

Johnny ruffled her hair. "You'd be some player, too! You're a tough little thing. I bet you'd take no prisoners on the pitch."

Zara beamed. Johnny always made her feel tough and strong. It was something he always commented on. And she was. Having worked on the farm since she was nine years old, she had developed strong arms and a lean torso. Her diet of meat, vegetables and milk had helped her grow into a healthy, athletic young woman. This wasn't praise that Johnny, widely regarded as the toughest man in the village, dished out to anyone. Even his entrance into the new world was tough and uncompromising. His entire family had been affected and he had to kill them all.

"Iain's pulled out of this trip. He's sticking around here to help Bow with finishing the flag." The flag was Matty's idea. It was to be hoisted thirty feet in the air above the school building. Bow had spent two months on it and it was nearly complete. The flag would read STILL ALIVE. Matty wanted it to attract any other survivors, or if any airplanes flew overhead. It would probably be futile. They hadn't seen a new survivor for sixteen years.

"I've had a chat with Matty and your dad. I'd like you to come with us. You'll miss Memorial Day but we can pay our respects out on the road."

Zara's eyes widened. She looked at Johnny, disbelievingly. "My dad said yes?" she asked, shocked.

"Yep. Zara, you're one of the toughest buggers in this whole village. And you ride that bike better than anyone. I'm not asking you out of sympathy and I'm not just asking you to train you up. I'm asking you because you're the best choice and you're ready."

"Aw, thanks, Uncle Johnny." She hugged him. "You don't know how much that means to me. Especially today."

"I think I do, honey. But remember one thing. I'm in charge. You do what I say. I made your dad a promise that I'd bring you back here in one piece and it's a promise I intend to keep." He ruffled her hair again.

"Yes, sir," she said with a serious tone. "I promise I won't let you down."

Johnny stood. "You'd better not. Nice singing voice, by the way. I've not cried since the day I buried my family back in '38. But you had me blubbing like a baby. Not ashamed to admit it either. She was a good woman. The best."

5

They set off two days later at sunrise. Zara packed her rucksack with the essentials. Raw carrots, cold lamb sandwiches and a first aid kit. She had a rolled-up mat and a sleeping bag strapped to her back. Bow gave her bike a comprehensive service and MOT, pumping up the tires and ensuring she had enough spare inner tubes, puncture repair kits and even a spare seat. Despite her strong protests, Mike strapped a fiberglass helmet to her head.

"Stay safe, darling. Don't make me regret saying yes to this. I went through too much to see you break any bones tumbling off this rusty old thing."

"Of course, Dad. Thanks for saying yes. You know how much this means."

"I do, but please be careful. Do whatever Johnny tells you."

"Of course, Dad. I love you." They embraced. "Always will."

"Just try to… expect the worst and maybe it won't seem as bad."

Zara knew what he meant. She had heard the stories about the dead. Dusty skeletons, still with clothing and jewelry intact. Bones sprawled across streets and in buildings, turning entire towns into charnel houses.

"I know, Dad. I'm ready for this."

"I'm proud of you," he said, his voice breaking with oncoming tears. "I did a good job with you."

"You're the best, Dad. I'll see you in three days. Hope Memorial Day goes well."

He kissed her in his exaggerated, cartoonish way that so often broke any tension, a remnant of the secret language that began when his wife was still alive. Zara grinned and mounted her bike.

The whole village had risen early to see them off, as they

always did. Johnny's reconnaissance trips were a big event. The villagers would spend the entire duration of their absence discussing what they might bring back with them: toys, tools, new clothes, new food. But mainly it was the stories that captivated and excited them – tales of adventure, stories of gruesome encounters with dead bodies and wild animals.

Johnny's four children were the most excitable. They all crowded round their hero as he mounted his bike. He ruffled their hair, one by one. That was Johnny's trademark display of affection, he was too manly for hugs and kisses but all the same, everyone knew what the hair ruffle meant. Cassie, Johnny's wife, hugged him and kissed him on the cheek. With all the losses they had suffered in the past, every second he was away from the village filled Cassie with worries and fears. He was too important to lose. Dave the dog jumped and barked. When the push bikes had been discovered, Dave had been relegated to the sidelines. There was no room for a dog who couldn't ride a bike, despite how much Johnny missed the hound's company.

Andy mounted his bike. He was a quiet soul. A media student at Windermere University, he was the only survivor that Mike Pilkington knew before that terrible night in 2038. Andy hadn't killed any twitchers that night, but he had shut himself in his university dorm room, hiding under the covers while his roommates pounded rhythmically and slowly on the door. Mike had come across him while he and Matty were clearing out the university campus, looking for bodies to move into the mass graves. They had hugged wordlessly and Andy had wept for hours. Andy had volunteered for the reconnaissance trips as he couldn't find a role within the village. He had no real life skills to apply to the new world. He wasn't strong, he couldn't cook and he knew nothing about farming. He helped Mike in the classroom after the school was established but stepped aside for Zara to help her father when she turned fourteen. Never one with confidence and self-esteem, even his experience of the terrible night felt cowardly compared to the heroics of others. He loved the community and everyone made him feel like a part of it, but he often felt inferior. Bow and Johnny were the big heroes, the strong characters of the village. Mike was the scholar, Matty was the leader. The two women that were around his age had already been snapped up, the others too young for him to have a relationship with, even in the future. Part of Andy's sadness came from the realization he would be alone for the rest of his life. Not alone really, he had a brilliant community and some amazing friends who he would die for. But he felt that he would always be half a person. An unfulfilled future stretched out in front of him like a long, dark path. The trips gave him some time away from the village and made him feel useful.

The bikes had been Andy's find, and when he saw how much joy they had given the whole village, he had beamed all day. It had been the best night of his life. Johnny had recognized this and given him his trademark hair-ruffle. "You did good, kid," he had told him. At 34, Andy was hardly a kid, but his heart had grown with pride at praise from one of the best men he'd ever known.

* * *

They waved Johnny, Andy and Zara out of the gates and saw them cycle westwards alongside the lake until they became three tiny specks and then disappeared over a distant hill. Matty approached Mike. He was always there when Mike needed some comfort.

"She'll be fine, Mike," said Matty. "You raised a tough 'un there, pal."

"I know, Matty. It's what she wanted. I just... you know."

"I know. You've protected her as much as you can. But you've got to let her go. And if she's gonna be safe under anyone's wing, it's gonna be our Johnny."

Mike nodded in agreement and headed to the school, where his class of seven children would be waiting for the first lesson of the day.

6

The classroom had been constructed by Bow, Mike and Samir in the summer of 2041, with a regular supply of materials from Johnny's reconnaissance trips. They had found a DIY superstore in Kendal and spent three months carrying materials backwards and forwards, using a handmade cart, pulled by horse. Mike loved it. He had stood in the finished classroom all day on its completion, admiring his new place of work. As head of education in New Windermere, this was his domain. He had been instrumental in the success of Windermere University and this was his chance to start again. This was his chance to make his mark on the new world. Each person needed a project to feel useful. Bow managed to have several on the go at once, it seemed, but all were concentrated on fixing, building and creating. Johnny was New Windermere's Francis Drake, travelling to distant lands to bring back strange and mysterious bounties that would enrich the lives of the community. Trish had her vegetables and the responsibility of feeding the village, a task that she excelled at. With Matty, she oversaw the animals and farming. Matty himself had the whole community to oversee. He was in charge, really, but he was too laid back to be 'the boss'. At seventy-two years of age, although still physically fit, he was a bit long in the tooth to be throwing his weight into manual tasks. He had a wise old head on his shoulders and it was put to good use in his role as Mayor. Cassie's project was healthcare. It was the big gap in the community. There were no healthcare professionals in their ranks. Even a nursing student or biologist would have been useful. Cassie had been a personal trainer in the Time Before so she took on the role of head of healthcare as she was the most qualified. Her expertise was based around fitness and nutrition, but she had little knowledge of illnesses, injuries or medicine. In the Time Before, Razor technology diagnosed all ailments, so there was a real dearth of medical knowledge even before 2038. Although they still trained doctors and nurses in the traditional way, to help operate and program machinery, their numbers had shrunk. In the new world, it was a skill that was needed more than anything.

Johnny had raided a local pharmacy so they had a healthy supply of pills and potions. As would be expected for the spouse of Johnny Jameson, Cassie was a strong woman. Even at forty-five years old she had rippling muscles in her arms thanks to a daily exercise routine in the gym. She kept herself in shape in the Time After, as she had in the Time Before. She had even continued part of her old role by taking physical education sessions for the kids as part of Mike's education program. The kids loved it and Cassie enjoyed teaching, carrying on that part of her old life.

Cassie's entrance into the new world came after she had plunged a kitchen knife into her husband's heart in their Carlisle flat. He had turned around in bed and tried to strangle her. She threw him off and ran across the hall into the kitchen where she grabbed a knife. As he approached, she tearfully thrust it outwards. He slid into it, gurgling. His white drool became thicker and redder and his bloodshot eyes rolled around their sockets before he fell backwards with a thump, dead.

After spending two weeks locked in her bathroom, she had wandered out of the flat, dazed, after two weeks with no food other than toothpaste, her ribs were clearly visible against her emaciated body. She had walked to her nearest diner, cooked a burger and eaten it greedily amongst the corpses slumped all around her. After a few weeks of walking she eventually came across Matty and Mike, digging mass graves. She had been suspicious of them, it took a few days for her to trust them, for them to convince her that they didn't have some hand in this terrible event. When Johnny arrived on the scene she fell in love with him within hours. They had similar trauma, having killed their spouses out of necessity. Cassie fell pregnant within weeks. They went on to have four children; James, Lorraine and the twins, Olivia and Louie. They were a formidable couple and had the respect of everyone in the village.

But the healthcare project was a tough one. When Penny Alabaster fell ill, Cassie grew frustrated and angry at herself for being so powerless to diagnose or treat it. No one blamed Cassie. Nana Penny had been old, that's all. At ninety-five she had come to her time. But Cassie was a perfectionist. When Iain had broken his foot, she attended to it every day to make it better, but she eventually realized that rest was the best recipe, with lots of painkillers. Cassie had delivered Nancy and Bow's children and Nancy had returned the favor, with a little help from Trish and Penny. Cassie had done a fine job for someone with no knowledge or training. She just prayed that she wouldn't have any mystery illnesses to contend with in the future. The village really would be in her hands.

* * *

Mike walked into the classroom to see his class sitting at their chairs. They were chatting noisily, excited about what Johnny, Zara and Andy would bring back. But most of all they were excited by Zara's inclusion in the trip. It gave them all hope that they could be part of it someday.

"Sir, Sir!" shouted Olivia Jameson. "How is Zara feeling? Is she excited, Sir?" Olivia was always the loudest in the class. She sat with Louie, her twin. They both had the solid frame that their parents had blessed them with. They were both highly intelligent. Olivia in particular was usually top of the class and always challenging and pushing accepted norms. She reminded Mike of Simon Churchill, his PhD prodigy. Mike felt a sudden and sharp prod of regret in his mind at the thought of Simon. He never had the chance to make it up with him after their argument sixteen years ago. And now Simon was probably dead. His thoughts were broken by Olivia's high-pitched voice.

"I wish I was going with her. My dad said she could be one of the best reconnaissance trippers in the future. She's my hero now, Sir."

Mike laughed. "She's always been my hero, Livvy. But we can discuss all that later. Today we're looking at algebra." The class uttered a collective groan.

7

Memorial Day came and went the day after the reconnaissance mission began. It was their sixteenth year of remembering the dead from that terrible night in 2038. They had quickly established a routine. In the assembly hall, people volunteered to stand up and share memories of the Time Before. Amusing anecdotes, emotional tales or memories of specific people usually dominated the event. A slap-up dinner followed, laid on by Trish, and the children wrote notes which were put in a glass bottle, to be taken by Johnny to the sea on his next expedition.

This year Samir shared a story of the Time Before. Samir was a quiet, well respected member of the community. He had been saved by his dog, Daisy, on the terrible night, as he was walking her after a late shift driving a taxi in Leeds. Sensing danger, the Staffordshire Bull Terrier went for the throat of an attacker, ripping it clean out of the man's body until his white Adam's Apple was exposed to the cool midnight air. Samir's assailant had continued to walk towards him, but the dog went for him again, jumping up and chewing the battered remains of the affected man's throat. This time the dog didn't let go until the man's head rolled loosely on his neck, mashed ligaments and chipped bones dangling out of the gory mess. Samir had run back home terrified and hid in his house with the dog until he ran out of food and water. When he came out he had walked for three days in a north-westerly direction. Not that Samir knew it was north-west. He just walked the dog and followed his instinct. He found a community already in its infancy and soon established his place amongst it.

As Samir stood up to address the crowd, everyone took notice. Samir, although well respected, was well known to be a quiet, hard-working man. He didn't have any particularly special skills, but he lent his hand to several tasks throughout the community. An able chef, he helped Trish in the kitchen, while he also wasn't shy of hard labor, helping Bow when any construction help was needed. Samir had even helped Mike in the school when he'd needed an extra pair of hands. Something Samir had never done before was to address the whole village. If he had something to say on this day of all days, it was going to be worth hearing.

He stood in front of the village community and was silent for a few seconds. Mike was about to stand and help Samir out when he opened his mouth and finally spoke.

"I used to drive taxis," he said. There was a low rumble of laughter to acknowledge the obvious statement that had come from Samir's mouth. In a small community that had been together sixteen years, everyone knew everyone's history and Samir's was no different.

"Of course, you all know that. But I just want to tell a story from my days as a taxi driver. It was back in '33. It was a brilliant sunny afternoon in Bradford. Some of you might remember that summer. It was the hottest summer in the UK since 1976 and Leeds won the FA Cup Final at Wembley Stadium. I was there, before you ask," he said and smiled, displaying a gleaming set of white teeth,

"If this is a story about Leeds United, Sammy, you can forget it!" Bow shouted.

"No, although maybe I'll tell that again later tonight, it is one of my favorites. No, this is a story about the Time Before and something I'm glad to leave behind. I had a fare that day from Bradford to Leeds. A group of three people, in their twenties. They were in the area for the weekend. Flash lot, each one had the latest RazorVision strapped to their heads. All the additional gear, y'know? The stuff you pay a lot of money for to modify it. They were projecting all sorts of stuff onto the street outside. I had to tell them to calm down as they could've been a danger to other drivers.

"So, after a few miles we get to Leeds City Center and we see something awful. I knew all the shortcuts, see. The back alleys, the rat runs, the cut-throughs. So, in one of these alleyways, behind some disused buildings, we come across something really bad. I mean something really, really appalling. Broad daylight, a man was attacking a woman. I don't wanna say too much with the young'uns in the room but let's just say he was forcing himself on this woman. So, I stop the car, pull the handbrake on and get out. I grab the man from behind. He's so busy doing what he's doing to this woman that he's barely even registered me there, even though he must've heard my cab pull up. He just tells me where to go. So, I grab the back of his head and punch him in the face. He runs away shouting abuse at me so I help the lady. He's had a bit of rope around her neck while he's been attacking her. He's pulled it so hard she's got rope burns around her neck, so badly burned it's deep red and weeping. She hugs me to say thanks but then I'm thinking about the man. Should I go after him? Should I find out who he is? So, I walk back to the car and remember the fare I've got. These three people, two of them men. What were they doing when I jumped out? Did they call the police? Did they jump out and back me up? Did they help me come to this poor woman's aid? Nope."

The room was so silent, Bow's belly made a hungry, gurgling noise that was audible to everyone in the room. He put his hand on his stomach and shrugged as a way of apology.

"What did they do?" young Jimmy Jameson asked, captivated by Samir's story of the Time Before.

"They filmed it. They had their RazorVision and they were filming what had happened. They let it play out in front of them like it was some kind of fucking film for them to enjoy. I'm surprised they didn't have fucking popcorn." Samir's face was red, burning with anger at the memory of the incident all those years ago.

"But, Sammy, to be fair, didn't they do that so the police

could catch him?" Cassie asked.

"Nope. They didn't want to get involved. I had to force them to send the video to West Yorkshire Police. Can you believe that? They had to be persuaded to help catch the man. As it happened, he was never caught. He just disappeared in broad daylight. But that always stayed with me. It made me realize what the world had become, what RazorVision was turning us into. A race of voyeurs who had lost all connection with human emotions. And that is why I value you all so much. There is so much here to be proud of. We have built something marvelous. So, I'd like to raise my glass and drink to New Windermere. The way life should be."

They raised their glasses and drank.

8

It took five hours to cycle to Whitehaven for the reconnaissance trip. Zara hadn't expected to see just how overgrown it was. Trish and Samir kept their village trim and tidy, but here, everything was wild. Grass stood four feet in the air, concrete from the paths and roads cracked, with huge weeds growing up from the crevices. Brick buildings crumbled, looking lonely and shambolic after nearly two decades without any human touch. She was glad that she'd prepared herself for the worst. Within twelve miles she saw her first corpse.

A dusty, dirty skeleton lay in her path, its yellowed skull appearing to gaze straight at her. Zara could see all the way into the black void of the empty sockets. The exposed teeth gave the impression of a terrifying grin. She slowed her bike but didn't stop to look anymore at the body.

Zara pedaled on. They continued in single file, with Johnny leading the way and Andy bringing up the rear. The sun was setting into the sea by the time they reached Whitehaven's west coast. There were more bodies. More death for Zara to look upon. With each body she passed, each grinning skull, each set of exposed ribs, she grew more resilient. She developed a coping mechanism where she would picture Nana Penny's face and hear her voice. *It's okay my angel. You can do this.*

They came to the beach and found a spot away from the tide, where they set up camp. They never set up camp indoors, the horrors of the buildings were too much, the feeling of death and decay hanging in the air like a tribute to the apocalyptic events of sixteen years ago. Johnny briefed them on what they needed. Clothes. Tinned beans. Bottled water. Paracetamol, Ibuprofen and as many antibiotics as they could carry.

"Any special requests?" Johnny asked them.

"Trish wants to see if we can find some sunflowers that we

can take back and plant. She thinks it'd be a nice tribute to Nana Penny," Zara said.

"No problem," replied Johnny. "Andy?"

"Mike wants some more books for the school library," Andy replied.

Johnny groaned. "He always wants books! Does he know how heavy they are? We'll grab one or two maximum if we can."

He looked at Zara. "How was your first ride out then, honey?" he asked.

"It was great," she lied.

"Those bodies," Andy said. "You never get used to them, Zara. Don't think it's just because it's your first time. You never get used to seeing them. All those bones ..."

"That's enough, Andy. We don't want to put her off do we?"

Zara gazed at the beach. A body was lying on the shore, the waves lapping and nudging it back and forth. A seagull landed next to the corpse and began pecking at its ribs. The seagull thrust its head back so it's neck and bill were at a full 180-degree angle. It screamed, a piercing yell that sounded horrible in the dim light with only the gentle rustle of the lapping waves to accompany it. She turned back to look at Johnny. His chiseled, handsome face was full of concern.

"I'm fine. Honestly, you don't need to ask. Ever since I was little and we used to dream about what this was like, I prepared myself for the worst bits."

Johnny's face changed and he laughed, tipping his head back in a way that reminded Zara of the seagull not fifty yards away.

"I knew you were a good 'un. Ha! You'll go far, honey. Good lass."

They ate their lamb sandwiches and crunched their carrots, washing it down with water from Lake Windermere. Trish, as ever, had done a grand job on the food.

"Okay, Zara, here's the initiation. Here's where you really become part of the club."

One of her eyebrows rose inquisitively. This was beginning to sound even more interesting.

Johnny reached into his bag. He rummaged in his backpack and pulled out a small, white tube. Zara had no idea what it was. She looked over to Andy who grinned broadly.

"Now, this is a reconnaissance secret. We don't tell a soul about this. Never have, never will. We risk the most out of anyone in our village and this is a little perk. It helps us sleep and relaxes us after a day on a trip."

He handed her the object. It was soft in her hands and around six inches long. It smelled strange, almost like the urine from the animals she tended on the farm.

"It's called cannabis," said Andy. "It's a drug, a bit like when Cassie dishes out the painkillers or the antibiotics to make you feel better. This helps make you feel relaxed and not at all bad."

Zara looked at Andy and then towards Johnny. "Is it safe? How do you take it?"

Johnny took it back off her and struck a match. He lit the end and took a deep breath. "You smoke it," he said with a muffled exhalation of thick, greenish smoke.

"Like I say, this is very much reconnaissance shit. You're one of us now. What's more, your dad would fucking kill me if he knew about this. In the Time Before, potheads – that's what they call people who smoke these – were seen as layabouts. On one of our trips I found a farm that grows pounds and pounds of this stuff." He handed the joint to Andy, who took two quick pulls. He passed the joint to Zara.

She took a drag and coughed out the green smoke. "Urgh, that is horrible! It burns your throat!"

"Just give it one more drag," Johnny told her. She did and coughed again, this time it took her over a minute to stop, which plunged Andy and Johnny into further laughter. When she stopped, she looked at the two of them. She felt different. Everything came into focus a little more. The lapping, rhythmic sound of the waves slapping against the shoreline sounded like silky whispers, as if some unknown spirit was divulging secret thoughts in a language she couldn't understand. Her head buzzed and her entire body began to tingle.

"Good shit, innit?" Andy asked.

Zara burst out laughing, tickled by the stupid phrase. Andy and Johnny, realizing the weed had begun to affect her, joined her laughter. They laughed until their sides hurt, each time one of them managed to stop, they were set off again by someone else who had begun giggling once more. They laughed for so long they couldn't remember what they were laughing at. Once the laughter had died down, they lay back side-by-side and stared at the stars.

"Do you think there's life up there somewhere?" Zara asked the two men.

"Got to be," said Andy. "It's infinite. Maybe there's another world that's just like ours. Maybe there's three of us looking a hundred million miles away, a mirror world to this one. But maybe the terrible night didn't happen and the Before is still the Now." He was getting excited at his own theory. "The other question, I suppose, is if there's life out *there*." He waved his arm towards the land. "On this planet. Are there other survivors? Who knows. If not, we went from eight billion people to eighteen overnight. But surely the person or people who caused it are still alive? But that's a can of worms for another time."

"What was it like?" Zara asked. "You know, in the Before."

Johnny sighed, resting his head on his hand. "There were more people," he said. And we all lost people we loved. The technology was amazing. All the stories you hear about cars that drove themselves and magic glasses. It's all true. But were people happy? I don't know. Looking back, the technology had kind of taken over real life. I've never been happier than I am now, life just feels better, purer. Like I've earned my happiness. And I say that from my heart. I just wish there were more of us to enjoy it."

Andy contemplated this. "It's a bit different for me. But... I've got to agree, there's something a bit more wholesome about things now. I tell you what though, I do miss the films."

Zara had heard all about films; like books but with moving pictures telling the story. Some films were projected all around you so it was like you were in the middle of it, participating.

"Johnny, if you had the choice, would you go back?" Andy asked.

Johnny contemplated this for so long Zara turned to look at him, thinking he'd fallen asleep or passed out from the weed. Eventually, he did speak.

"Yes and no. I miss the people I knew back then. My wife, my kids, my brother, my friends. But I love Cassie and the kids. I love my new family and that includes the two of you. For me, the Before is the Before. So, to answer your question, no. I wouldn't go back."

Zara listened intently, Nana Penny's last words echoing in her head, merging with the whispering of the waves and repeating to her, *don't go back. You'll want to but don't go.*

Zara lay awake for an hour before she slept, thinking about their secret. Although she had enjoyed smoking with Andy and Johnny she made a decision not to do it again. She had been brought up in a community without secrets, one where everyone was in it together. She wouldn't tell anyone about Johnny and Andy's secret, but she didn't want to be a part of it herself any more. She hoped they would understand.

Zara slept and dreamed of the grinning skull that she'd seen on the cycle path. Its black eye sockets glared straight through her eyes and into her soul. The awful grinning mouth moved, the jaw fell with a dusty crack from its top half. Its voice was inhuman and haunting, pushing out the words with a wispy, watery mutter. *Don't go back.* The seagull landed on the skull's head and looked straight at Zara, it's bright yellow eyes piercing her so intensely that it forced her to look away. It thrust its head back to align it in that same straight line and released a bloodcurdling scream that sounded like a thousand souls yelling in tormented agony.

She awoke with a start and regarded her companions. They were both fast asleep. The sun was beginning to rise over towards the land where they'd cycled from. She looked over towards the sea and her heart jumped. Approaching the dock, less than three miles down the coast, was a huge iron ship.

9

Zara woke her companions. Sleepily, Johnny gazed at the large, grey vessel. His eyes widened and jerked back to Zara, who was smiling broadly.

"Jesus fucking Christ. Oh, my days." He leant forward and gave Zara a smacker of a kiss on the cheek, not unlike her father's cartoonish efforts. He jumped on Andy and did the same to him. Andy, laughing, pushed the big man off.

"Human beings! Human fucking beings. This is big, Zara. This is big big big." He stared at the grey, floating hunk of iron as it coasted towards the dock. "Looks military. Shit, I wish I had binoculars on me."

Andy's grin took a downward turn. "How do we know if… you know. If they're OK. If they're safe."

Johnny looked at them both. "We don't. We approach the ship. And we do it carefully. We expect the worst. But if it's the US or UK military, I would bet anyone's money they're here to help."

They packed up their camping equipment, mounted the push bikes and made their way towards the dock. They didn't make good time, subconsciously moving slower than before as they contemplated the magnitude of what lay before them. A ship, probably military, had come to the west coast of England. Would they take over? Would they take them to a new community? And would the New Windermere survivors even want to leave their beautiful lakeside home? These questions bounced around Zara's mind as she followed Johnny's large, muscular frame, the sea breeze blowing her hair sideways across her face.

They were one mile away when they heard a crunching, crashing sound and saw the ship hit the pier. The small white lighthouse crumbled inwards and fell into the sea. The three cyclists stopped in unison and watched, open mouthed at the carnage before them. The ship stopped dead against the stone pier.

As they approached the vessel, the letters on the hull read *USS New York* and the unmistakable stars and stripes on the US flag waved from the flagpole in the middle of the ship.

"Americans!" said Johnny but his earlier happiness had faded and his optimism had waned. The ship had crashed. Was anyone at the helm? Was this military ship going to be a ghost ship, just another charnel house floating along with its rotten stench of the dead?

They cycled up the pier, the long grey mass of the ship looming larger as it grew closer. They could hear the ship moving, great iron screams echoing from its large body.

Johnny turned to Zara and Andy. "We're gonna go on board," he told them. "It might not be pretty on there."

"But how could it have sailed here without a captain?" Zara asked.

"New York's over there, past Ireland," Andy said, pointing over to the west, beyond the sea's horizon. "It could've just floated over in the last few years."

Zara slumped, her body language defeated. *Of course, it was too good to be true,* she thought.

The crash had left a section of the pier that rose up against the hull of the ship, giving them easy access to board. Johnny led the way, with Zara in the middle and Andy at the rear, in the familiar formation. They had all packed weapons. Zara felt her belt and her fingers brushed against the bulge of the hunting knife that Johnny had given her before the trip. It gave her some reassurance, but her heart was pounding in her chest all the same.

They jumped aboard and walked slowly towards the door that led to the inside of the ship. Johnny drew the knife from his pocket. He opened the door with a stiff kick and walked in. Zara and Andy followed.

The ship had a clean, chemical smell but it was still there, that sense of decay, in the undertones of the ship's atmosphere. *There is death on this ship,* thought Zara, her shoulders slumping, resigned. It didn't take them long to find their first body. Slumped in the ship's sick bay, the skeletal remains of a man lay on the floor, his US Navy uniform surprisingly intact over the bony remains. Other bodies followed further down the corridor. One of them hung from a noose, swinging creakily from the iron pipe above.

They walked on, Johnny with the knife drawn in a defensive position, ready for attack. But there would be no attack here, Zara realized. There wasn't one living soul on board.

Despite the corpses it contained, the haul from the ship was good. Several weapons, tins of food, bottles of antibiotic pills, morphine and bandages were gathered. Johnny also grabbed the military uniforms, the heavy boots were especially handy. To make it even easier, they had come across large containers that could be attached to jacks on wheels and pulled through the corridors. They each filled one. They would be able to attach them to their bikes for the journey back, although as they were so heavy, it was likely to slow them down considerably.

As Zara filled her container with dozens of tins of beans, she saw Andy smiling in the doorway of the kitchen's stock room. There was a crashing, tearing noise that sounded synthetic somehow. "Come in, Zara. Come in, Zara Pilkington," Andy said. He was holding a small black box, and he spoke into it. "Walkie-talkies! These are like out the Stone Age! These military Yanks must not have trusted new tech," he said.

"What are they?" asked Zara. "What do they do?"

"They let you talk to each other within a distance. For example, if I was the other side of Lake Windermere to you, we could speak into these and hear each other."

Zara's eyes widened. She had heard of all the possible communications available in the Time Before. Conversations you could have with people on the other side of the world where you could *see* them as well as hear them. This wouldn't let them do anything like that, but it was a start. She laughed as her mind began to run through the possibilities that this discovery presented. "We've got to tell Johnny," she said. They both raced down the corridor to find him.

Johnny was in a place labelled the "communications room." His two companions bounded through the door. "Johnny you'll never guess—" Andy's words were cut short by what he saw in the room. Johnny was scribbling intensely with an old pencil onto a small notebook. Next to two slumped corpses in uniform, the emblems on their shoulders making Zara think they must have been a high rank, there was a holographic projection of a man in a suit, talking.

Andy gasped. "That's Eric Morantz. He was president of America. In the Time Before." Morantz's thick New York tones were solemn and grave, his face drawn and pale. He adjusted his tie, nervously.

"Men. Women. I'm broadcasting this to all military. I'm in the White House bunker. There are a few of us in here. Not many survivors. We are in the midst of a great disaster. There have been many, many deaths. Violent, unexplainable deaths at the hands of regular people. If you are still out there, if you have survived, come to Washington DC and we will look to start over again. We have a plan. We have identified the source. A video was created and seen by three billion people, causing a terrible change in behavior. We think this was a deliberate attack. The video was from Rick Razor, of Razor Incorporated, in London—" President Morantz stopped his sentence and looked into the distance. Zara's heart jumped as she thought the man was looking directly at her. There was a piercing sound of a gunshot. Another gunshot and another. "He's twitching! Vice President Cutter is—" The president's words were cut short once more but this time a bullet hole had appeared in his forehead, snapping his head back and exploding holographic blood across the room. The president's image slumped lifelessly on the floor. Vice President Cutter stepped into the hologram view. His face was pale, drawing a stark contrast to his red, bloodshot eyes. His head jerked a couple of times a second with considerable force. White drool slobbered out of the man's gaping mouth, dribbling down his neat tie. The saliva flicked sideways with the twitch of his head. His breathing was fast, like a man who had just finished strenuous exercise. In his left hand, he held a gun. A few seconds more twitching and drooling and Cutter lifted the gun to his mouth and pulled the trigger. Blood and bone burst out the back of his head and Cutter's twitching body was thrown backwards against the wall. He slumped onto the floor in a pool of blood. Johnny switched off the transmission.

* * *

They stood in silence. Zara's mouth gaped open. The men in front of her were there, as real as any living person she'd met. She'd seen the president gunned down right in front of her at the hands of the vice president. But she knew this footage was sixteen years old, roughly the same age as her. She knew that the president must have broadcast it to every US military base and vessel, to get a message out.

"How did they...? The power? I thought it was off?" asked Andy, amazed.

"Back-up generator. Not much power but enough for emergencies. Just for this projection, a direct line from their president," replied Johnny. "Wow. If you told me twenty years ago that I'd see the president shot in the head right in front of me by the vice president, I'd have called the men in white coats."

"What do you think he meant? About Rick Razor? The video. Do you think it's like what Mike has always said about the cause of all this? Him and Iain always said it was the video. We all thought it was terrorists or some kind of virus. Or both. Does this mean Mike and Iain had it right?"

Johnny shrugged. "I really don't know. I've written it all down after watching it twice. If you don't mind, I really don't want to see that again."

Zara agreed by nodding, although she felt a twinge of disappointment. The hologram was the most amazing thing she'd ever seen. A remnant of the Time Before had been right in front of her, bringing all those stories about the technology of the old days to glorious life. She knew about the references to Rick Razor and the video though. Her father had told her several times, and it was well known that he believed in his theory that somehow a bizarre video had influenced the behavior of everyone who saw it. There had been large holes in his argument though. People seemed to go through physical changes when they were affected, with viscous drool, twitching and bloodshot eyes being the main symptoms recorded in Mike's report. How could a video cause that? Also, Mike himself had seen the video but was unaffected, as had several others in New Windermere. Some kind of virus immunity would make sense but immunity to some kind of magical video? Very unlikely. But the American president's last words had seemed to corroborate Mike's theory, no matter how absurd it sounded to the other villagers, including Zara.

"I'll call a meeting as soon as we get back," said Johnny. "We've got some top notch supplies here too. Successful trip?"

Andy and Zara nodded. Johnny ruffled Zara's hair.

"You did good, kid. I know you're disappointed that we didn't see anyone alive. But this is the world that we live in now. It's a new world with reminders of the old world all over. If you expect anything more, if you hope for a better place, you'll be disappointed. It's the hope that kills you. Why do you think we've never gone very far over the years? What we have at Windermere is as close to perfect as we can get."

Zara nodded. "Thanks for bringing me, Johnny."

As they jumped off the ship, down onto the broken pier, Andy put his arm around Zara. "He's not just saying that, you know. You've been brilliant. It's not an easy job, this. You're a natural. I think we're gonna do just fine on these trips in the future."

He smiled sweetly and Zara saw a twinkle in his eye. At 34, Andy was eighteen years her senior, and technically old enough to be her father, but at that moment she felt a surge of attraction for him. He was lean and good looking, with an introverted way about him that she found appealing. *Maybe when I'm older something could happen?* she thought to herself. She jumped forward and gave him a peck on the cheek. "You're not so bad yourself, Andy Pratt," she said and walked ahead of him, to fall back into the single file formation they had stuck to for the entire trip, dragging her container behind her.

Andy felt the sudden chemistry between them and daydreamed about a possible future together. He had no idea that within twenty-four hours he would be dead.

10

The journey back to New Windermere took over two full days, partly because of the extra weight from their bounty from the ship, but partly because of Andy's accident.

They were less than half a mile out of Whitehaven when he came off his bike. A simple fall would have been manageable. Zara herself had fallen off her bike several times back in the village, but Andy had been unlucky. His bike hit a rock on the road and his entire body had been propelled over the handle bars. His leg had scraped against a jagged steel rod that had marked the edge of the path and ripped away the skin all the way to the bone. Andy screamed in agony. There was so much blood. Zara wrapped it up with thick layers of bandage and covered it with antiseptic cream. They had to jettison a few tins and other items so that Andy could sit in the container, with Johnny pulling on the bike. Andy's bike was left behind but Johnny would make plans to return and pick it up again. Even for Johnny, a muscle-bound hulk of a man, pulling Andy on top of his existing load was a big effort. Andy's screams continued for hours, until he passed out with the pain of his injury.

After a long, hard slog, they came to the New Windermere gates at dawn, exhausted. Mike rushed to see them. He had been nervously awaiting his daughter's safe return. Mike grinned widely to see his daughter's face at the gates, her muscular frame heaving with heavy breathing from the exercise. Mike's face dropped when he looked to see the load that Johnny was pulling.

Andy was unconscious, and his wrapped-up leg had large, dark patches of blood soaking through from the gaping wound underneath. Mike opened the gates and grabbed Andy by the shoulders, Johnny taking the other side. Zara grabbed his legs, careful not to put any pressure on his wound. Andy's head lolled and he groaned with confused pain. Inside the dorm, they placed him on his bed and Zara went to find Cassie. Cassie, on seeing Andy's state, put her hand over her mouth and shrieked. This was beyond her expertise. She carefully removed the bandages from Andy's leg, releasing a strange, nutty smell into the atmosphere. The wound was deep and unsightly. Fresh blood poured from the gash and Cassie could see the white patch of Andy's shin bone, a shiny contrast to the different layers of red blood and raw pink flesh.

Cassie soaked a cloth in antiseptic and gently dabbed the wound. Andy, now awake, released a long, high pitched scream. Cassie replaced the bandages with fresh ones, which immediately became red with the increasing amount of blood flowing from the wound.

"This will help," said Johnny who stood at the door with a small bottle in his hand. "Morphine. For the pain." He looked at Andy's pale and drawn face and grimaced.

Cassie took the bottle and tipped some of the liquid into the cap. "How much?" she asked Johnny.

"Damned if I know but enough to get him to sleep. He's been through a lot. If that leg gets infected… well, we'll cross that bridge when we come to it." Johnny fingered the huge hunting knife that was harnessed to his belt.

"Do I dilute it?" Cassie asked her husband.

"God knows," Johnny replied. "But that looks fine. Bottoms up."

"God, Johnny this is a mess. This is why you shouldn't go too far out of the village." Cassie tipped the morphine into Andy's mouth. It had an immediate effect and he stopped wheezing, his eyes closed.

They left Andy sleeping and Johnny called a founders' meeting. Matty asked Johnny to chair the meeting on his behalf, realizing that he couldn't direct something that he didn't know about. Trish, Samir, Mike, Bow, Nancy, Iain, Matty, Mike and

Cassie joined them in the meeting room. It was agreed that Zara, although not an official founder, should join them to talk about what they had found on board the USS New York in Whitehaven.

"Okay," began Johnny. "I've called this emergency board meeting for one reason – to tell you what we saw in Whitehaven. I think it's something you're going to find really interesting."

Johnny filled the founders in on their trip, leaving nothing out, other than the joint they'd shared on the beach three nights before. Zara chipped in with any details she felt were left too thin. They covered the huge American ship, the dead bodies and the bounty they had gathered. Zara brought up the walkie-talkies, which even Johnny was amazed at – with the president's message and the injury to Andy, they had forgotten to fill even him in on that little gem.

"Walkie-talkies!" exclaimed Bow. "Wow. That's brilliant. God bless old technology. We could use them for—"

"That's not all," Johnny cut in. "You need to hear this first." Johnny told them about the message from the American President and his death by gunshot to the head; the vice president being affected and his grim suicide. He finished with the mention of Razor's video, that Morantz had revealed as the cause of the disaster, just before his demise.

The room fell silent. Johnny glanced over at Mike. Bow's eyes followed Johnny's and Cassie and Nancy followed suit. Looking down at his hands, taking in the information Johnny had unloaded, Mike raised his eyes to see the entire room looking at him.

"The president. He said it was the video that caused it?" They all knew he'd passionately pursued this whenever the cause of the disaster had come up in conversation. "And the president's dead. Wow. This is really big. And he said it was Razor? Rick Razor?"

"More or less," said Johnny, looking over at Zara, who confirmed the comment with a brisk nod.

"Did he say why?" Mike asked.

"No," Johnny replied. "But if I remember what Rick Razor was like, he had a big ego and lots of money. If he was a psycho, maybe he's done something to wipe people out. Maybe he's sat in his tower right now, lording it over this destroyed world."

"There was something about that video though," Iain chipped in. "I know we've been over this before but it made me feel different. Mike, you felt the same."

"Who knows?" Trish added. "I know one thing. This doesn't really get us anywhere other than knowing a tiny bit more. And now that poor boy is laid up with his leg in a mess."

"Cassie," Matty said. "Have you got an update on Andy?"

"He suffered a severe laceration on his shin. It's gone through right to the bone and I think it's infected. He's been loaded up with morphine and I've wrapped and raised the leg. He's not in a good way."

"Will he make it?" Nancy asked.

"I think so," Cassie replied. She locked eyes with Johnny. "It depends on the infection. Worst case, I suppose, the leg might have to go below the knee. But I wouldn't be sure about how to do it."

"Okay," said Matty. "But be careful with that morphine. If he's on a course of it he'll need to treat it carefully. People can get reliant on that stuff."

Cassie's face went a shade of white and she audibly gulped. Zara looked down at the table, thinking guiltily about the cannabis she had smoked on Whitehaven beach.

The meeting ended without any real action point, but Johnny was pleased to get the information off his chest. As they had talked about the president's message, it was obviously of a huge magnitude, but it seemed frustrating that they couldn't actually act on the information. Bow slapped his best friend on the back as they walked out. "Tough trip, pal. You did good, Johnny. Don't put the boy's injury on yourself. Tomorrow I'll take a look at those walkie-talkies."

"Cheers, Bow. It means a lot."

Mike was next to approach Johnny. "John, I just wanted to say thanks. You know. For looking after Zara."

Johnny laughed and clapped his hand on the nape of Mike's neck. "Looking after her?" he said, amused. "Mate, she looked after me. She's got more balls than any man I ever met. She'll go far, believe you me. I don't know what would have happened if she hadn't been there."

Mike beamed. He caught up with Zara who was walking back to the living quarters and gave her a long hug.

"I'm so proud of you, Zara. We all are, but after all we've been through, I'm just so glad to see you."

Zara looked at her father through exhausted eyes and stifled a yawn. "Thanks, Dad. I suppose I just wish Andy hadn't got injured. It's a nasty one."

"What was it like on the ship?"

"It was awful. I mean, the bodies. Some of the things I saw."

"I know, I know," said Mike, thinking about his experience with Matty, clearing the dead from the streets. "You don't need to say anything. Go to bed. It looks like you need a nap."

"Thanks, Dad. Love you."

"Love you, too," he said and planted his cartoon kiss on her cheek. Zara grinned and walked to her quarters.

* * *

Cassie went straight back to check on Andy. He was sleeping. She went to check his leg and flinched when she saw the empty bottle of morphine on the table next to his bed. *You left it within reach,* she thought to herself. *You fucking idiot. You stupid, stupid bitch.* She rushed over to his body and checked his pulse. But there was no pulse to check. She tipped his head back to do mouth-to-mouth but when she saw his eyes she knew. He had swallowed enough morphine to kill two men. Even if she brought him back, they didn't have the expertise or the equipment to fix him. Andy was dead.

11

Andy's funeral, the second in a week in New Windermere, was a more somber affair than Nana Penny's. They found a tree overlooking the lake. It was a tall one and stood alone, leaning, with a couple of branches dipping into the water, as if to tentatively sample its temperature. It seemed apt somehow. They buried him there, repeating the circle from Nana Penny's ceremony, holding hands. Nancy, Bow's wife, sang *Let It Be* this time, Zara was too upset. Matty said a few words about Andy, recounting anecdotes about his time as a member of the community. Johnny was quiet and contemplative while Cassie was drawn and pale.

There was another wake, but this was altogether more quiet and mournful. Whether it was the aggregated sadness of two funerals taking place within a week, further decimating their numbers, combined with Andy's relative youth, Mike wasn't sure. No one was sure whether it had been an accident or suicide. Had Andy simply been overwhelmed by pain and glugged the deadly dose of liquid morphine? Or had he intended to end his own life? Andy had always been a withdrawn character, out of everyone in the community, he was the one who was an outsider. They had loved him all the same but he didn't have that outward connection like the rest of them, the burly respect that Johnny commanded, the useful knack that Bow had of making something out of nothing, or the steady, wise dependability of Matty West. But his death had knocked them out of kilter. And it had knocked Cassie the most. She blamed herself for Andy's death.

Cassie had barely spoken a word since she found Andy's lifeless body. She had wept for hours. And when the tears dried up, silence had come. Giving only monosyllabic answers to anyone's questions, Cassie's face became older. She had stopped eating and her increasingly gaunt face thickened the pits of her wrinkles. Cassie had fallen into a deep, black depression.

Nobody else in the village had blamed her, of course. Johnny, if anything, was angry at Andy for his selfish actions. It wasn't an anger he could really express outwardly, other than in his and Cassie's private quarters. It wasn't the done thing to criticize the dead. He also partly blamed himself; Andy had been under his command at the time of his accident.

Mike sat at the wake, looking around the room. There weren't many conversations taking place. He yearned for the time before Nana Penny's passing. Those sixteen years without a single loss, they were like utopia. He felt that he'd seen enough darkness to last him a lifetime during that black night in 2038. But it seemed to be coming again, in a horrible crashing wave. He could have coped with Nana Penny passing on at the age of ninety-five but this was a tragic end to a young man's life. A young man he was fond of and had known, albeit vaguely, in the Time Before. But Mike's feelings of grief were tinged with additional feelings of relief and, subsequently, guilt. It could have been his own daughter that had suffered a bad injury and died. Mike was eternally grateful that it hadn't been the case, even if it did mean another member of the community had met an untimely death.

Ten minutes into the wake, it was with some surprise that Cassie walked up to the lectern in the corner, preparing to speak. Johnny, realizing this, attempted to encourage her down, but Cassie ignored her husband and began to speak, the population of New Windermere looking on in silence and cautious wonder.

"Hi, everyone. As you probably know, Andy was in my care when he died. I made a mistake and he overdosed on morphine." There were grumblings of disagreement in the room.

"No, don't be stupid!" shouted Iain.

"It was my fault. I take full responsibility for the death of our friend. So, I have made the decision to step down from my position as head of healthcare. And if anyone from the village so wishes, I will accept any punishment that is deemed appropriate."

Johnny walked up to his wife and led her away from the lectern and out of the room. She looked on the edge of sanity.

Mike approached Matty, who was standing in the corner of the room with Trish. "She shouldn't blame herself," Matty said as Mike approached.

"Of course," Mike replied. "I don't think anyone else thinks it was her fault other than Cassie herself. But it does raise a question. If we accept her resignation, which I suppose we have to, who will be in charge of healthcare?"

Matty scratched his ear thoughtfully. It was what he did when he was thinking something over.

"There's no one. Hell, we gave Cassie more than she could handle. I mean, did she ever really want the job? Was she comfortable with it? I don't think so. We all have a responsibility to fix this, Mike."

Mike looked at Matty. The week had been a bad one. Probably the worst since their new community was formed.

"We need someone," he told Matty. "If only Windermere University had been a medical school!" he said, not without humor.

Matty slapped Mike on the back. "And if only you'd been a professor of medicine instead of that technology shit," he said. "Look where that shit's got us!" He laughed abruptly and stopped, remembering the sobriety of the day's events.

Mike looked at him and raised his finger, waving it at Matty like a scientist who had just connected the dots in his brain to find a solution to an impossible problem. "That's it! Matty, can you call another founder's meeting? Tonight? I've got an idea."

12

They gathered in the meeting room. All the founders sat, gloomily, but Mike's eyes betrayed a sparkle of optimism that he'd tried in vain to disguise. Feelings were still raw from Andy's death, not to mention the revelation about the American president's demise.

Matty, as always, opened the meeting. "Well, as you know, today has been a sad day. And we have had much to discuss over the past week. Yesterday's events were upsetting for everyone involved." He turned to Cassie. Her gaunt face looked completely colorless, almost transparent. "Cassie, on behalf of all the founders I would like to apologize. We placed a responsibility on you that not one of us was qualified to do. You have done a brilliant job, everyone can vouch for that. And over the years you have saved lives and you have brought new lives in to the world. If Andy wanted to kill himself, he would have done it by any method. If he didn't then it was his mistake, not yours. Everyone here appreciates the work you have done in the village. It's with a heavy heart that I accept your resignation."

Johnny sat, nodding and clasping his wife's hand. Cassie simply stared ahead. "Now," continued Matty, "I think Mike would like to run an idea past everyone." He put emphasis on the word *idea* in a way that Mike did not feel was entirely supportive.

"Okay," Mike began. "Cheers, Matty. I'd just like to add to Matty's comments about Cassie. Cass, you did a better job than any one of us could have. I would've crumbled delivering babies, treating knocks, bumps, Iain's broken foot a while back."

Cassie's eyes met his and she offered a brief, weak smile. Johnny squeezed his wife's hand and winked at her.

"And I also agree about your resignation. Looking back, Cass, I don't think you were ever fully comfortable taking the role, you kind of just got it by default. I've seen you working with the kids on the PE lessons and you're fantastic. They love you and you seem to really enjoy it."

For the first time, Cassie's eyes brightened up. She nodded jerkily, her eyes filling with tears.

"So, I've got a proposal. I want you to take my job as head of education. And I'd like to take Andy's place on Johnny's reconnaissance team. Starting next week for a special mission."

Johnny looked at Mike through squinted eyes. "Interesting proposal, Professor. Can I ask why I should take you instead of someone else? Bow, for example."

"You know I can do it, Johnny," he replied. "I'm as fit as anyone else around here. Bow's needed around the village for maintenance and he's still building the washrooms near the lake."

Bow nodded in agreement. "Fine by me, John. Mike, what's this special mission. Are you ready to enlighten us?"

"Sure," Mike replied. "We need a new head of healthcare. Not just any of us, but someone with medical qualifications. A nurse? A doctor would be even better. Even a vet would be handy. So, let's go and find us one. Let's go and look for one and bring them back here to work."

Bow laughed harshly. Johnny and Cassie looked gloomily at each other, as if in resignation.

"So, you want us to go out there somewhere, find a fully qualified doctor and bring them back to the village. Mike, have you been at the whisky again?" Bow asked, snorting as he spoke and wiping his eyes from the laughter. "And how will you identify this medic? Will he be wearing a white coat with a stethoscope around his neck?"

Mike nodded. "I see what you're saying, Bow, I know it sounds crazy. But there's something you're forgetting. Newcastle is about a day's bike ride from here. Newcastle has a medical school, a vet school and a nursing college. It's got five fairly large hospitals in the area. So, it's not exactly a sure thing that we'll find anyone over there. But there were two out of eighteen survivors over here that were from Windermere University. Maybe there's a doctor over there. Really, it's the only thing our village is missing. The only gap to ensuring our future survival as a community of people." He looked at Johnny who was rubbing his chin. "What do you say, Johnny? I know it would be the furthest any of your trips will have gone. But think of the possibilities if we bring a doctor or a nurse back with us? And at the very least, maybe we could bring back textbooks. Maybe one of us could learn. Your Livvy is as bright as a button."

"It's a long trip, Professor. Lots of danger, a big city like that." Johnny whistled as if to imply something unlimited, an unknown but vast quantity. "It would be some mission. And one you would have to take without me."

Mike's face dropped. "Why? Johnny, we couldn't do this without you. It would be like playing in the World Cup without your star striker."

Johnny looked over at Cassie. "I can't leave her, Mike. I can't leave Cass in this state."

Cassie looked over at her burly husband and spoke for the first time since she had stood at the lectern at Andy's wake. "No. Johnny, you have to."

"Cass, I can't. I can't leave you."

"You must. For me, for the village. For Andy. Mike's right, we need to do something. You'd be doing it for me. I'm feeling sorry for myself, but I'll be fine. I've got Nancy, Trish, Matty, Bow. I'm not going to let you sit this one out just because I'm down in the dumps. Are you listening to me, Jonathan Jameson?"

Johnny looked around at the familiar faces in the room. "Well, it looks like my wife has returned, ladies and gentlemen. I'm in."

"One catch though," Cassie added. "Make it your last trip. I can't afford to lose you, Johnny. We need you here."

* * *

They spent the next few days arranging the plan. It would be Johnny, Mike and Zara to go on the mission. The route to Newcastle was quite straight, the A66 cutting a wide path through the North Pennines. With the wind on their backs and minimum stops they could make it in less than a day. However, Johnny conservatively planned for a four day round-trip. They would take the walkie-talkies in case they were split up or had to investigate anything. Cassie would head up the school and the remaining villagers would share the farm work. When they arrived in Newcastle they would begin at the medical school before looking at the nursing college, then the veterinarian college and finally the hospitals. Mike hoped they wouldn't need to go to the hospitals. They were ugly places, full of clinical death at the best of times but with the world the way it was now, who knew what untold horrors lurked in the wards and in the corridors.

As had become routine, Bow checked the bikes thoroughly and Trish packed their backpacks with meat, bread and vegetables. This time they took a handgun each, part of the bounty from the USS New York. After Andy's death, the send-off they received was more downbeat than usual for a reconnaissance trip. There was a darkened element to the journey now, the likelihood of tragedy all too real, the danger all too apparent. Mike looked over at Zara and felt a pang of relief that he didn't have to say goodbye to her this time. He wasn't sure if he could do it again. Indeed, Cassie hugged Johnny hard and didn't want to let him go. His four children held on to his legs. The adventure stories they had craved now seemed too scary, too full of dark possibilities.

Mike and Zara received well wishes from all their fellow villagers and it was Matty who spoke to them last.

"It's a good thing you're doing here," he said. "I wasn't sure about your idea at first. A big trip so soon after Andy. But it's for the village, for the community. We'll all remember this." He hugged Mike and kissed Zara on the cheek. "And bring us back a doctor. You do that, the whiskey is on me."

"Yeah, and the first job they'll have will be to check your liver," Mike replied. They both laughed, Matty grabbing his belly in a mocking tribute to Mike's joke.

Mike, Johnny and Zara burst through the gates on their bikes, trailers in tow, each looking at the road ahead. The magnitude of what they could achieve, balanced with the dangers that faced them, reverberated around their minds.

13

Three hours of cycling, in which barely a word passed between them went by before Mike spotted the airplane in the distance. It had landed square on the road, cutting across the tarmac like a huge barrier, hunks of debris scattered in the area around the place where the plane had made its impact.

It was Zara who saw the first sign of death. A woman's skeletal remains lay thirty yards in front of her. The skeleton was still strapped to the airplane seat, its lower half completely missing.

The belongings of passengers were everywhere, along with their bones. And the shoes. *So many shoes,* thought Zara. She felt these were more upsetting than the bodies and the bones. More personal somehow. They approached the plane and Zara noticed how the crash had actually scorched the entire road, turning it a deep black color. Going around the plane would be impossible, there were deep ravines either side of the wreckage. They would have to go through the plane to continue their journey, boarding through a large crater in one side of the vehicle and hoping there was an exit point at the other side.

Johnny led the way, climbing up and over into the long body of the plane, hoisting his bike onto his shoulders. He signaled to the others that it was safe. Once Zara and Mike had climbed up, they assessed their surroundings. There were more corpses in the passenger seats and smashed glass littered the aisles. Dried blood covered the seats and the floor. Zara noticed a skeleton with a plastic knife buried into its eye socket. They all turned around, wide eyed and alert.

There was a rustling noise coming from the far end of the airplane.

Johnny approached carefully and drew his handgun. Mike and Zara watched on, holding their breath, not wanting to make a sound. Feelings of excitement and anxiety filled the air. Would it be a survivor? Someone, like them, who had come aboard the plane, looking to make their way across this ruined world? Would they be friendly? Or would they be wild and violent, not used to interactions with other humans. The few seconds of wonder felt like hours as they waited to see what the cause of the rustling noise was.

Johnny made it halfway down the aisle when he saw what had caused the movement. There were two green eyes, sparkling between two seats, eyeing him warily. Johnny craned his neck to see more. His body relaxed and he turned to Mike and Zara. "It's a dog! A German Shepherd! I used to have one when I was little. Tex, he—"

Johnny was cut off by the dog bounding towards him, its sharp teeth exposed within its snarling, angry mouth.

"Johnny, look out!" shouted Mike, but it was too late. The dog knocked Johnny over and was snarling in his face. The handgun flew under one of the seats. Johnny had just managed to push his hands out in time, holding the dog's face six inches from his own. He could feel the dog's warm, rancid breath on him. Johnny was panting with the exertion of keeping the dog's jaws at a safe distance. The dog's green eyes were locked with his own. Johnny felt the deep, black pupils testing him, challenging him. Its razor-sharp incisors dripped with hot drool. He saw a large tick nestled on the dog's furry back.

Mike and Zara both ran to help him. The dog sensed their oncoming movements and looked up, snarling. Johnny sensed his chance with the dog's break in concentration and put his hands around the dog's furry neck. With one hard twist of his forearms, Johnny broke the dog's neck. With a loud crunch and a soft yelp, the dog crumpled backwards, its head slumped between two airplane seats. Johnny closed his eyes and exhaled loudly.

"Jesus fucking Christ. That'll teach me to underestimate

something. That was tough. It looked just like my old family dog."

"Is it dead?" Zara asked. She peered over at the dog. It lay still, its large head twisted at a right angle to its neck. "I guess it is."

"Gone feral, most likely," Johnny said. "Been living off the land and who can blame him? Poor bastard. Just looking for his next meal. But we need to be careful. There's probably more around. And they'll be hungry, just like him."

They stepped over the dog's body. Johnny forced the door to the cockpit, where the windscreen had been completely smashed. They climbed out and jumped down onto the other side, throwing their bikes onto the grass to avoid damage.

The rest of the day went by without further incident. They had to weave in and out of cars. Some were parked and abandoned. Some were crashed. Some had the dusty remains of their drivers still behind the wheel.

How great would it be to just jump in one of those cars? Mike thought to himself, feeling the burn in his muscles from the cycling. Of course, none of the cars worked any longer, as all Razor technology was broken or switched off. Even vintage cars were unusable as all petrol and diesel supplies were kept in holdings supplied by Razor Technology: supplies that would be no longer accessible.

They found somewhere to camp just outside Durham. Trish had worked wonders once more. Rabbit with herbs and leeks. Big hunks of bread with cheese. They carefully rationed their portions and ate. Zara wondered if Johnny would break out the cannabis as he had on the first night she had spent away with him. She was pleased when he didn't.

Johnny was preoccupied but Zara knew why. "She'll be fine," she told him. "Auntie Cassie is the strongest woman I know, Johnny. She had a shock, that's all. We'll make sure she pulls through. And the teaching job will keep her busy."

"You're a good girl, Zara," Johnny replied. "Mike, you've done a good job with this one. If Cassie's the strongest woman in the village, this one isn't too far behind," he ruffled Zara's hair in the way only he could.

"It wasn't just me that brought her up," Mike said. "We all did it, Johnny. Me, you, Bow, Cass, Nancy, Penny, Samir. We all did it."

Johnny raised both eyebrows and nodded. "And now we're old farts, she'll get to look after us!"

They all laughed. After a short silence, Zara spoke.

"Thanks, guys. I know everyone talks about the Time Before. But I really couldn't imagine growing up in a better place. I've got the best family anyone could ask for."

They were interrupted by a rumbling sound. A flurry of legs and antlers mingled together as a herd of several dozen deer passed them. Zara smiled at the sight. There was something so natural, so beautiful about them. Within seconds they were gone, disappearing in the distance beyond the brow of a grassy hill.

Mike thought back to their mission. If they succeeded, if they found a doctor in Newcastle and persuaded him to come and live in Windermere, their little utopia on the edge of the lake would be complete.

14

The next day went by with more of the ghastly dead bodies but little in the way of interest. The decayed, cracked road sprouted long reeds of grass which the three cyclists had to slalom around to avoid. After a few more hours of riding, they came to a river, which they followed for several miles. The river reminded Zara of home, the water much like the tranquil sheen of Lake Windermere. They crossed it, over a stone bridge, Zara looking down warily at the large cracks, exposing the flowing water below. There was a good ten-meter gap between the three companions and Zara occupied her usual berth in the middle of three, with her father at the rear in place of Andy. *Andy,* Zara thought. *Poor Andy.* He had been a sensitive soul, one of the quietest people in the village. Zara had always liked him, hell, she loved everyone in the village; they were her family. But Andy, distant, introspective Andy, had been as close as their community had come to an outsider. The trip to Whitehaven had made Zara see Andy in a different light. He was kind and funny. She had grown to like him and even felt a hint of attraction towards him, despite the not insignificant age difference. And now Andy was dead, lying in a grave beside the tree that leaned into the lake. Zara sighed. She had no male peers. Johnny had Cassie, Bow had Nancy. The Jameson and Bowskill children would probably match up with each other when they were older. But Zara was alone. She glanced back at her father and realized he was in the same position, without a spouse. It was something she hadn't really considered before, that her Dad might be lonely, yearning for company. But all the females in New Windermere were spoken for. She broke out of her daydream as she noticed that Johnny had stopped ahead of her. He was pointing across the river at a large, odd-shaped glass building.

The building was magnificent. It reminded Zara of the campus at Windermere University, where her Dad had been a big shot in the Time Before. It was curved and covered in paneled glass, which reflected both the sunlight and the water in a sublime mixture of blue and yellow. Zara's mouth gaped and a warm feeling rose in her heart as she saw what Johnny was pointing at. Painted on the side of the glass building, in giant black letters, was one word. One word, five letters that conveyed so much. It meant hope, companionship, a future. It meant their mission might be a success.

ALIVE.

Mike joined them, pulling up his bike. His eyes gleamed and his whole face was beaming. Johnny glanced at Zara. "Don't get too excited, Professor. Your daughter and I have been here before." And they had, Zara remembered glumly, recalling the death she had witnessed inside the USS New York. "That sign could've been there for a while," Johnny added.

"Still, there's a chance. Newcastle Medical School isn't far from here. There's a chance. Even if there are more survivors, Johnny, we haven't seen any other humans from outside the village since all this happened. Sixteen years. You've got to let me get a little excited at this, John," Mike said. His eyes were wide, almost manic. Zara's thoughts returned to her father's loneliness.

"Hope," Johnny said, sighing. "It's the hope that kills you, Professor."

No," Mike said, almost shouting. "It's the hope that keeps you alive!" He pointed at the building. "I bet that we find good people up there, medic or no medic, and that we're better off because of it."

Johnny laughed. "And if they're bad? If they're all toting machine guns? If they're feral cannibals, waiting to boil us in a pot and eat us for supper?"

"Okay, you got me. You're an old cynic, Johnny. All these missions have made you mistrust everything. Come on, let's go and see."

Johnny nodded. There was a white bridge, shaped like a crescent with a noticeable bend. They rode their bikes over the bridge and found themselves at the foot of the curved glass building. Leaving the bikes behind, they climbed stone steps, dodging the large cracks that had formed in the concrete. They reached the imposing doorway. Johnny pushed the door open.

The inside of the building was wide and spacious.

"Used to be a music venue, I think," Mike said, his voice bellowing louder than he expected, accentuated by the curved ceiling.

Something occurred to Mike: he hadn't seen any human remains for the last two miles. This place looked clean and tidy and it smelled nice. It was a smell Mike recognized. Before he could identify it, Johnny looked at them both with excited eyes. "Popcorn!" he shouted. "I smell popcorn!"

Zara was confused. She didn't know what popcorn was, but she sensed that it was somehow a good thing. Johnny, as usual, led the way, quickening his pace in pursuit of the source of the sweet smell. He burst through a door, followed closely by Zara and Mike. The door led to a balcony, looking down at a large room, shaped like an auditorium, with several seats facing the front. They gaped in awe and froze at the sight below them.

There were two people in seats, looking at a raised platform. On the platform, a woman lay on the floor, a dagger protruding from her chest with a patch of blood growing on her white t-shirt. On top of her was a man, his head leant back. They were both dead. Zara screamed, the acoustics in the auditorium causing the sound to shoot jaggedly around the room. The people in the seats looked up, shocked at the sudden entrance of the three intruders.

15

It was Mike who first realized what they had stumbled upon. When the two 'dead' people on the stage had stood up and jumped up and down in excitement at seeing new faces, Mike had burst into hysterical laughter. The people below them had just finished a performance of William Shakespeare's *Romeo and Juliet.* Juliet had plunged the dagger in her own heart while Romeo had poisoned himself seconds before Mike, Zara and Johnny had burst through the door. Zara, unfamiliar with the work of Shakespeare, took a while to understand but joined in the laughter all the same.

"Hey. Hey, come down and join us," the man dressed as Romeo shouted. "We'll meet you at the bottom."

Johnny led the way again, although his hand brushed the handgun strapped to his belt.

They descended the stairs to meet the group. They were the first live human beings that they had seen outside their community in twenty years and Mike rushed down the stairs excitedly, almost knocking into Johnny. Zara, still raw from her experience on the ship, walked tentatively.

They met in the auditorium. Shaking hands and hugging. Johnny loosened up. The fast and rhythmic North East accents of the new group were friendly and reassuring. Johnny soon forgot about his handgun. Halfway through the introductions, Mike remembered the purpose of the mission.

"Are any of you a doctor?" he asked the actress playing Juliet, a middle-aged black woman, who introduced herself as Vanessa. She had thick black hair and bright white teeth, displayed in a dazzling smile. Everything about Vanessa's face conveyed friendliness and warmth.

"Well, you've certainly asked the right person," she replied in an accent that was two-thirds African and one-third Geordie.

"In my previous life, I was a junior doctor. Sophia over there is a nurse. Why do you ask? Do you need help?"

Mike's answer wasn't verbal. He grabbed Vanessa and launched her upwards, before planting a giant kiss on her cheek. "Yes!" he shouted, his voice echoing in the vast room. "You hear that, Johnny?"

"Okay, Prof, I admit it, you were right," replied Johnny, smiling.

The next few hours were a blur as they experienced new people for the first time. They sat in the auditorium seats and asked each other their stories, how they came to survive in this new world and their theories on what caused the events of 2038. And they ate popcorn, something Zara thought tasted like light, fluffy balls of heaven.

The building they found themselves in was the Sage Gateshead, over the river from Newcastle-Upon-Tyne. The survivors had come from all over the surrounding area, as far south as Middlesbrough and as far north as Northumberland. Much like them, the Gateshead survivors had cleared the bodies from the surrounding area soon after they emerged from hiding. Once each week, they performed a play from the works of Shakespeare, in an attempt to use entertainment to ease boredom and to give them a project to work on – to put the building to its intended use. *Everyone needs a project*, Mike had thought to himself. As was to be expected, each of the four survivors in Gateshead had a tough survival story. Vanessa had hidden in a secure room in Newcastle General Hospital as murder and suicide broke out in an ugly wave on each floor of the large facility. Paul, a small, intense-looking man of around forty years old, had been forced to throw his girlfriend out of their apartment window. "She just kept coming at me," he told the group, shaking his head at the memory. Vanessa grabbed his hand as he told the story, offering him some comfort.

Mike filled them in on their mission: Andy's death, Cassie's resignation and the lack of any medical knowledge in their community. He glanced at Vanessa during his speech and she didn't look away. Mike thought that was a good sign. Zara filled them in on the message from the president, news which stunned them into silence.

"The video," remarked Ronnie, who had been playing the part of Romeo on stage. "But... I saw it. How come I'm okay?" They all spoke in agreement that they had seen it and not been affected.

"I don't have the answers for you, I'm afraid," replied Mike. "But I do think it was the cause."

"Whoah," Ronnie said. "I thought it was some kind of disease."

"Us too," added Johnny. "Well, apart from the Professor here, the technology hotshot."

"Never trusted that Razor guy," Vanessa said. "They should never have let one person have all that power. Something like this was bound to happen at some time."

Silence passed between them for a few seconds. They all looked down at their hands awkwardly. There was an elephant in the room. Paul was the first to bring it up.

"So then. You've come here to find a doctor. And you've got one. So, what happens now? We leave here and live happily ever after with you?"

"Yeah..." Mike replied. "That's about the size of it. Look, we're all survivors here. When's the last time someone new came on board with you lot here."

Ronnie looked upwards, thinking. "I'd say about three months after it first happened."

"Exactly," said Mike. "This is amazing. We weren't sure we'd find anyone here. But when I saw your sign, 'ALIVE', I just knew. Something just felt right. Our community in New Windermere is good. It's got room to grow, places to live. We have a farm, fresh vegetables. Clean water from the lake. A school, a little town hall. We've got a good thing going over there. A real community. We want you to be a part of it."

"But you don't have a doctor? No real healthcare available," Vanessa replied.

Mike nodded and shoveled a handful of popcorn into his mouth.

"Well. We'll need to discuss it amongst ourselves, Mike," Vanessa continued. "But I've got to admit, it sounds pretty good."

The two groups split off, allowing the Gateshead survivors to talk about the opportunity that awaited them in New Windermere. Mike was anxious. He was desperate to bring them home. And not just to include a doctor in their population. He was energized by the new people and he saw the same reaction in Johnny and Zara. They were fascinated by their new friends and had already talked for hours, effortlessly. Mike felt they would be good additions to their community.

After an hour, Vanessa came up to Mike, leading the small group that made up their community.

"Professor Pilkington. You've got yourselves some new residents in New Windermere. But on one condition."

"And what's that?"

"This man Bow you talk about. The man you say could build anything. Would he build me my own doctor's surgery?"

"Vanessa, for you, I'd build it myself with my bare hands."

"It's a deal," she said and offered her hand out to Mike. There were smiles all round the group, although Johnny thought he detected some malice in Paul's expression. It didn't surprise him. He wasn't sure how he'd react himself if people came to take them to the other side of England. After all, who needed who the most? It had been their need for a doctor that had brought them here in the first place.

Mike shook Vanessa's hand. "Excellent. Okay then. Now we just need to work out how to get back without any bikes."

"Ah, worry no longer. There's a vintage bike shop over the river. We've got one each already."

Mike, Johnny and Zara all looked at each other and laughed. The mission was going perfectly. *Too good to be true?* Mike thought, and brushed the thought away as quickly as it came.

16

They carried several supplies, Johnny, Mike and Ronnie hauling the trailers behind their bikes. A day's riding took them to the eastern side of the A66 road at Barnard Castle, where they set up camp in the grounds of the castle itself. There was still some rabbit to share, and the Gateshead survivors brought popcorn, which Sophia heated in a makeshift pan. They sat in a circle, eating and chatting.

The mood in their temporary roadside camp was jovial, despite the numerous bodies they had seen since passing Durham. It was something they had come to accept. Mike wondered to himself whether the skeletons would ever disappear, whether they would decompose and be sucked back into the earth. *Maybe archaeologists thousands of years in the future will attempt to study all the bones and piece it together. Maybe they'll do a better job in finding out about it than we have,* he thought to himself.

After they had eaten, Ronnie pulled out a pack of cigarettes and handed them around the group. Mike and Johnny took one, but Zara refused, thinking about the cannabis she had smoked with Johnny and Andy a few days earlier on Whitehaven beach.

Mike lifted the cigarette and lit it, Ronnie holding the match under his face. The lit cigarettes sparkled in the darkness, like dancing fireflies. The embers of the cigarettes glowed and lit up the faces of the smokers.

"Okay, story time. Anyone got a good one?" Vanessa said. She had also refused a cigarette. Working in a medical profession, seeing exposed blackened lungs, various cancers and smoking-related amputations had put her off for life, even in this barren world.

There was silence for a few seconds. Zara, Johnny and Mike looked at each other, bemused. This group had different routines and it felt like they had been thrust into a strange new world.

The survivors in Gateshead were flamboyant. Their culture was heavily reliant on expressions, the arts. It made Mike feel comfortable and he realized that any form of entertainment was missing from the New Windermere community. This new group would not only add healthcare, but they would also inject fun and art. It was a thought that warmed him.

"I got one," Ronnie said, his bright white teeth exposed in a mischievous grin as the glow of his cigarette lit up his face. He looked at the cigarette. "It's about smoking actually."

Vanessa groaned. "That dirty habit. You're obsessed!"

"Haha. No, it's not what you think. Are you ready, kids?"

They all nodded, the red cigarette ends bouncing in unison. Sophia nudged Zara. "Ronnie's stories are the best. He's a natural comedian."

Zara looked at Ronnie. His entire aura seemed to center around joviality. He was always looking for his next joke to make people laugh. His hair flopped over his forehead and his cheeks were soft and pink, giving him a permanent youthful look. He held his cigarette expertly, flicking the end with grace and precision at regular intervals.

"Okay, here we go. So, as you know, I smoke a few cigarettes a day," he began.

"A few!" Sophia interrupted. "You smoke like a chimney!"

"Okay, okay. Sophia, it's my story. Are you gonna let me tell it or not?"

Sophia looked down, feigning sadness at her castigation.

"So, one day I wake up and I tell myself. *This is the day I quit.* I've been coughing for a few weeks and my new girlfriend's complaining about the stale smell I always have on my clothes. My teeth are going a bit yellow. I can't even go to the cinema without wanting the film to end so I can fill my lungs with this horrible stuff. So, I just quit, there and then. I stop for good. It was easy."

"Yeah right," Sophia said, then slapped her hand over her

mouth when Ronnie glared at her.

"Well, it *was* easy. I went two weeks without even fancying one. Even went on two nights out, got pretty hammered and still didn't have one. I'd quit. So, what did I do on the night when two weeks had passed? I celebrated. Bought myself a pack of ten and smoked right through them. I'd done it, see? I proved to myself I wasn't addicted, so I started smoking again."

The group laughed at Ronnie's twisted logic. This time it was Vanessa's turn to speak. "So, you're a non-smoker because of those two weeks?"

"No, of course not. I soon became addicted again. The point is, I quit and didn't even fancy one. But the idea of smoking as a treat for quitting, it was like I was proving to myself that I could smoke without being a smoker. Does that make sense?"

They all laughed raucously. They were wiping tears from their eyes.

"Well, that was my first attempt to quit," Ronnie continued. "And I have to say it would have been successful if I didn't have my little reward to mark two weeks smoke-free. Attempt two was, how could I put it, much less successful. I booked myself into a hypnotist. If I couldn't stop smoking using my own willpower, maybe I could be hypnotized to do it. So, I meet this woman and go into this small, dark room. She puts this weird music on and starts talking in this strange, low voice. I just kept bursting out in laughter. At one point she got, like, really angry and told me to take it seriously. So, I did. All I heard was her talking. I was expecting to go into some kind of trance, where I could reach the deepest parts of my mind, all that weird shit. But nothing happened. She asked me to visualize the damage each cig was doing to my body, to imagine the smoke blackening my insides and causing tumors to instantly appear. I closed my eyes tight and imagined it, these fleshy lumps just *growing* inside my neck, my chest, even my balls.

"So, I'm sat there, eyes shut tight, picturing these horrible tumors infecting my body, imagining my black lungs. Then this woman clicks her fingers and says, *"You're back with me."* Back with me? Like I'd ever left in the first place. The stupidest thing was, I didn't have the heart to tell her it was a crock of shit. That I'd just spent half an hour of my life with my eyes closed picturing horrible things inside my body. I'd paid a hundred quid for the privilege. It was stressful, y'know, to maybe tell this woman she wasn't good at her job when she took herself so seriously, but I kind of felt ripped off at the same time. So, I paid her the money, walked out of the building, made sure I was at a safe distance and smoked seven cigarettes in a row. For the stress, like."

For the second time that evening, they all howled with laughter. Mike's eyes dripped with tears, which he had to wipe away with the sleeve of his shirt. Johnny threw his head back and released a booming laugh that came straight from his stomach.

"And, I suppose that day I just gave up giving up." He put out his cigarette and lit another. "And, given what's happened to the world, I think there's a lot worse hobbies to take up. So, cigarettes in the air, everyone. Drinks in the air to you non-smokers," he looked at Zara, Vanessa and Paul through squinted eyes, feigning anger. He affected a grand, regal voice. "I propose a toast, to the cancer sticks. May our lungs be blackened and our tumors grow. But we shall say at the end, that it was certainly worth it."

When the laughter subsided into a few chuckles and sighs, Johnny spoke.

"I got one about a hypnotist too. I won't tell it as funny as Ronnie here, but it just reminded me of something, in the Time Before."

"Go ahead," Ronnie said. "Do your worst, big man." Ronnie lay back, taking a heavy drag on his cigarette. "No pressure," he added. "But I *will* mark you out of ten."

"Right. So, it must have been about 2030, I went to this comedy club with my wife. They had this hypnotist up, and he was making people do all sorts of daft stuff. One man was hypnotized to think that everyone apart from him in the room was naked. You should've seen him, he was grinning like a schoolkid. No one in the room was allowed to let on that they knew. He kept staring at this beautiful blonde girl in the audience and the more he did it, the more embarrassed she got. Ah, it was so funny. But then he gets me and my wife on stage. He hypnotizes us both separately. Just like you, Ronnie, I'm shutting my eyes tight. I'm not sure if it's working. I'm trying to relax, trying to make it take effect. He's telling me, *"Your wife is a dog,"* and the audience are in hysterics at the double meaning. I resist the temptation to open my eyes and have a go at him. *"Your wife is a dog,"* he repeats to me. *"She's a big, black Labrador. She wants to go for a walk. You're in a park. Take her for a walk. When I say "walkies," you will think she is a dog."*

Zara was listening intently, she'd never heard Johnny tell this story. The idea that people could manipulate the minds of others was fascinating and as alien a concept to her as the stories of RazorVision and self-driving cars. She looked at the rest of the group. They were all smiling apart from her father and Paul. Mike stared at Johnny as he spoke, it looked as if the cogs of his mind were working overtime. Paul had a glum look on his face. Zara noticed that his eyes would flick to Vanessa every few minutes.

Johnny continued his story. "So, then he goes to my wife and tells her, *"You're a dog."* Then he tells her that I'm playing games with her, she needs to go on all fours and run around me."

"Did it work?" Zara asked, fascinated.

"It did and it didn't," Johnny replied. "As soon as the hypnotist said the word, my wife went down on all fours, running circles around me. She was barking and her tongue was lolling out her mouth. She panted when she stopped still. She even went on her hind legs and looked up at me with her tongue still hanging out." Johnny sighed comically as the others laughed loudly.

"That's some story, big man," said Ronnie. He leant forward and shook Johnny's hand. "The King is dead, long live the King. Ladies and gentlemen, I've been usurped. There is a new King of Comedy in town," he yelled to an imaginary crowd.

"How did it affect you?" Mike asked, his face focused in a serious manner. "Did you go along with it."

"Well, that's the worst bit," Johnny replied, "it didn't affect me at all and I didn't even go along with it. I just stood there like a lemon as my wife ran around on all fours. Shit, it was embarrassing. The most embarrassing moment of my life. I had to just turn around and tell the hypnotist that it hadn't worked. I couldn't pretend. That's what reminded me of it, Ronnie. When you said you pretended so you didn't hurt your hypnotist's feelings. That's what I should've done. Why didn't I do it?"

"You're about twenty-five years too late to worry about that, big man," Ronnie answered. "What did the hypnotist say?"

"Well, he didn't seem to mind. The fact that I stood up there, totally unaffected, seemed to make it funnier for the audience. I was the straight man and my wife was the funny one. She was mortified when she realized later. She said she was aware of what she was doing but that it just felt like the right thing to do. The hypnotist just said that it actually happens quite a lot, that around a quarter of all people are immune."

"I'm immune too," said Vanessa.

Mike grabbed Vanessa's wrist in a move so abrupt that it made the rest of the group jump.

"That's it!" he shouted. "That's why we survived. The president was right, the video hypnotized everyone apart from us."

The group all looked at him, open mouthed. "Do you get it? Why didn't I realize it before? Everyone in this group saw the video. And we didn't get hypnotized. We were immune!"

Zara looked away from her father's excited expression. He was wrong about one thing: she hadn't seen the video.

17

They discussed Mike's theory and all agreed it was probably right. It was further evidence that the intelligence provided to the president before his death was correct. Rick Razor was most likely the cause. The video had been on his network. Only he had the power to control technology in that way.

Mike remembered Simon's anger at him the day before his wife turned. He had blamed Razor for all the world's ills, the widening gap between rich and poor, the availability of unlimited data on every one of its five billion users, including the thoughts inside their heads. Maybe Simon was right. But why would Rick Razor have used a video to effectively wipe out the world's population? Had he been compromised by a terrorist? Mike thought not. Death by video hypnosis would be too elaborate a plan for the average terrorist. Had Razor been a psychopath all along, building up his empire in order to wipe it clean? Was Razor himself even alive? These questions raced around Mike's head as he sat in a circle with his fellow survivors.

Ronnie, true to character, lightened the mood. "Well I think this calls for another toast." He lit his fourth cigarette of the evening and held it in the air. "A toast to all of us. We're all shit at getting hypnotized. And now, we're still alive because of it. To us, and our underdeveloped, unhypnotizable little minds."

The group all laughed hard at that one, apart from Paul. Paul's eyes were locked on Vanessa and Mike. He had noticed, as had some others, that Mike held Vanessa's hand in his.

Mike spoke. "In all seriousness though, that's not the only reason we're still alive. If around a quarter of people can't get hypnotized and another few million people didn't use Razor technology at all, that still leaves quite a few people who wouldn't have been affected. And that tells you all you need to know about how this happened."

"How so?" Sophia asked. "Should there not be a lot more survivors?"

Johnny smiled without humor or happiness. "Anyone not affected, I suppose, was killed by the affected. We've all got a story about killing a loved one or hiding away for weeks or months on end. We all climbed mountains to survive. I think there will be other survivors but I bet those who weren't affected were mostly murdered."

Murdered, thought Mike. A brutal, cold word that conjured up images of blood and death. His own wife had tried to kill both himself and Zara. He shuddered at the memory.

"That's right," he said to Johnny. "It was genius really. Evil genius. Whoever did this, if it *was* Razor or not, they wanted to make sure everyone was gone, erased from the world. The affected were hypnotized to kill the unaffected. When there was no one left to kill, the affected killed themselves. It's a perfect solution. Well, if your solution involves killing the world."

"And we bucked the trend," Vanessa added. "We avoided the hypnosis and then the killing."

"But there is still one big question," Mike continued, pointing one finger in the air. Zara rolled her eyes. She'd seen her father act like this several times in the classroom. It was his academic theory mode. He was excitable, each additional sentence adding to his enthusiasm until it became a spiral of revelation and his ideas developed further. "We've worked out the *how* but what about the *why*? What possible reason could anyone, including Rick Razor, have to wipe out humanity?"

They discussed it at length, with various reasons ranging from aliens to good old-fashioned psychopathy. They talked for hours and Sophia dozed off. "I think I'll turn in too," said Johnny. "It's been a hell of a day."

"Too right, big man," said Ronnie. Johnny glowed. He hadn't dished out his trademark hair-ruffle yet, but everyone could tell he liked Ronnie's breezy humor. Earlier, Ronnie had told them how he escaped. A drama student at the local college, he had been on a night out. He'd dodged five attackers and hid in a sewer, surrounded by the putrid smells of human waste, while rats, sleek from the liquid waste they lived in, scurried past his body. Johnny felt that even at this point, this low, difficult situation, seventeen-year-old Ronnie would still have cracked a few jokes to himself. The famous British 'gallows humor' was an apt phrase for someone like Ronnie.

Mike, still buzzing from his discovery, didn't feel tired at all. "I think I'll go for a walk round the castle."

"Be careful, Dad," Zara said.

Vanessa looked at him. "Do you mind if I come?"

The rest of the group looked at Mike in anticipation of his answer, including Zara. Paul's eyes narrowed.

"Of course not. The more the merrier." He grinned.

Zara snuggled into her sleeping bag and watched them walk into the distance. *He's found someone,* she thought, not without a touch of jealousy.

"I just felt I had to process this somehow," Mike told Vanessa when they were out of sight of the rest of the group. "I've been an academic all my adult life, I suppose I'm always looking for answers. The others, they're interested, but I suppose I just see it as a mission. I can't live my life without finding out. I just can't."

Vanessa took his hand as they walked. Mike had only known this woman a matter of hours but he felt a deep connection with her. In the old days, before he met Charlotte, he never felt that way about anyone. Even when he met Charlie it evolved over a matter of months. But, whether it was this setting in the new world or whether it was something chemical between them that would have happened in any time or place, he wasn't sure. And at this moment in time, he didn't care.

"In your old job, you were an expert on technology?" she asked.

"I suppose I was more like *the* expert," he replied. "I followed

Rick Razor's career. I taught people on the history of social media, the sociological impact of his technology and the potential for future developments. A bit embarrassing now, really. I must have been pretty shit at my job!"

Vanessa squeezed his hand. "I'm sure that wasn't the case."

"Maybe not. It's funny though, the night before it all happened, I had a strange conversation with one of my students. My *best* student. He was looking at the impact of Razor Technology on the Third World. If it could help, or if it was making things worse. He seemed to have decided on the latter. I had a huge argument with him about it, where he told me I was blinded by technology. He seemed to have found something out about the way the data was being used. Maybe he knew something about this. It was the last time I spoke to him."

"Did he die?" Vanessa asked.

"I assume he did. I mean, I never saw his body, but between us we buried thousands of people over the years. And the more time went on, the harder it was to recognize people." Mike shivered, recalling the hundreds of bodies he personally dragged to their graves: so many oozing, rotting corpses, the stench of death polluting his senses.

"Can I ask you a question?" Vanessa enquired.

Mike nodded.

"Did you not agree with him? About the gap between rich and poor? About the negative impact of Razor Technology on the Third World?"

"Not really. I suppose I just believed that Rick Razor was working hard to fix it."

"I disagree, I'm afraid," Vanessa said, looking not at him but straight ahead. "I'm originally from Lagos in Nigeria. I've seen the effect of Razor Incorporated from both sides. I've seen the rich become richer and the poor become poorer. I've seen RazorVision, used free in the west, unavailable to people in the slums. Apparently, they thought it'd be dangerous for it to be distributed there. And I've heard rumors of data and money being used for political gain, even war. It's never been an equal world, but Razor made it worse and worse. And if he was responsible for this then I wouldn't be surprised."

Mike thought about this before he spoke. "Yes, I understand what you're saying, completely. I suppose I just thought it would spread around the world eventually."

"Eventually!" Vanessa spat out the word. "Like people in Africa are an afterthought. Someone to take care of once the fat cats in the west have been fed. Sorry, I don't mean to have a go at you. It's just that, one of the best things about this new world we're in is the lack of technology. People were indifferent to the world around them. What would happen if people went to a concert, visited a famous landmark? If you rewound twenty years and stood here, in front of this beautiful building, what would the tourists have been doing? Looking and admiring with the naked eye? Or would they have RazorVision strapped to their faces? Why did we need to enhance the world all of a sudden? Is our planet not good enough? If we'd had this conversation all that time ago, would we be having it face-to-face, alone? Or would we be interrupted by a newsflash or some god-awful machine telling us that we'd burned sixty calories or walked four-point-five bloody miles?"

"You were a traditionalist then? In the Time Before?" Mike asked.

"No I wasn't a fucking traditionalist! I was me. A human being. I used the technology like everyone else. But I just saw an obsession. Why should anyone know all those things about me? My height, my weight, the number of alcoholic units I had every week, the number of hours I slept? My thoughts? Whose hands would that fall into? People, organizations could tell where I was at any time with the minimum of effort. Is it any wonder the world pretty much ended when we all gave one company so much power?"

"Ah but you're forgetting the good that was done too," Mike interjected. This was an argument he used to have regularly in the Time Before. "Suicide detection saved thousands of lives. Anti-bullying techniques made sure the products weren't being used to pick on people, or minimized it at least. All the relationships that were started by people networking with Razor Technology. The eradication of obesity."

"And where did you get that information from?" Vanessa asked. "How do you know it wasn't propaganda? Did you know a suicide that didn't happen because of Razor? Did you know of any bullies who stopped picking on people because Razor employed a new head of bullying? *Think*, Professor. You're an academic man. Should you not question things? Challenge the status quo? I think your student was right, you've been blinded by the technology. You made the mistake that generations before us have made, you believed the hype. You were sucked in by the convenience. The shiny new things at your disposal, and the improvements to your cushy western life."

"Wow," Mike exclaimed, but he couldn't follow it up with further words. He was speechless. After all his years as a respected lecturer, he never had anything explained to him as convincingly as that about Razor Technology. This beautiful doctor from Lagos had turned his whole belief system upside down.

"Sorry if that was harsh," she said. "I'm just passionate about it. The world has so much beauty and I just felt that we were plunging further and further into darkness."

"No. No, you're right. I'm passionate too about it. It's just what you said. I think you're right. I really think you're right."

He pulled her hand around and spun her into a tight embrace.

"Professor!" she said, smiling. "Where did you learn that move?"

"Us dusty academics didn't just bury our heads in books you know."

He leant into her and kissed her. It was the first woman he had kissed in over sixteen years. Her lips were soft and sweet. He felt her tongue enter his mouth. It felt heavenly. When they broke off, they looked into each other's eyes.

"Vanessa, I'm not normally cheesy with stuff like this, but ever since we first met in Gateshead, I just felt something between us."

"Shut up and kiss me, you idiot," Vanessa replied.

When they had finished their long, slow kiss, Mike leaned back, grinning and looked Vanessa in the eyes. "Wow. I've got to tell you. Since my wife, you're the first person I've kissed."

"And she'll be the last, you fucking pompous prick," said a voice from the shadows.

It was Paul. He was pointing a gun straight at Mike's head.

18

"Paul, calm down," Vanessa said. "Please. Put the gun down."

"Wh–What's going on?" Mike stuttered. "Are you two together?"

"Not anymore," Vanessa said.

"Ah, right," Mike said. He stretched his hand out in an attempt to calm Paul, but Paul's eyes were wild, his face strained in intense focus.

"Fuck you. You prick, who do you think you are, coming here and taking us away to your fucking commune. How do we know who you are?" Paul yelled.

Vanessa tried a different approach. "Paul, you know you're not going to do anything with the gun. Whatever we had, it ended over a year ago. Go on, put it down. Look at yourself. You're not going to use it."

It didn't work. Paul raised the gun and pulled the trigger. With a loud crack, the bullet flew upwards towards the castle and smacked a dusty hunk of stone. "You believe me now, Vanessa? I'm serious. I'll either take one of you, or both of you. You lot from Windermere think you're so great, don't you? With your shit-stinking farm and your boring fucking lake. And we're coming over to *you* because you happen to need a doctor and a nurse. But what about me? What good am I to you? I was unemployed in the old world. I was a fucking junkie. The only reason I survived this shit was because I'd spent three days wrecked out of my eyeballs. What good is a dickhead like me in your new world, your u-fucking-topia by the lake? Not much. As soon as you settle them in, you'll get rid of me. But I'm not going to let that happen."

His manic eyes shifted from one of them to another, back and forth. When he spoke, large globules of saliva flew out of his mouth. "I'll fucking kill you!" He raised the gun, Mike and

Vanessa hugged each other and squeezed their eyes tight. When the shot came, with another deafening crack, it whizzed over their heads. Mike opened his eyes to see Johnny jumping on Paul's back and wrestling him to the ground. The others emerged from behind them, looking on in terrified awe.

Johnny picked the gun up off the ground, which had spun away and landed on the grass.

"I wasn't ready for this today," he muttered.

Paul jumped up behind Johnny. He had drawn a small, sharp knife from his sock. "Fuck you. Fuck all of you," he shouted.

As Johnny spun round to look at him, Paul planted the knife into his chest with considerable force. Johnny gurgled. Blood dribbled out of his mouth and streamed out of the wound, splashing onto the grass below. His eyes were wide with shock. Mike gasped. Zara screamed Johnny's name. Vanessa's eyes filled with tears. Ronnie stood, silent and frozen, his jaw gaping open.

Johnny fell forward, the knife's handle sticking out of his chest rammed even further into his body on impact with the ground. He gurgled once more and then fell into silence.

Paul picked up the gun that lay beside Johnny's dead body. He waved it around the crowd. "Fuck you all. Wankers. See you all in hell." He tittered manically, still waving the gun. For the second time that night, Mike squeezed his eyes shut, unsure if he would open them in this life or the next.

Paul put the gun to his own head and pulled the trigger. The top half of his head simply collapsed with the force. Red, pink and white matter burst out of his skull and splattered onto the ground, the hot gun smoke lifting thickly from the mess into the night air. His lifeless body crumpled onto the floor.

Vanessa wailed. "I'm so sorry," she shouted at no one and everyone. "I should've seen it. I knew he didn't want to come. I knew he wasn't right."

"Shhhhhh," Mike said as he put his arm around her.

Zara sobbed as she looked at Johnny's body. She had loved him as an uncle but she had respected him as the man he was; an adventurer, a man who literally went to the ends of the earth for the community. Her sobs grew louder when she thought of his children. Olivia and Louie, Lorraine and Jimmy. And Cassie. Poor Cassie who had blamed herself for Andy's death. She would blame herself again. They were supposed to be going back to New Windermere with fantastic news but instead they were returning with tragedy once more. She crouched down next to Johnny's body and hugged him, her tears dripping onto his back.

19

The journey back to Windermere was almost silent. Mike cycled hard, taking his emotions out on his bike. He kept glancing back to his trailer, where Johnny's shrouded body lay. It was only when they stopped to repair Sophia's flat tire that Vanessa came and spoke to him.

"It sounds obvious now, but Paul was a bit unstable. When he came to us he was all over the place. I helped him get through the heroin withdrawal. Administered methadone, made him comfortable. He was a good man but he'd lost his way. I knew he still liked me but I just didn't see this coming."

Mike hugged her. "Don't beat yourself up. Just leave things to me when we get there. Johnny was probably the most respected man in the entire village. It's going to be hard for them to welcome newcomers when they've lost such an important figure, and that's me being honest. And we've recently lost two others. But trust me, we will get there. I promise you."

"I'll hold you to that," she told Mike. "Thanks. I just wish it could've been so much easier."

Mike leaned forward and kissed her on the forehead.

* * *

Their arrival in New Windermere had been even more traumatic than Mike could have imagined. Of all people, Cassie and her children came to greet them first. Cassie had looked around and smiled at the sight of other people. She even shouted to her children that there were newcomers. But then she realized that her husband was missing.

"Johnny? Johnny? Where's Johnny?" Each time she said his name, it got louder, more desperate. Until the name was snorted, accompanied by tears and snot. Mike caught her eye. He shook his head, solemnly which reduced Cassie to her knees. Her children surrounded her, asking, *"Mummy what's wrong? Where's Daddy?"* But Cassie couldn't answer. The answer was unspeakable.

The rest of the day was gloomy and awkward. Vanessa made herself at home, setting up her office and treating some minor injuries to children. She checked over Iain's foot, which had been suffering from severe cramps, causing him agony. But the other newcomers didn't know where to put themselves. Ronnie had been hit the hardest, his jovial, comic persona was no good in this environment.

Mike requested a private meeting with Matty. They walked over to the south bank of the lake, where they shared one of Ronnie's cigarettes.

"Matty, we've got a challenge here," Mike said. "We got what we went for. But what happened to Johnny was a travesty."

"You can say that again," Matty scoffed.

"This has got to work. We went for a reason, to bring back a doctor. And we came back with a doctor, a nurse and another survivor. We succeeded."

"It sure as hell doesn't feel like it, Mike."

"I know, I know. But these people have been through the same as us, Matty. They've had to battle through this shit too. They've seen their loved ones die. They're survivors like us. We can't let Johnny's death be for nothing. The rest of the village have got to accept them as their own. They're just like us. Nothing more, nothing less. And we need them more than they need us."

"Rumor has it you've grown quite attached to our new doctor?" He glanced sideways at Mike and drew on his cigarette.

Mike looked away. The evening breeze blew across the lake. Two ducks glided along, their reflections glistening in the rippling water.

"That's right. I can't deny it. But why am I justifying to you, Matty? I brought back a doctor and a nurse. I found survivors. The first new people we've seen in over sixteen years. There was a nutter amongst them and he nearly killed me. He nearly killed Vanessa. But he killed Johnny and then himself. It's something I'll carry with me for the rest of my life. Why him, not me? But I'll tell you something, Matty. I stopped feeling sorry for myself the day I buried my wife under that weeping willow by the lake. I stopped apologizing for the actions of others when me and you buried all those people in that mass grave. These survivors I've brought back are human beings. They're us. They're me, you, Zara, Cassie. And we *have* to welcome them. If our community means anything to any of us it has to be open. It has to welcome people, no matter what the circumstances. Otherwise, what are we? We may as well join the animals on the farm."

Matty took a drag on his cigarette. This time it was longer and made the embers glow a bright orange. "You're right. Of course, you're right," he said. "I'll call a meeting and formally introduce them." He eyed Mike cautiously. "There will be a backlash, you know that? It's hard to welcome newcomers when people you love have gone. Like it's some kind of swap. And we all need to be there for Cass and the kids. They're a mess. She'd only just picked herself up after Andy, and now this."

"Of course. Goes without saying."

"Right then, let's go and try and fix this shower of shit. Let's get our village back the way it was."

"Matty," Mike said. "That's not all."

Matty eyed him with mock disdain. "Whatever else could be the matter? Shit."

Mike filled Matty in with his theory about the video. The hypnosis. The immunity. When Mike was finished, Matty looked up at him.

"Jesus. That's some news you've brought back. Some news. One thing at a time though, Mike. I'm an old man now, you know. One thing at a time."

They walked back to the village, the moonlight illuminating their path.

20

Johnny's funeral was somber. The newcomers from Gateshead attended, at Cassie's request, but stood towards the back of the group. Mike's heart warmed when Cassie invite them to join hands around the tree. The one they chose was a good hundred yards outside the village gates. Louie and Olivia had chosen it especially, after Cassie had told them to find a tree that represented their father. It was a balsam poplar, wide and expansive, with auburn leaves decorating its chunky branches. Mike thought it was apt that people would need to walk outside the village to remember Johnny, given his pioneering adventures. He wasn't sure if the twins had done that deliberately or subconsciously, but he liked the idea. And now he felt that Cassie's action in including the newcomers in the ceremony was a fitting tribute to Johnny. He wouldn't have wanted any animosity at his own funeral. Johnny had been a warm man and was keen to include everyone.

Tears formed in Mike's eyes as he remembered Johnny. He was a paradox: one of the hardest, toughest people he'd ever met, but also, a gentle, thoughtful man with a keen sense of adventure. Even in the new world he wouldn't be confined to one place. He had helped develop the village into what it was today, the community had grown around this gentle giant.

Mike looked over at Cassie, who caught his eye and offered a sad smile in return. They were a good match, Johnny and Cassie, and they had produced four wonderful children. *What were the chances?* Mike thought. Fate was both wonderful and awful. These two tough, warm survivors had found each other and created a family, a fairy-tale ending. Except it wasn't. Johnny had been murdered by an unhinged lunatic at the age of forty-two. The situation was a mess and it would take some repairing. They would have to be closer than ever as a community.

He glanced at Vanessa. She had tears in her eyes. Mike guessed she was having the same guilty thoughts that were running through his own head. But at least he was back home, with his own people. Vanessa, Ronnie and Sophia were intruders whose entrance into their world brought tragic news. And it was one of their own who had caused the damage. Mike spotted Jimmy, Johnny's eldest son, glaring at Vanessa. *There's some work to be done here,* he thought.

Zara sang. She felt like she owed it to Johnny, this generous man who had shown so much faith in her. She had come back twice with bad news. Maybe she was a bad omen? Nana Penny's funeral had been under two weeks ago and this had been the third funeral in that time. It was a trend that she hoped to see the back of.

At the wake, Mike noticed more narrowed eyes shifting towards the newcomers. Iain looked over a couple of times, turned back to Samir and they both whispered to each other. Jimmy and Lorraine sat together. Mike was sure he could see one of them pointing at Ronnie and Sophia and scowling. He found Matty and Trish who were pouring out measures of whiskey. With three wakes in a fortnight and the stress of losing friends, Matty's stocks had reduced at a fast rate. Mike felt an icy sting of poignancy. It was one of Johnny and Andy's reconnaissance missions that brought the boxes of whiskey back to the village.

"Matty," Mike said, placing his hand on the mayor's shoulder. "We need to do something. Vanessa and the others, they need to be integrated somehow. I can feel it in the air, the animosity. If Cassie can be civil to them, everyone can."

"Mike, I know this is your mission, but you can't force it. These people are outsiders. It'll take time. Things'll be pretty raw for a while, but especially today."

"If we don't do something now it could get worse. If not now, then when?" Mike asked.

Matty sighed. "Okay. I was going to say a few words. I'll try and get the message across subtly. But you've got to appreciate, Mike. This will take time. We're tight knit and we've lost one of our own. You can see why people aren't exactly rolling out the red carpet."

"No one's asking that, Matty. But we need these people here. If we lose them, we lose any hope of a future in this village."

"I'll see what I can do."

Matty distributed the whiskey in small tumblers. Mike took his and nodded briskly at the old man. He thought back to the night in their motorhome where they'd shared whiskey and Zara had a capful to help her sleep. It had been a good night amongst all the terror. Matty cleared his throat to get the audience's attention.

"I'd like to say a few words about Johnny. It's a difficult one for me. We were very close. The whiskey you're drinking was his bounty. A lot of this village was built with the rewards of his reconnaissance trips. We used to joke about Johnny and Bow. We have that saying, *Johnny takes it, Bow makes it*." Everyone turned to look at Bow. Nancy hugged him as he hung his head, wiping his eyes. Bow had been hit hard by his best friend's death. "We used to call them the *Twin Towers*," Matty continued. "But one thing's for sure, he died doing what he loved. Out there on his adventures, bringing things back for us to enjoy."

"He was murdered," came a shout from the back of the room. It was Iain. "He was knifed by one of them!" He was pointing towards the three newcomers. "Johnny didn't come back. And we swapped him for these fuckers. I say we send 'em back."

A few groans of agreement echoed around the room.

Mike closed his eyes tight. This was exactly what he'd feared. This friendly, close-knit community had turned dark very quickly. Zara grasped his hand. Mike opened his eyes and looked over worriedly to Vanessa. She was looking towards Matty, emotionlessly.

"Now come on, Iain, that's not fair," Matty continued. "We

need to welcome new people. It's exactly what we wanted. It's—"

"It's a load of shit!" shouted Jimmy Jameson. "My dad's dead. Because of them." Mike groaned. Matty wasn't doing a good job with this.

Vanessa walked forward. Ronnie tried to hold her back, saying, "No, Vanessa, come on. Let's go, we're not welcome here. Let's go back home."

Vanessa ignored him and walked to the front of the room, holding her whiskey glass in her hand.

"Hi, everyone. I've introduced myself to most of you, but I think the time has come to tell you a little bit more." The room stood in silence. Mike saw Iain's eyes narrow. Jimmy sat down by the side of the room.

"I feel a lot of hate in the room towards us," Vanessa continued. "But I also feel love, towards each other. You should be proud of this wonderful community you've built. When we were invited by Mike, Johnny and Zara, it wasn't an easy decision to come. We had built our own little community. Nothing like this, but it was there. We had a routine, a system. We loved each other as you do in this community. When strangers came, we welcomed them, but not without suspicion.

"Caution of strangers is an instinctive human trait and rightly so. It protects us against danger. Unfortunately, one of our party had been troubled. He had a disease of the mind. I'd worked hard to fix him. It had worked, I rid him of the evils of heroin. But the mind is a delicate organ. Moving away from our tiny community had a bad effect on him. Johnny died a heroic death, saving both me and Mike. You will think badly of Paul who caused this. I will mourn him and a day will not go by that I don't blame myself for both of their deaths. But please do not see us as the enemy. We are the same. We survived against the odds, hiding in terror as the world around us crumbled into chaos and murder. As you may know, I am a doctor. Sophia over there is a nurse," she pointed to Sophia who waved, uncomfortably.

"Ronnie over there is the nicest, funniest person you could meet. We are all sorry about Johnny, more than you could ever know. We may only have known him for a couple of days but he was an excellent man. We grieve for your loss and that we weren't able to get to know him better."

Mike looked around. The hostile atmosphere in the room had not disappeared. But he could sense that it had lifted slightly.

"When I look at you all here, on this sad day, I see a community so close, so loving. I really think we can contribute. If we are not wanted here we can walk away. We can find our own way in the world and move on. As a young girl, when I moved over here from Lagos, I experienced some awful comments because of the color of my skin. They hurt me deeply. Why would someone hate me because of something I could not help? Why would they be so horrible? But I realized, they didn't hate me because of the color of my skin. They were afraid of what I represented. They were scared that someone from a strange land, who looked and sounded so different from them, could come to their place and change the way they lived. But I came with love then, and I come with love now. So, if anyone in this room would like me and my friends to leave, please say so now. If just one person speaks up, we will walk out of those gates, take our bikes and set up home elsewhere. We will leave with only our good wishes to your beautiful community."

Mike looked around nervously. Vanessa had set the stakes too high. Surely one of Johnny and Cassie's children would say something. Surely Iain or Samir would speak up, or even Bow. Mike looked at young Jimmy. Tears were rolling down his cheeks. Iain and Samir were silent, gazing at their newcomer. Cassie, like her son, was crying.

Vanessa looked at her audience. She wasn't sure how long to wait to see if anyone had anything to say. It was Bow that spoke first. He walked to the front of the room.

"You're welcome here, Doc. Don't let anyone tell you anything different. A lot of emotions here today. Johnny was the best man I ever met. I'll miss him like hell. Maybe Johnny died for a reason, Doc. To bring you here. This village was created in exactly the spirit you were talking about. So, if no one has anything else to say, I'd like to propose a toast. To Johnny. A great man whose death brought light into our community."

They all raised their glasses. Tears grew in Mike's eyes. He never saw this coming, in fact he had expected the worst. Bow, not a man known for his ability to articulate his feelings, had just won over the whole room. Vanessa, Ronnie and Sophia were staying. Not only that, they were going to be accepted.

21

The months passed and the newcomers gradually became more integrated into New Windermere life. Vanessa and Bow worked on the doctor's surgery. After losing Johnny, Bow was pleased to have a new project to occupy him. Sophia also worked with Cassie on a stock-take of drugs, medicines and first aid materials. Although most of the drugs and medicines had gone well past their expiry date, they found that they still worked most of the time, although sometimes the dose needed to be slightly larger than it said on the bottles' faded labels. Cassie continued in her role as head of education, a job she thrived in as she slowly came to terms with her husband's death. She loved the school and the company of the children. They had renamed it the Johnny Jameson School. Mike thought that the new name gave Cassie comfort and encouraged her to spend more time at her place of work.

It was Ronnie who integrated the quickest. The kids in the community loved him. Even Jimmy, who had been so hostile to begin with, wanted to spend as much time as possible with the funny, charismatic newcomer. Ronnie entertained them no end, doing impressions, spinning out his child-friendly stories. They had never heard a Geordie accent before, his jumping, almost musical tones had the effect of making his stories even funnier. Ronnie even quit smoking, after Vanessa had warned him about his growing responsibility as a role model. Ronnie had not seen a living child since he was a teenager. Now he was thirty-six he found he was a natural. The children surrounded him everywhere he went. Although Ronnie possessed no immediately obvious talent, he helped Bow's construction efforts for a while, but Cassie decided he would be better served in the school. He worked every Friday where he taught them games and read aloud books. They were slowly working their way through J.K. Rowling's *Harry Potter* series and Ronnie read it brilliantly, adding his own unique touch of flair to each character's voice, even carrying out the actions when he felt it added to the story. The children roared with laughter each time. They would eagerly anticipate each Friday when he would come in. Even Zara, who kept her job as a teaching assistant to help Cassie, would look forward to *Ronnie's Fridays* as they came to be known.

It was one of these Fridays that Mike found himself walking through the village to see Matty. After three deaths in their small community, life had settled down in New Windermere. But something burrowed away in Mike's head – a sense of unfinished business, of something missing. It certainly wasn't his love life. Mike and Vanessa became a couple almost immediately. They now shared their living quarters and were deeply in love. After Charlie, in this world almost completely devoid of people, Mike thought his chance of love and companionship had disappeared. But he was in heaven with her. Vanessa had been concerned about Zara's opinion and approached her before she moved in with Mike. The two women had walked together by the lake.

"I love your dad," Vanessa had told her. "We're thinking of moving in together, but I wanted to ask you first. I would do anything for him. And because I love him, I care deeply about you, too."

"You don't need to ask me," Zara replied, "but I'm glad you did. You're a good woman, Vanessa. You and Dad deserve happiness. I'm really pleased."

They spoke for a long time, walking by the lake. They came across the weeping willow that stood over Charlotte's grave.

"I'm not sure if my dad has shown you this before," she had said to Vanessa. Her blank expression said that he hadn't.

"Vanessa, meet my mother. Mother, meet Vanessa." She giggled awkwardly, unsure whether her joke was too morbid for Vanessa to laugh.

"Wow. Nice to meet you Mrs. Pilkington." Vanessa stepped forward and kissed the tree. "I'm sure I'll do you and your husband proud. As well as your beautiful daughter."

Zara welled up. "Thanks, Vanessa. I come here every morning to talk to her. To try and remember where I came from, I suppose."

"I understand," Vanessa nodded and placed her arm around Zara's muscular shoulders. "You bury people underneath trees. Mike said that it's become a tradition, that the tree represents the person. I like that, Zara. I really like it. There's something spiritual about it."

Zara nodded. She didn't realize it was anything new or different, having visited her mother's tree for years. She had factored the other trees into her morning routine, too, kissing each one, always ending with Nana Penny. How she missed her Nana: her sense of fun, her wisdom. Zara had felt lonely since Penny passed away. She enjoyed spending time with the other villagers including her dad and Vanessa. Zara also helped Cassie through her grief, supporting her in the school and helping out with the children. But seeing her Dad and Vanessa so happy brought her own lack of company even clearer into view in her own mind.

* * *

Mike found Matty helping Trish on the allotment. He bent down to help him dig up some potatoes.

"These have got a shepherd's pie written all over them," he said.

"That's right, Mike," Trish replied. It's gonna be the biggest one yet. Got the finest lamb and some of my best veg for the side."

"I can't wait for that," said Mike, licking his lips. "I was wondering if I could borrow your husband for a bit."

"Borrow him? You'd be doing me a favor! He's more of a hindrance than a help round here."

Matty stood up, scraping his hands together to remove the soil. "Okay, Mike. This sounds serious. I hate your serious conversations. Why can't you be like young Ronnie?" Matty said, half-jokingly.

"I wish you could be more like him too, you miserable old bastard!" Mike replied, laughing.

"Get away, both of you," Trish said. "Leave the hard work to the hard workers. You two layabouts go and stare at the lake and blow hot air. We could do with it, it's chilly at the minute."

They walked out of the gates, following the curve of the lake's bank until they came to Johnny's tree. Mike put his hand against it and gently felt the carved letters that spelled out Johnny's name and the dates of his time on earth.

"So," Matty asked. "I might regret asking this at some point in the future, but what is it you've brought me out here to chat about?"

Mike breathed in deeply. "Another mission," he said.

Matty grimaced. "I thought as much. We don't need any supplies at the moment. We've got our doctor and nurse. We've got a school. We've gone months without anything bad happening, touch wood." He reached across and patted Johnny's tree's thick trunk. "What are we looking for this time?"

Mike looked out on the lake, watching a seagull swoop on some baby ducklings, the mother noisily shepherding them to safety. It took him a few seconds to think about his response. Finally, he spoke.

"Answers."

22

Matty called a founder's meeting. In the spirit of inclusion, Vanessa, Ronnie and Sophia had been added to the board. Matty asked Bow and Vanessa for an update on the doctor's surgery. It was nearly complete, they announced, proudly. It would be operational within a fortnight. Sophia would handle appointments. All interactions with the doctor would be confidential.

Cassie gave an education update. She made sure Ronnie was thanked formally in the meeting for invigorating the classroom atmosphere and helping develop an interest in reading amongst the children.

Finally, Matty handed the floor to Mike. Mike gulped, aware of the enormity of what he was proposing.

"Since we lost Johnny," he began, Cassie's eyes dropping at the mention of her husband, "there've been no reconnaissance trips. We have a lot of things here at the moment so it's not really been needed. We *will* need to pick them up again. But that's not the point of me talking at this meeting today. I want to go on a mission. It will be the longest one yet. Probably the most dangerous. I want to go to London."

"Why?" Cassie shouted, her eyes filling with tears. "Have we not lost enough? First Andy, then Johnny. Who'll be next? What could be worth it to go all the way down there? Have you not seen enough death already? We're happy. We're fine." She sat back and folded her arms, petulantly.

"This will just be me. I'm happy to go alone. I've got to go and find answers. If Razor caused this, he'll still be alive. I want to go to RazorTower and find out why this happened to our world."

Cassie looked at Vanessa. Mike had pre-warned her about what he would say. "Don't look at me, Cass. I've tried to talk him out of it. It's a suicide mission. If I could stop him, I would.

Trust me."

Bow spoke. "Say you're right. You go and find Razor and he's sat there in his big swivelly seat, lording it at the top of his giant tower. He's done this for shits and giggles, he's wiped out the world 'cause he's a bit of a prick. What will we gain from this knowledge?" Ronnie stifled a laugh at this ridiculously simple perspective.

"I know where you're coming from. But I just feel that I've got to try. I've been thinking about this ever since we found out that we were immune to hypnosis. Ever since the president's message, I suppose. It's who I am, I'm an academic, I find things out. And what can we learn from it? Everything. Why do people study history? The World Wars? The Egyptians? We need to know where we came from. We need to learn about the events that shaped our future. I want to write a book about it. We'll teach our kids about it. Tell them exactly why we find ourselves in this situation. Maybe Razor's still got his technology up-and-running. Imagine what we could do with—"

"What could we do?" Nancy said. "What possible good could any of that technology do? Do you think we're ready for that? You think RazorVision glasses would go down well here now? We've been burned by Razor's gadgets and I don't want this village to be duped by all that again."

The room nodded and muttered in agreement. "Okay," continued Mike. "I agree with that. But it still doesn't change anything. I want to go down and find out. Otherwise it will eat away at me for the rest of my life. You don't like it? Believe me, I wish I was happy to stay and just shrug it off. But that's who I am and that's all I've got."

Vanessa spoke. "I've made a decision too. I'm going with him."

"No!" shouted Cassie. "My husband died bringing you here. Bow has worked his ass off building you a surgery. You were supposed to be the savior of this village. I'm not going to let you go on this trip. You just said it yourself before, it's a *suicide mission!*"

"It is if he goes alone," Vanessa replied. "We'll be stronger together. And Sophia is more than capable of working in the surgery. She will be able to deputize in my absence. A trip to London and back should only take a couple of weeks, even if we stayed in London for a few days. It's a straight run, too, and fairly flat. We can stick to the motorways."

"No," said Mike. "I can't let you come. I can't—"

"That's the deal, Mikey," Vanessa interrupted. "You go with me or you stay here. I'm not taking no for an answer."

Trish groaned. "You two are as bloody stubborn as each other. Christ, give me strength. Is anyone else gonna go with them then, while we're talking about it?"

Ronnie raised his hand.

"No!" shouted Cassie once more. "I can let the doctor go but I can not let you go, young man. This village has lost enough already. You are not breaking those children's hearts. They love you, you big ugly lump. Don't think for a second that you're going to leave them."

"Jesus," Ronnie said. "I was only gonna ask if I could go to the toilet, Cass."

The whole room exploded into laughter. Under the table, Mike and Vanessa squeezed their hands together.

* * *

The first person they spoke to when the meeting was over was Zara.

"I want to come," she said. Vanessa smirked at Mike. She was certainly her father's daughter.

"No," said Mike. "It's too dangerous. I can't risk you again."

"Dad, you need me. I've been on two tough trips. After Iain, that makes me the most experienced reconnaissance tripper out of everyone in this village. It's not a case of you risking me. It's a case of me risking you two, letting you go without me. Anyway, we've been through too much to let Vanessa go just like that."

Mike's face strained into a grimace. She had him there. "Are you sure you two aren't related?" he asked, laughing. "Okay, you're in."

It was welcome news for Zara. The village was doing well, the community had settled down. But she yearned for something more – for an adventure, for some company. Johnny's reconnaissance trips had given her purpose, made her feel alive. Both trips had ended in disaster. But this had more at stake. She could find the man who murdered her mother and created the desolate world in which she lived; the man responsible for all the skeletal remains that she had seen scattered across England, the ever-present reminders of death that still haunted her dreams. She walked back to the school for the afternoon shift, nervous excitement bubbling in the pit of her stomach. She glimpsed Nana Penny's tree fifty yards away, its branches swaying lazily in the early afternoon breeze. As if to reassure her dead grandmother, or possibly to reassure herself, Zara said softly, "Don't worry, Nana. I'm not going back. I'm going to find out what happened to us. Watch over me, Nana. Like you always do." The tree's branches dropped still for a second before taking up their slow sway once more.

When Zara walked away, Vanessa put her arms around Mike's shoulders. "Well, it looks like it's going to be a family affair then, Mikey-boy," she said.

He kissed her hard on the lips. "I love you, Vanessa," he said when he pulled away. "But are you sure about this? It's going to be dangerous. People here love you and everyone knows how important you are to the future of this community."

"Well you'll just have to keep me safe and bring me back then," she said and jabbed him playfully in the ribs.

"Ow!" he said, laughing. "You know I broke them a few years

back!"

"Ah it's no bother. I'm a good doctor, I'll just patch you up again if I break you."

"When do you want to leave then, V? Shall we drop everything and go now or wait a while? It's up to you. Doesn't bother me either way. I'm just glad we've made the decision."

"I think we should stay for the opening of the surgery at least," she said. "I'm not going to completely abandon my duties. I want to make sure Sophia has everything she needs first."

"A couple of weeks then?"

"How about three weeks today?"

"Fine by me. Why the extra week?"

"There's something I'd like to do first. Before we head off."

Vanessa lowered herself to the ground. "Professor Michael Pilkington. Will you do me the honor of being my husband?"

Mike grinned. "My God. Yes. Of course, yes!"

He pulled her to her feet and hoisted her into the sky.

23

Mike and Vanessa were married by the lake in early summer. Ronnie gave Vanessa away, cracking jokes the full length of the walk to Vanessa's amusement and irritation. Zara was chief bridesmaid, while Cassie took the role of the reverend. It was a beautiful, sunny day. After the grief and despair of three funerals, the wedding was a blessing on the community. Tears of joy and happiness replaced the tears of loss. The whole village attended. Afterwards they sang and danced. Matty had opened old bottles of champagne that he had been keeping for a special occasion. And none could be as special as this, New Windermere's first official wedding.

Zara sang at the reception. It was a love song that Nana Penny had sung to a young Zara to help her get to sleep. The song was called *Time After Time* and told a story of how someone would be there no matter what. Zara thought it was appropriate, not just for this occasion of love but also for the journey they would endure together and the peril that lay ahead.

She received a warm round of applause for her performance, Ronnie drunkenly yelling for an encore. The children screamed for Ronnie to stand up on stage and read something. He surprised them all by giving an off-the-cuff, poignant speech about finding love, a bright light even in the darkest of times. The children, who had expected a comedy routine, were even more captivated at Ronnie's change of pace. He, too, received a warm round of applause. Cassie, who had warmed to her charge even more than the children, stood at the front of the crowd, clapping loudly, a beaming smile on her face.

At Vanessa's request, to remember the lost villagers, they placed a bunch of flowers, specially selected by Trish, at the foot of each tree that stood over a grave. Vanessa had worked out the order. They walked, in a procession, to Nana Penny's grave first. Vanessa laid the flowers and each villager kissed the tree in turn and said a few private words. Even the newcomers who did not meet Nana Penny joined in. They visited Andy's grave, the leaning tree dipping into the pond, and repeated the gesture before moving on to Johnny's grave, where Cassie hugged each of her children emotionally, and then on to Charlotte's. Vanessa hugged Charlotte's tree firmly, causing Zara to burst into tears. They finished by visiting each mass grave to lay flowers. Vanessa knelt down at each one, everyone else following her lead. She wanted the dead to join in her happiness, the blessing of the past to move on with the future. Her wedding day endeared her even more to the villagers, the hostility of her entrance to New Windermere now a faded memory. The villagers saw her for what she was: a strong, spiritual woman with a high regard for the history of their small commune. She had become one of their own and they loved her for it.

At some point in the evening, the men and women split into two groups. Zara had thought it an odd, antiquated tradition but loved spending time with her new stepmother. She enjoyed seeing the happiness on Cassie's face, too – Cassie, who had been through so much with the death of Andy and then her husband. Zara thought much of that was down to Ronnie, whose entrance to the village had energized and refreshed so many people. Zara wasn't sure if there was anything romantic between the two of them and, with Cassie's tragic past, she didn't want to ask. But she knew that Cassie loved him dearly. The color had returned to her face and Zara was glad to see it back.

Mike sat on the grass with the males of the village. They smoked Ronnie's cigarettes and faced the lake which was glistening in the early summer light.

"So," Ronnie said. "All downhill from here, Prof. Ball and chain and all that."

They laughed raucously. Mike looked over at Matty. He'd been quiet, considering the happy occasion. *Something is on his mind*, Mike thought to himself.

Bow slapped Mike on the back. "I wish Johnny was here to see this. He'd have been proud of you today."

"I think he was here in some way or other. Without Johnny, I wouldn't have found Vanessa."

Bow nodded and glanced over at Johnny's tree, the large, colorful bunch of flowers sat by its bulky trunk. Bow went there every day. He talked to his best friend about his worries, his day, any amusing incidents that he thought Johnny would have loved. There had been even more funny stories to tell since Ronnie joined their ranks.

"Hey, do you remember that time the kids challenged him to carry that massive pile of bricks?" Bow asked. "It was like that old strongman contest they used to do in the Time Before. Your Zara had marked out about twenty meters for him to carry them. He nearly did it, too. But a brick fell off the top of his pile and landed on his foot. It swelled up like a football and he had to delay his next reconnaissance trip by two weeks. Cassie hit the roof!"

"I only knew him a couple of days," Ronnie said. "Seemed like a great man. I'll always be grateful to you all for bringing me here. This messed up world makes sense up here with all of you. Do you know what I mean?"

They did.

* * *

After another hour of lively chatting and sharing stories, Matty grabbed Mike's arm. "Mike, can I have a word. Just a quick one. Let's go for a walk."

They made their way to the lake, aimlessly wandering.

"Something on your mind, Matty?"

"Yeah. In truth, this little something has been on my mind since 2038 when I drove over the A66 with half a tank of diesel in the motorhome."

Ah, the motorhome, Mike thought. He had enjoyed a good night in the motorhome when he'd met Matty and Trish. It was the first time he could see some kind of future in this desolate world.

"What is it, Matty? A problem so old can't be doing you any good. A problem like that can eat you from the inside. Tell me."

"It's my son. I don't think I've talked about him that much really."

Mike remembered that Matty had mentioned his son a couple of times, but never in depth. It wasn't always wise to ask people about their past life in case the nerves were still raw. In Matty's case it seemed they still were.

"Mike, we had a son and daughter-in-law and a gorgeous granddaughter, little Evie. They were our world. Trish kisses Evie's photo every night. Once, a few years back, we were ready to pack our things and go. Just to make sure, to find answers. Sound familiar?" Mike nodded. "We just had to know whether they were alive or dead. But, we just couldn't do it. At our age, the journey would have killed us. And that effort just to find out our son's little family were lying there, a pile of bones in rotten clothing. Had they gone out when it happened? It might have been like finding a needle in a haystack."

"Of course. Matty, you should've told me. We've been friends a long time now."

"I couldn't, mate. Sometimes things have to stay between a man and his wife. Every man fights his own battle in his head. Sometimes he lets others in when he needs a hand solving it. Sometimes he fights it alone and wins. Sometimes the battle lasts a long, long time."

"And you're letting me in now?"

"Mike, I want you to do me a big favor. When you go to London, follow the M40. It's a pretty straight run once you get down the M6. You'll find a town called High Wycombe in

Buckinghamshire."

"I know Wycombe."

I'll draw on a map where the house is. And I'll write down a description of what they looked like, what clothes they wore, jewelry they had. Just in case. If you could just check the shops and bars nearby too. It probably won't be nice."

"Matty, I think I stopped worrying about what's nice around April, 2038. Of course I'll do it. I owe you my life."

"Good. *Good.* Trish will be happy. And when you come back, don't sugar coat it. We want to know the truth."

"Yes, of course. You know I'm a bad liar anyway."

Matty put his hand on Mike's shoulder. "One more thing, Mike."

"What's that?"

"If you do find them, give them a proper send off. Under a nice tree. Bury the bodies."

Mike leaned forward and hugged him, squeezing tight as salty tears rolled down the old man's cheeks.

24

The doctor's surgery was opened three days after the wedding. It had been another happy time in the village. Matty, Vanessa and Sophia all gave speeches. Sophia's speech included some health tips. She didn't want all and sundry making an appointment for a simple wasp sting or a nettle rash. Matty made sure to thank Cassie for her work in setting up healthcare for the village.

The schoolchildren had helped design health posters that were stuck to the interior walls of the surgery, instructing people to wash their hands before eating and to sneeze into a tissue. Bow had done an outstanding job on the construction. The building was small, with a waiting room, two smaller rooms and a large, locked storage room for medicine and health materials. It carried a new smell of pine, and the wood was varnished and shiny. After her speech, Vanessa had run over to Bow and hugged him, kissing him firmly on both cheeks. She had suggested that they name the surgery after him, but Bow, a man of unfaltering modesty, refused. They had simply named it "New Windermere Doctor's Office." They didn't have to wait long for their first patient. Olivia sliced her finger open helping Trish chop carrots and was rewarded with a plaster and a pat on the head from Vanessa.

Sophia kept health records for all residents, spending two days carrying out one-to-one consultations. It made Mike proud; he knew Vanessa and Sophia would secure the future of New Windermere, that they would fill this one remaining gap. And in introducing the newcomers, he had also found a gem in Ronnie. He had instilled a sense of fun, humor and artistic expression that the village hadn't previously experienced. The culture of New Windermere was changing, and for the better.

He made a promise to himself that this trip would be the last out of the local area. There were still some reconnaissance missions to try locally, where there wasn't as much danger. Survive this trip and he would come home and retire with Vanessa. They could even look to build their own house, closer to the lake. And one day, two trees would stand, side-by-side, with Mike and Vanessa's names carved roughly into the bark. The thought, although it held its own darkness, made him smile.

* * *

It was another week before they set off. Bow fine-tuned the bikes while Trish prepared a huge feast for the long journey. The night before they left, Ronnie, Cassie and the kids set up a performance in the town hall. It was the story of *Harry Potter and the Philosopher's Stone.* Louie Jameson took the titular role, with Livvy taking up the part of Hermione Granger. Cassie, appropriately, was cast as Professor Dumbledore, while Ronnie played Snape and a host of supporting actors. Ronnie, predictably, was outrageously flamboyant.

Zara loved it. Harry Potter had been one of her absolute favorites and to see it acted out in front of her, *for* her, was fantastic. She spent the duration of the play in tears, unsure whether from laughter or at the sentiment of the performance. There was so much happiness in the room. Zara beamed, thinking of how the village had risen from the darkness of a few months ago. She felt sad to leave at this happy time, but something still felt empty. Although her passion for answers about Razor didn't come close to matching that of her father, she still felt a burning desire to spread her wings. Seeing her father so happy made her realize that she wanted to have children of her own. It was a purpose that burned through her every fiber. The thought of her life ending without reproducing made her feel empty, creating a desperate, sad void in her heart and mind. They had travelled to Newcastle and found six people. Surely, in London there would be more life, perhaps even more developed than theirs. Zara would come back to Windermere, but maybe not immediately. Maybe she could stay in London, if the community was right. These thoughts buzzed through her head as she sat watching Livvy jump around on her broomstick.

When the play ended, the audience gave a standing ovation. Bow announced loudly at the end that his next project would be an outdoor theatre, so they could host weekly performances. They all cheered, but none louder than Ronnie.

* * *

The next morning, at sunrise, it was time to go. As was tradition, the whole village came to say goodbye. Mike noticed that many people made the same joke, telling Zara to look after her father rather than the other way around. There was some truth in it. Zara was tough and adventurous: her arms and shoulders thick with ropey muscle. Her physical make-up was more akin to Johnny and Cassie rather than Mike and Charlotte. She had grown into a formidable, respected member of the community.

"Bring her back," Sophia told him, pointing to Vanessa. "I can't do this by myself for too long. Otherwise I'll be demanding a pay rise," she joked.

Cassie hugged all three of them, squeezing each one into a tight embrace. She leaned forward and whispered in Zara's ear, "Johnny, Penny and Andy will be with you all the way, remember that." Both women burst into tears.

Matty and Trish were the final people to say goodbye. Mike had filled Vanessa and Zara in on the extra stop in Wycombe. It was Trish who spoke first. "Good luck, Mike." Her face was drawn and pale. "Bring my babies back if you can. If you can't please just… make sure they're happy. At rest."

Mike hugged her.

"You're a good one, Mike," Matty said. He gave him a firm handshake, which Mike pulled into a hug. "Stay safe. And when you see Rick Razor, kick him in the balls from me. Never liked that smooth prick."

Mike nodded. With all the distraction of the stop in Wycombe, he had almost forgotten about Rick Razor.

Mike, Vanessa and Zara pedaled out of the gates and by the lake, towards the south. Matty watched them go before turning to his wife. He hugged her, tears welling in his eyes. "When he comes back we'll know. We'll know a lot of things."

Part III

Answers

1

They cycled hard. It took a full day to reach the M6, with its glorious views of mountains and lakes, down towards Lancashire. There were several cars on the road but Zara avoided looking at the horrors contained within the rusting hunks of metal. But that was one of the blessings of travelling on a motorway – the death was contained and out of sight.

They set up camp just north of Preston, tucking into Trish's package of egg sandwiches and cheese. The mood was reflective. There was a mellow feel to the evening, matched by the purple sky and the balmy summer temperature.

"Last night was so good. So funny," Vanessa commented.

"Yeah, that's one of the best nights I've had in the village," Mike said.

"One of the best nights in my life," Zara added.

"I used to go to the theatre a bit back in the Time Before," Mike said. "Last night reminds me of how much I miss that kind of thing. Entertainment. With all the talk of getting healthcare sorted out, we've managed to get Ronnie in to sort out the fun and games. Buy one get one free, if you like."

Vanessa hit her husband playfully. "Oi. You didn't buy me, you ignoramus. You're right though. Those plays helped keep us alive in the North East. Kept us sane."

"What do you miss most about the Time Before?" Zara asked.

"Wow. That's a big question!" Mike replied. "I never thought I'd be able to cope without my RazorVision, but you know what? I'm not sure I even miss it at all. I miss my little world of academia – the university, the students, my colleagues. I miss having something to learn."

Vanessa looked at him suspiciously. "Au contraire, Professor. I think you're learning all the time. It may not be something that you get a certificate for, but you're becoming wiser all the same."

She paused and then looked at Zara. "To answer your question, I don't miss a thing other than the people I lost – my friends, my family in Nigeria, of whom I have no news. I would miss the culture, but I enjoy the fact that we are creating our own. I would miss my job, but I have an opportunity to build my career again. I have new adventures in front of me. I think that we all have a new appreciation of life. That's something that the old world lost and the new world has gained. And that's a blessed gift we mustn't lose again."

Zara looked at Vanessa, wide-eyed. She was reminded of Nana Penny's last words, *never go back.*

"On my first trip with Johnny and Andy, they let me into a little secret. They smoked cannabis on every trip they took. I tried some." She wasn't sure why she felt the need to tell her father and stepmother this, but it felt good to get it off her chest. "I didn't like having a secret. I wasn't really used to it. But we did talk for a long time after we smoked. The conversation was really deep."

Mike raised his eyebrows. "You smoked weed? Zara, I'm not sure if I agree—"

"Shut it," Vanessa interrupted. "You told me about when you were younger. You can't talk."

Mike shot a scolding look at Vanessa, but soon loosened up as he realized she was right. "Okay, okay. Point taken."

Zara raised an eyebrow. "Looks like Johnny and Andy weren't the only ones with secrets, Dad. In all seriousness, all I've ever known is the village, our community. I sometimes wonder if there's more. What I'm missing. I love it, I really do but sometimes I just get the urge to get out. That's why I was so happy when Johnny asked me to go on that trip. But Andy died and then Johnny. I was wondering if I was some kind of jinx. This trip... I just hope..."

"Don't even think it. Don't even mention it. There's really no such thing," Mike said, interrupting his daughter.

"You're not a jinx, my darling," Vanessa said. "Why do you think you're here? On another trip? And maybe this journey to London will satisfy your need to seek other places."

"Maybe," Zara replied and nodded.

Mike screwed his face up for a second, his possessive paternal instincts wanting to keep her from any harm that an over-zealous sense of adventure could bring.

They slept. Zara dreamed once more of a grinning skull. The dreams were always more intense, more real when she left the village. This dream was in a desert. A figure walked towards the skull from a distance. The figure was jerking wildly, the whole body convulsing. As it came closer she realized it was female, with dark hair. Zara saw white drool cascading from the woman's mouth. She looked closer and saw that she was looking at herself. This altered version of Zara stamped hard down on the grinning skull with a dry crunch and unleashed a horrible high pitched cackle. Then she spoke in a man's deep voice. "You are going back. You will go back. You will die, bitch. Go back. Die. DIE!"

She woke up, clammy, her skin covered with goose bumps. Vanessa and Mike were asleep. She peered across at the road and saw nothing. Frightened to experience the nightmare again, it took her another hour to get back to sleep.

2

The next day they made good time once more, reaching Birmingham by early evening. After another night's camping, they switched roads to the M40. A few more hours and they would be in Wycombe.

Mike looked ahead at the long, desolate road winding in front of him. *Matty, I hope to God I've got good news.* If not, they would need to find a tree and three spades. Or, even worse, they might find nothing. And even if they found skeletal remains, would Mike be able to identify them from Matty's description of their clothes? He wasn't so sure.

Vanessa, sensing her husband's contemplation, grabbed his hand. "Big day, eh?" she said.

"You can say that again."

"Whatever's down there. We can handle it. We've both had to handle worse, I'm sure."

He squeezed her hand tighter. "Yeah. Thanks. Let's go."

It was early evening when they arrived in High Wycombe. Their pace had slowed the closer they came to the town. Mike reached into his bag and pulled out a map that Matty had given him with clear directions to his son's house.

They came to the street where Henry West lived with his wife Yasmin and daughter Evie. Evie would be twenty-one now. The house, number eighteen, was a nice semi-detached one on the edge of town. Mike's heart was beating faster and faster as he approached the door. He gave three heavy knocks. No answer.

"What do you think?" he asked Vanessa and Zara.

Vanessa grimaced. "We've come all this way. If it was around midnight it all happened back then, there's a chance they might be inside. In bed."

"I was afraid you might say that. Okay." He grabbed a loose brick from a wall in the garden and held it over his head, ready to smash the glass panel of the door. "One, two—"

"Stop!" shouted a voice from the distance. "Who the fuck are you?"

Mike dropped the brick and turned, shocked. There was a man running down the street towards them, holding a knife.

Vanessa raised her hands. "We're looking for Henry West," she said, calmly. "Do you know him."

The man stopped in front of her. The look of anger on his face gave way to confusion. "That's me. Shit. I haven't seen another living soul for years. And you come here looking for me? What do you want? How do you know my fucking name?" His eyes were manic and his hair and beard were wild and untamed. His scrawny body was dressed only in a pair of dirty shorts, his bare, bony chest almost concave. His accent was strange and feral. But, somewhere, underneath the matted hair and the unkempt, dirty appearance, was someone who had the same nose, mouth and face shape as Matty West.

Mike laughed loudly. "Oh my God! Your dad is gonna love us. He's going to be so happy you're alive."

"My dad? He's alive? He's okay?" Tears welled up in Henry West's eyes.

"Not only that," Vanessa said. "Him and your mum sent us down here to find you. To find out if you, Evie and Yasmin were alive and well."

At the mention of his wife and daughter, Henry's eyes dropped and his shoulders slumped. Vanessa and Zara looked at each other, worriedly.

"I take it… it's not good news?" Mike asked. But Henry did not answer. "Oh, I'm sorry, mate. I'm so sorry." He held his hand out and Henry gave it a dry, limp shake. Henry put his knife down.

"Here. I should invite you in. Let me just get my key. I want to hear some more about my old mum and dad. Come in."

3

Henry West's house matched his appearance; it was messy, erratic and a musty, unpleasant smell hung over it. They pulled up four battered chairs to sit and talk.

"So, where you guys from?" Henry asked his visitors.

"Windermere," Mike replied. "Well, we call it New Windermere now. We've got a little community there. Your dad's the mayor. Your mum's in charge of the farm and the food."

Henry rocked in his seat and unleashed a laugh, wild and manic. "That *definitely* sounds like them. My old man always had to be in control. And my mum, well. She always did like to put on a good spread."

"They'd love to see you," Vanessa said. "They miss you terribly."

"Can I offer you a drink?" Henry asked, looking at each of them in turn jerkily. "Sorry, you must excuse me. I'm not much of a host. I wasn't expecting another human being to come and knock on my door with a brick."

Although Henry was smiling, his clumsy attempt at humor unsettled Vanessa.

"Henry, please tell us. What happened to your family?"

Henry shook his head like a small child warding away bad thoughts. Vanessa peered down at his face and realized he was crying and drooling at the same time.

"It's okay," she continued. "You don't have to talk about it, if it's too painful."

"Drinks!" Henry exclaimed. He walked through the dank mess into the kitchen.

While he was gone, Zara, Vanessa and Mike eyed each other worriedly. "He's not right," Vanessa mouthed, to which Mike shrugged his shoulders.

"What can we do?" he replied.

Henry returned with four bottles of beer. He opened each one with his teeth, an act which made Zara cringe, like someone scraping their nails on a hard surface.

"Bottoms up," Henry said. "To my old mum and dad. The hardy old buggers survived the end of the world and came up smellin' of roses."

From nowhere, a scream rose from the direction of the garden.

"What was that?" Zara asked.

"N-n-nothing," Henry replied. "Just one of the sheep from nearby," he said, unconvincingly.

"It sounded like it came from the back garden," Mike said, standing up.

"No. No, it w-was a sheep," Henry repeated.

"Henry, what's out there?" Vanessa said.

Zara looked at Henry's face. Behind the dirt, behind the matted facial hair, she saw a look of fear.

"Nothing. Please, it's nothing. I think you should go now."

"Henry, there's something you're not telling us," Mike said. He walked over to the kitchen and saw the closed back door.

Another scream sounded out, this one louder, more anguished. Mike walked through the kitchen and approached the door. Vanessa and Zara rose to their feet and followed him.

"No!" Henry yelled. He was crying, sniveling, with snot and saliva dangling in a thick string from his overgrown beard. "Please no. You won't understand. You won't—"

"What won't we understand?" Zara yelled over her shoulder as she followed Mike and Vanessa. She felt her heart beating faster.

Mike opened the door and stepped outside, hearing Henry's shout as his feet touched the long grass in the large back garden.

"I couldn't watch them die! You've got to understand!"

Mike looked to the bottom of the garden and gagged. Slimy, acidic fluid rose from his stomach, burning his throat. He turned and vomited into the grass. He looked up again, just to confirm what he'd seen.

Twenty yards in front of him, at the bottom of the overgrown garden, were two metal cages. Each one contained a naked woman. Both were twitching in unison, staring at Mike with bloodshot, vacant eyes, drool pouring out of their gaping jaws. Their faces were gaunt, the contours of their skulls jutting out of their blotchy skin, which hung thinly from their faces. Both women had lank, dirty hair hanging to their thin waists. Various scars, some healed and some fresh, covered both their bodies.

Mike felt dizzy and held on to the garden fence to steady himself. It was the first time he'd seen anyone affected since the terrible night it all started. Since the night his wife had tried to kill him and Zara. He vomited again, although the heave, which began at the pit of his stomach, brought up nothing but gloops of thick saliva.

Zara and Vanessa followed him and stopped so abruptly at the sight of Mike doubled up they all nearly crumpled into a heap together against the fence. Vanessa looked at the bottom of the garden and brought her hand to her mouth, muffling a small cry of anguish. Zara looked up and gasped.

With Mike and Vanessa frozen to the spot, Zara slowly approached the cages. She had heard so much about the twitchers, thought so much about the death of her mother. About the end of the Time Before and the start of the new world. The devastating change in human beings who were affected. The murder in their eyes and the other-worldly effect it had on their entire demeanor.

She approached the cages and saw that one woman was older than the other. They were Matty's daughter-in-law and granddaughter alright. As she approached, she saw the two pairs of eyes follow her in a flickering, unfocused fashion. The older of the women jumped forward and grabbed the cage, hissing. Saliva flew out of the woman's mouth and landed in the long grass, draped thickly between the reeds. Zara approached slowly, her head cocked to one side in fascination. She raised a hand. It was all she thought to do to communicate. The flickering red eyes looked at her raised hand and jerked back to Zara's face. Zara was shivering with fear. Despite the cool breeze in the air, she felt a bead of sweat form on the right side of her temple and begin to roll down the side of her head.

The younger woman now ran towards her and flung her whole body against the side of the cage. She shrieked, loudly, causing Zara to flinch and then shudder, almost echoing the intense jerking of the two affected women. The screams were loud and Zara detected sadness and misery in the noise. A sound of utter despair.

"I'm Zara," she said, her voice shaking. "Yasmin? Evie?"

Still jerking, the two affected women cocked their heads to the side simultaneously, like dogs trying to understand their owner. Zara could hear their heavy breath in their chests, rattling and throaty.

"Can you understand me?" she asked.

They still didn't answer. Evie jumped towards her again and rattled the cage with her bony hands. Her mother followed suit, grabbing the cage and shaking it. They both screamed, louder and sharper than before. Zara stepped backwards, shaking.

"It's time for you lot to go now." Henry's emaciated figure stood in the back doorway. He was carrying a shotgun, resting the barrel on his thin left forearm. "So go. Fuck off! Leave us alone!"

4

"Come on now, Henry," Vanessa said in her calm voice. "This isn't right. You can see that, can't you? Keeping them caged up. They look in pain."

"What do you want me to do about it?" Henry asked. "What would any normal man do with his wife and daughter?"

Mike thought back to his own wife. Would he have killed her if she hadn't fallen to an untimely, or was it *timely*, death? Would he have put baby Zara out of her misery if she had been doomed to a life of twitching and snarling, a drooling, violent vegetable? He couldn't answer. But he did know a few people who had killed their loved ones, their children, their spouses when it came to a question of live and kill, or love and die. He guessed a lot of people in the world had loved and died. People currently buried in mass graves.

"Henry. What happened? How did you catch them without... without..."

"Took a whole lot of strength. Had these cages in the back garden for the dogs." He gestured to the cages which held the two women. "Took a whole lot of strength," he repeated.

"How do they still survive?" Zara asked. She was still staring at the two women. She couldn't take her eyes off their quivering, alien-like forms. These people, these *affected* people she had heard so much about. She felt like a scientist making a discovery. Zara locked eyes with the younger woman. She was only a few years older than Zara herself, had just been five when she was affected. She stared at the woman and Zara was sure she sensed a sadness deep behind the blank, expressionless and unfocused eyes. A black sadness, so terrible and full of despair that it forced Zara to look away.

"I fed 'em whatever I could find," Henry replied. "Tins of beans. Tins of corned beef. Anything I could find. I sprayed water into their mouths from bottles. They don't drink until they're on the verge of death, then some kinda instinct takes over. Same with food. Don't eat much."

Zara noticed the sharp ribs protruding from the bodies of both women. Even the younger of the two had saggy skin and her breasts hung loosely, like old lengths of thin dough. The older woman urinated, standing up, without breaking expression. The urine cut into the grass and Zara could smell the thick rancid odor. Zara glanced behind the woman and saw two separate heaps of feces. They looked relatively fresh but not healthy. She turned her attention back to the two women. Their skeletal bodies looked grim; they both seemed close to death.

"They're like animals," Zara said. "They're not like humans anymore." She began to cry. She cried for the loss of life she was seeing in front of her eyes. Once, when she was younger, she had seen two pigeons fly into the window of the town hall. She had rushed outside to see if the birds were okay and saw that one had died instantly. However, the other was still alive, its body crushed and useless, but its long neck rose from the smashed body, its head looking around. The pigeon's head looked unharmed, as if the message hadn't made its way to its tiny brain that it would soon die. The living pigeon scared Zara more than the dead one, and the feeling of discomfort stayed with her for weeks afterwards, inhabiting her nightmares in various terrifying forms. It was the inevitability of the pigeon's fate that had disturbed Zara the most, the fact she looked upon both life and death in the same vision. Eventually, Bow was called to put the pigeon out of its misery. It was a feeling that came back in Henry West's back garden, looking upon Yasmin and Evie West's inhuman bodies and the sadness in their eyes.

"You need to use the gun," she said.

"W–what?" Henry asked. "What do you mean?"

"You need to be fair," Vanessa added. "What would they

want, Henry? This is no life for your wife and daughter. Your family left a long time ago." Vanessa stood and placed her hand on Henry's weak, shivering forearm. "Come back with us and see your mum and dad."

Henry, shivering with the grief and the weight of the heavy shotgun in his scrawny arms, began to cry. He dropped the gun and hugged Vanessa. "There, there," Vanessa said. "You've been through enough. I don't know how you've done it for all these years, but you have. You're a good man, Henry West. A good man to look after your wife and daughter all this time. But now you need to say goodbye."

Henry pulled away from Vanessa. "No. I can't. They'll get better. We'll get help. We can all help them."

"Look at them, Henry," Vanessa waved her arm in the direction of the cages. "Look at their suffering. Look at their lives. They've been like this since 2038. Let them go."

"I could let them go. I could let them out. But they'd kill themselves eventually. I had to stop them lots of times —"

"No," Mike interrupted. "Henry, there's only one way to stop it. You need to stop their suffering."

"I can't!" he shouted, desperately. "I can't do it." Stringy saliva flew from his mouth as he spoke.

"I can," Zara said. They all looked over to her, mouths open with surprise. "I will. You've all been through hell already. I'll do it."

Mike's eyes narrowed and he looked at his daughter sternly. "I can't let you, Zara."

"It's not negotiable, Dad. It needs doing. I can't explain why, but it just feels right that I'm the one."

Mike locked eyes with Vanessa. She nodded. "If you're sure."

"Love, please. Let me do it. I don't want you carrying this," Mike said to his daughter.

"No, Dad, go inside. I can handle it. It's for the best. Sometimes life is worse than death."

Mike nodded and went inside with Zara's words echoing in his head. *Sometimes life is worse than death.*

5

Mike walked into the messy living room and sat down. Henry had his head in his hands and was sobbing wildly, muttering indecipherable sentences to himself. Vanessa held his hand and whispered soft condolences to him. They all flinched, Henry with his head still grasped in his hands, not looking upwards, as a shot cracked and echoed loudly. Henry's sobs turned to wails and Vanessa squeezed his hand tighter.

Zara looked at the older woman's crumpled body. She had shot her in the chest with the powerful weapon, and the force had thrown her back into the far end of the cage. She had landed in her own shit, the final indignity of the woman's life. Zara was sure she saw something in the woman's eyes return to normality, even in the face of this violent and sudden death. The woman had not flinched or displayed fear at the gun barrel that had pointed at her. Had she embraced it? Zara wasn't sure. She turned to Evie, who had looked over at her dead mother as she had fallen, but the sight had not captured Evie's imagination for long. She was now twitching, looking forward at Zara once more, her red eyes full of sadness and pain. Zara thought once more of the pigeon, its yellow eyes twitching unknowingly side-to-side while its ruined body lay below it.

Zara levelled the shotgun. It was heavy but she was strong enough to raise it. This time she aimed for the affected woman's head. She wanted this to be quick. Evie's jaw opened and hung for a second. *She's going to say something!* Zara thought to herself.

"What? What is it?" she asked, frightened.

"Uhhhhhh. Uhhhhhhhhhhhh," Evie muttered. Zara looked into the woman's eyes and once more saw despair. She raised the shotgun and fired. The recoil jarred her shoulder in a painful jerk. The bullet blew the top quarter of Evie's head off, blasting skull, brain and blood all over the thin metal squares of the cage.

She fell to her knees and then backwards, her sagging breasts parting sideways and her eyes rolling upwards so only the blood-smattered whites were visible.

Zara sank to her knees on the grass and began to cry, thinking of the blurred lines between life and death and contemplating her own existence. It could have been her growing up, living her life in an unknowing mess, defecating and twitching, thinking only to kill someone or kill herself. It could have been Zara, like the pigeon, living a fraction of a life, unaware of the horror that her own body was causing her.

Zara left the shotgun propped up against the house and, after a deep, slow breath, walked inside. Henry was still sobbing loudly in the living room, Vanessa comforting him with softly spoken words, as only Vanessa could. Mike sat in silence. He looked up when Zara entered.

"It's done," she said.

"We heard the shots," Mike replied, nodding. Seeing his daughter's red, wet eyes, he stood up and hugged her strongly.

"We need to dig. I promised Matty and Trish."

"*Matty and Trish,*" Mike thought to himself. "*What the hell am I going to say about this? What can I say to them?*" But there would be plenty of time and other worries to pass through before Mike needed to worry about that particular quandary.

Henry looked up and sniffled. "The garden. I want them to be buried in the garden."

Mike and Zara dug the grave with spades from Henry's tiny, dilapidated wooden shed. It was hard work and they needed several breaks. Henry was too weak and full of grief to help. Vanessa sat with him while he wept intermittently. When the holes were dug deep enough, Mike and Zara opened the cage and took Yasmin's body. Henry was told to go inside, he didn't need to watch his wife and daughter thrown into a hole in the ground. "You should come back when we call you," Vanessa said.

When the bodies were in the graves, Mike, Zara and Vanessa set about covering them with the displaced dirt. They were halfway through the task when they heard a sound of metal on concrete. They all looked up in unison to see Henry holding the shotgun.

"I can't let you do it," he said.

"Henry, it's done. This is the way to say goodbye."

"No!" Henry shouted. "I can't see them go. I won't let you take them."

"Henry, you're not making sense. Please, put down the gun," Mike said.

But Henry lifted the gun towards them. Tears were rolling down his cheeks. In one fluid motion, he spun the shotgun round so that the thick end of the barrel was in his mouth.

"No!" shouted Vanessa.

There was a loud bang and a smash as the bullet careered through the kitchen window, taking half of Henry's head with it. His body fell backwards and the shotgun crashed onto the concrete floor.

Zara looked at Vanessa and they both looked at Mike. Mike sighed with the painful agony of a man who had seen too much, experienced too many painful moments.

"What will I tell Matty and Trish?" his thoughts repeated again. But there would be an answer. *Sometimes life is worse than death.*

6

The trio continued their journey down the M40 in near silence. The sun set to the western side of the road, its warm rays casting an orange sheen on everything it touched.

Zara's legs burned with the effort of cycling. When the sun disappeared behind the distant horizon, Vanessa suggested setting up camp and resting for the evening. Mike agreed, and Zara felt a surge of relief. She had built up a reputation, even with her own father, of being a strong and competent woman. She didn't want to compromise that by being the first to admit she was exhausted. Part physically tired from the exertion of riding a bike across hundreds of miles of motorway, part mentally drained from the trauma of shooting two affected women dead.

Vanessa shared out tins of beans, which they ate cold with their hands.

"I'm not sure I want to be sleeping next to you, Michael Pilkington," Vanessa said.

"What do you mean?" Mike asked.

"Well, you know what you say. Beans, *Beans good for your heart. The more you eat, the more you fart.*"

"You're eating them too! My good lady doctor, I do believe you need to heal thyself."

"Ah, but ladies do no such thing, Professor."

"I rest my case, Vanessa. For you are no lady."

Zara watched the jovial exchange between her father and new stepmother and smiled without humor. Mike looked over, noticing her melancholic mood.

"Tough day, love?"

"You can say that again," Zara replied. She looked down into her empty tin and wiped her hands on her jeans, smearing dark orange tomato sauce across her pocket. "I'd heard so much about people who were affected, I just never thought I'd see it. It just gives me a whole new appreciation of things, I suppose."

"Appreciation of your own life?" Vanessa asked.

"Yes and no. Yes, appreciation that I didn't end up like that when I was a few weeks old. But also, appreciation of what you all went through that night. I just can't imagine how bad it must have been. To see people you loved looking like that. To have to defend yourself against them. I just don't know how you did it."

"Is that why you felt like you had to do it, in Henry's garden? To have some kind of parity?" Mike asked. "Because you really didn't. There's no atonement needed. We've all been through the mill here."

"Yes, that's exactly the reason. I suppose I felt I owed it to you. To all of you."

"Well I disagree," said Mike. "But I was proud of you today. I'm not sure I could've done it."

"Me neither," said Vanessa.

"More importantly, though," Zara added. "What are we going to tell Matty and Trish? They were so upset when we left. How can we tell them that all three were alive and now they're buried in Henry's back garden?"

Mike sighed. Zara's words had echoed the exact thoughts that had been dominating his own mind over the last few hours.

"I really don't know," he said. "But Matty was the first person I met after the world changed. I was holding you in my arms and he knew straight away what kind of horrible time I'd had. He was the first person I told what had happened. What I'd been through. In the Time Before, you wouldn't have dreamed of telling people that you'd killed their granddaughter and daughter-in-law and that their son had killed himself in front of you. But in this world, I suppose it goes with the territory."

"Trish and Matty will accept what we tell them," Vanessa said. "But I feel we owe them the truth. They were all in pain and now they're not. There's some victory in that. We delivered them peace and if we hadn't come along, they would've continued the way they were until they died a painful death. Would Matty and Trish have preferred that?"

Zara thought of Bow putting the pigeon out of its misery. One thing she loved about Vanessa was her pragmatism. She always seemed to view a situation from afar, a perspective that was calm, logical and clear.

"Where would we be without you, Earth Mother," Mike said, as if reading his daughter's mind.

Vanessa hit her husband playfully. "Shut up! Don't tease me!"

Zara looked at the two of them. "I really envy you two, you know that?"

"And why's that?" Vanessa asked.

"You've found each other. In this world where nearly everyone has gone, you've found happiness in each other. After all the death you've both gone through, you've found a reason to make everything make sense."

"You're not making much sense!" Mike joked, awkwardly.

"Thank you, Zara," Vanessa said. "Can I ask you something, though?"

Zara nodded.

"What do you want out of life? You were quick to leave the village on this mission. What is your goal?"

"I suppose I'm still working it out. But I look at the two of you and I suppose I want what you have. I just don't know what my purpose is."

Vanessa burst out in laughter, rocking to the side and holding her stomach. Mike squinted at her in surprise and confusion. Zara looked in bewilderment at her usually stoical stepmother.

"I'm sorry, I'm sorry. It's just, you sound like nearly every teenager I have ever spoken to," Vanessa said. "No, sorry, that came out wrong. I don't want to make what you're saying sound trivial but I suppose it's quite reassuring to know that you are just like a normal confused teenager, even amongst all this chaos."

Mike nodded. "You'll find your feet. All this is normal, even in an abnormal world like this one."

Zara yawned and stretched her arms. "Okay I'll take your word for it. Anyway, I'm tired. Good night."

They turned over and slept. Zara lay with her eyes open for half an hour, contemplating the day's events and what the future could possibly hold.

7

As they travelled in the cool morning air, Zara noticed a large queue of cars ahead.

"Dad, what's that? Why so many cars?"

Mike chortled, creating a knowing, cynical sound. "That, my dear, is the M25. One of the worst motorways in Western Europe. Home to gridlocked traffic, road rage and not much else. Even in this world it seems that the traffic is still waiting."

They continued down the road. As the cars came closer, Mike sensed that something was different. These cars didn't look like they had been suddenly abandoned. They were facing the wrong way, for a start, pointed towards the edge of the motorway rather than the usual direction of travel. It looked more like a barrier. Just as Mike saw it, he felt his bike whizz away from under his body and a strong net engulf him, becoming tighter and tighter. He fell to the ground and hit his head, when everything went black.

"Mike! Mike!" It was Vanessa. She was shaking him, slapping his face gently. "Wake up." His eyes slowly came into focus to see Vanessa's smiling face. He saw a group of faces behind her. One was unmistakably that of his daughter while the rest were strangers: three males from what he could make out. His wife and daughter seemed safe. He put his head back to the ground and closed his eyes. Everything went black once more.

When Mike awoke, Vanessa and Zara filled him in on what he'd missed. The men, a group of three Londoners who had survived the terrible night in 2038, had set up a trap for any animals who happened to wander along the M25. It was a clever mechanism, strung between two cars, that sprang a net to catch their prey. Vanessa and Zara had been untangling Mike from the net when the men had come along, expecting to see a deer or a sheep. Instead they had helped cut Mike free and invited them back to their camp for a dinner of beef and onion stew with cans of lager. The lager was out-of-date but still tasted good. They lit a fire on the roadside verge and warmed themselves as the sun set.

* * *

The men were Greg, Don and Chris. They all carried an extremely masculine swagger, very different to the academic world to which Mike belonged. They called themselves the "M25 Engineers" and were experts at building and making contraptions. After Vanessa had attended to Mike's bruised head and ensured his concussion would not have any longer term affects, Chris walked him to a car, around a hundred yards from where they had camped.

"Now I know you are gonna love this shit!" Chris said. His cockney accent reminded Mike of his own roots: made him feel like he was home. He breathed in deeply. Even the air felt like his own. Maybe he had missed London more than he thought.

Mike screwed up his face at the sight of the car. It was a Kia Sportage, an old one, from 2021.

"What's so special about this?" Mike asked.

"Oh, you probably seen plenty of cars on your way down here," Chris replied.

Mike nodded.

"Well, have you seen one like this before? Get in." He opened the driver side door.

Mike eased himself into the car, careful not to knock his bruised head. Chris walked to the other side of the car and sat in the passenger seat.

Mike looked at Chris, his mouth turned down in confusion. "So...?" Mike asked.

"You know how to drive? Like properly drive? Not that GPS shit."

"Yeah, I think I remember," Mike said.

"Well, knock yourself out," Chris said, handing Mike the key.

"What are you on about? No car has worked since the night it all happened."

"Trust me," Chris said, grinning.

Mike looked down at the steering wheel. Surely these men couldn't have got a car working? This was an old one, pre-RazorCar but still, all fuel was out of commission since it was locked down with Razor Technology. He put the key into the ignition and turned it. The car spluttered. He looked at Chris who grinned still.

"Try again," Chris said.

He put his foot down on the clutch and turned the key again. It spluttered again and then hummed. The hum turned into a purr and the whole car thrummed, ready for action.

Mike looked at his passenger, incredulously.

"It works?"

"It works."

"How... how..."

"We got our hands on some fuel. Found a tanker on the M25 transporting it. Punched a hole in it, and managed to store it. Obviously, we can't use any RazorCars but there's still a few old-schoolers knocking about. Go ahead. Drive back to camp."

It had been a while, but Mike moved the gear stick into first and put his foot on the accelerator. The car groaned loudly and jerked. He had left the handbrake on. He pushed the handbrake down and the car jerked forward, lurching like a kangaroo.

Chris slapped his legs and guffawed loudly. "Must've been a while, pal. You drive like my grandma!"

After a couple more lurches, he managed to make the car glide smoothly back to where they had walked from. He pulled up with a slight jerk next to camp. Zara and Vanessa were staring open mouthed as Mike opened the car door and stepped out.

"That's how I roll," Mike said, laughing.

They continued talking into the night. The three men had met in London. They had been wandering individually around the North West London area and happened to find each other. Mike was surprised to hear that they had seen other survivors, mainly in central London.

"There aren't loads," Greg said. Greg was the skinniest of the three and the only one without tattoos. He wore thin glasses and an oily black vest. "But if you go to the center, you will see people. Some, you wouldn't want to see."

"Affected?" Mike asked. "Like, twitching?"

"No. None of them anymore. Just some people are friendly and some people not so friendly. No laws now, pal. When there's no laws, anything goes for some people."

"You hear anything about what started all this?" Vanessa asked.

"Heard a few rumors," Don replied. Don was the biggest of the three men. He had large, chunky arms with huge tattoos stretched across them in the shape of skulls and various script-like sentences which Mike couldn't interpret. Don had a twitch in his eyes, every few seconds he would blink quickly. He also had a habit of picking his nose and flicking the findings in full view of his guests. "You seen the video?" he asked.

Mike's eyes widened. "Yes. Yes, we all have. You think that's what did it? Some kind of hypnosis?"

"Don't think it. We know it is. We seen the video," Don replied.

"Yeah, I know, as I said, so have we," Mike said.

"No, I mean, we *seen* it. You wanna see it?"

"What?" Mike asked. "What the hell are you talking about? How could we—" Mike cut off his own sentence as he looked towards the car. An hour ago, he wouldn't have believed he would be driving. Now this man was telling him that they could play videos.

"How could you have the video?"

"We don't have much power," Don replied. "But we got

enough."

Mike was fascinated. "You could really do that? You can make RazorVision work even after all this time?"

"Not exactly. Bear with me a second. Chris! Do your stuff." Don gestured at his skinny friend. Chris stood and walked over to a pile of machinery ten yards behind their camp. He came back with an old car battery, a few wires and a pair of RazorVision glasses that looked like they'd been rebuilt and modified in some way. He set them down at the floor and pointed the glasses at the side of the car. He picked up the wires and placed them by the battery, sparking the glasses into life and projecting a moving image onto the vehicle.

It was grainier and had less color than before but to Mike it felt like he had only seen it days ago rather than all the years that had actually passed. But it was the same video.

The same patterns from nearly two decades ago swirled in front of his eyes. Flowers morphed into buildings, buildings morphed into cats, cats morphed into birds, birds morphed into knives, knives into eyeballs, colors morphed from green and purple to yellow and red to deep red to bright pink, pulsing and swelling. It cut out.

"That's all the power we can use at any time," Chris said. "Weird, 'aint it?" That's what we think caused it. We reckon it was put out deliberately."

"Rick Razor?"

Chris looked at Don, raising his eyebrows. They both looked at Greg.

"You a fuckin' detective?" Don asked. "I didn't expect you to say that. Jackpot. Razor. Yeah it was him."

"How do you know, like? For sure?" Mike said.

"We know," Greg replied. "I went all the way across there once. Canary Wharf. Seen someone who worked for him. They'd got out, escaped from the Tower. Said Razor did it. Did it all. Creating some kind of super race. That's what he said."

"And he used the video to wipe everyone out?" Vanessa asked.

"You got a better explanation?" Don spat. He looked at Vanessa in a lingering way which Mike didn't care for.

"I believe you, we all worked out that we're immune to hypnosis. Guess you three are too."

The three men nodded.

Mike said. "That's where we're headed, Canary Wharf. We came to find answers."

Don released a loud, booming laugh. "Respect, pal. I respect that. But the only answers you'll find are what I've just told you."

"We just need to know. I want to look him in the eye and know," Mike said.

"Okay, its well after midnight. If you three want to sleep here, we'll set up across the motorway. I don't tend to sleep much these days," Don said.

* * *

Don and Greg stood and made their way across the motorway, leaving Zara, Mike, Vanessa and Chris. Chris was fiddling with the car battery. "Sorry I just need to fix this up a bit," he told them. "Am I alright to stick around for five minutes?"

"Sure," Mike said.

"Chris, do you mind me asking, if you have fuel to use some of the old-style cars, why don't you drive up and down the county? You could pick up survivors, build a community. Start again."

"We just wanna concentrate on technology for now," Chris replied. "Don's got visions of turning everything back on eventually. Imagine having that power – being the person that switched it all back on. There's loads of treasure out here, mate. It just needs the right key to unlock it."

"What would you do? If the technology goes back on?" Zara

asked. "Like, what difference would it make?"

"Oh, so much. We could build our own city without all the manual labor involved. We could watch videos, *create* videos. We could touch base with the world. Any survivors in the USA? No idea. We could try and find out though. All those unmanned airplanes? We could just use GPS to get somewhere. It won't take us long to get back to where we were."

"I'm not sure I like the sound of that," said Vanessa.

"What, you like living in this empty place?" Chris asked.

"We come from different worlds," Mike added before Vanessa could answer. "We have a great community in the Lakes where we bring up families, we have education, even healthcare. We could do with some engineers."

"It's funny you should say that. We could do with some women!" he sniggered.

"I was going to ask about that. In this new world you're going to build, will it just be the three of you? I'd put you all around thirty to forty. Your little empire isn't going to last too long."

"There are others in London who'll join us. Maybe we'll do what you said and drive a bus around, picking people up. When the tech's back on we could even get trains up and running." He looked at Vanessa and Zara and his face became strained. "Be warned though. Don and Greg haven't been *with* a woman for a few years. Just be careful. It's a different world now."

"What do you mean?" Zara said.

"He means to be careful of their advances," Vanessa replied. "I don't think they'd be interested in me anyway. And Zara's too young."

They all settled down for bed, Chris making his way over to the far side of the motorway to join the other engineers. It took Zara three hours to get to sleep. She felt strange, like some kind of buzz had entered her entire body, making her feel too energetic to nod off.

8

Zara awoke early and sat up. She could hear a beautiful sound, some kind of music. The sun had not yet risen but she felt wide awake. She saw Don, Greg and Chris up already. Or still up from the night before? She wasn't sure.

She walked over to them. They were drinking cans of beer. "Either that's breakfast or you weren't joking when you said you don't sleep much."

"You can sleep when you're dead," Don replied, yawning. "Anyway, I tend to snooze in the afternoon."

"What you listening to?" she asked."

"It's a CD player. We dug it out of an old truck and managed to give it a bit of power."

"What's a CD?" she asked.

"Compact Disc," Chris replied. "It's basically a shiny disc with lots of ridges and indentations. A laser passes over and interprets every notch as music."

"Wow, that's unreal. Was that Razor Technology that came up with that?"

The engineers all looked at each other and burst out laughing. "No, it sounds pretty cool but it's been around for nearly a century," Chris said.

She looked at the small machine. The sound coming out of it was exquisite. A woman's voice, melodic and powerful, yet sad and haunting at the same time, sang through the device. "It's beautiful," she said. "Who is singing? Is it someone alive."

"Doubt it," said Don. "It's Adele. She was big a few years ago. Came from Tottenham, not far from here."

"So, she sang this years ago, and we're listening to it now?" She thought of the message left by the US president from beyond the grave. "There's so much about technology that I don't know. Some of it hurts my head to think about it."

Don offered her a beer and she opened it, sitting next to them against a rusty car. "If everything does get switched back on, what would it be like? I heard there were a lot of bad things before. Things that should change if we did go back?" She was thinking of Nana Penny's last words, not for the first time.

Greg shrugged. "We're human beings. Technology supercharges things. Man has flaws, needs, desires. Give a man a telephone and he'll use it to meet those needs. His flaws will be channeled through this device. They'll spread wider. You can't change humans. And I'd rather live in a world with technology than this shithole. Let people get on with their own stuff."

"Wow, that's deep, Greg," Don said. "You need to lay off the beer. Anyway, darling. Let's talk about you. Why you up so early? Wet the bed?" He sniggered childishly, an action that contrasted with his burly, hulking figure.

"Just felt a bit weird. Head was buzzing a bit. I usually sleep better than that."

"Maybe you saw three good looking lads over here and wanted to come and warm us up on this cold morning, eh?" said Greg.

"Not on your life," she replied, enjoying the attention. "When we come back from London, you should come up to our village. It would be good to have you around. We've got someone who builds things, but he doesn't do anything with technology. You'd get on and—"

"Not interested in the countryside," Don interrupted. "We're more city lads. No good turning anything back on if we're stuck by a lake. Thanks anyway."

"Maybe you can just get to know us right here?" Greg said. He was looking at Zara with sparkling eyes. Chris shifted awkwardly in his sitting position.

Zara ignored the question. "It's beautiful up there. The air feels a bit heavier down here. The lake is just gorgeous. It sparkles in the sun."

Don scoffed. "Spare us the poetry, love." He grabbed her hand and forcefully put it on his crotch. "Let's get down to business before Mum and Dad wake up. There's a bed set up in a camper van down there. Give the three of us a go. It's been a while so it shouldn't take long. What do you say?"

She felt the hard bulge beneath Don's faded, battered jeans and froze with fear and confusion. It was something she'd thought about, daydreamed about. Her first sexual experience. And she was enjoying the attention, the feeling of being desired, of being wanted. But she pulled her hand away as quickly as the thought came. It felt wrong this way. Don's approach felt dirty, sordid and forceful.

"No thanks. No. I've never..."

Don interrupted. "You're a virgin!" He turned to Greg and Chris. "She's a virgin, lads! Well that seals it." He stood up.

"Don, not like this. Her mum and dad are—"

"Shut it, Chris, you geek," he replied, angrily. "If you don't fuck her, I'll cut your fucking balls off, you useless prick. Man up."

Zara felt fear and dread overcome her. She looked over at her dad and Vanessa who were sound asleep at the far edge of the motorway. She opened her mouth to shout but Don put his large, sweaty palm over her face before any sound came out other than a quiet, muffled whimper. He dragged her towards the motorhome, with Greg grabbing her legs and Chris walking nervously behind. Don's hand was covered in oil and smelled strongly of petrol, making Zara feel dizzy.

Don threw her in to the motorhome. It was dirty, with a mattress dominating the middle of the small room inside. Utensils and rags littered the floor, along with old magazines with naked women on the covers. He pushed her onto the bed and began ripping her clothes off. Zara began to cry. She was strong, but Don was stronger and Zara was numb, frozen into inaction. She could barely even speak in terror. He ripped her top, jeans and underwear off, until Zara lay on the dirty mattress completely naked. She covered her breasts and crotch with her hands and tried to turn over.

"Well look at that!" Greg said. "That is a nice body. And she's turning over too! You can see how she likes to take it."

Don tittered. "Okay lads. I'm going first on this. It's gonna take a real man to break her in."

"Okay," Greg said. "But I'm off second. Chris, you can have thirds. Should be well and truly warmed up by then."

Don took down his jeans. Zara, in a moment of clarity, opened her eyes, which had been shut tight, anticipating the horror which was to come, and looked at the floor next to the mattress. There was a small pair of metal scissors next to her head, tucked under the cupboard.

She looked up at Don. He was completely naked. His body was muscly and rugged with several scratches and scars, along with his untidy tattoos. His penis bulged out in front of him and he held it in his large, dirty hand. "Here we go," he said. He turned around to his companions, who had walked to leave the motorhome. "No," he said. "Chris. You stay and watch. You're not bottling this one."

Seeing the break in his attention, Zara grabbed the scissors and stabbed them to the hilt at the back of Don's foot. She heard a loud snap as his Achilles tendon tore in two, lashing it back all the way up his leg. The back of his foot separated in a 'v' shape, red tissue and white tendons were exposed, close to Zara's face. Don screamed in agony and fell on the mattress, clutching his leg.

Greg ran in and pushed past Chris. "You bitch. You fucking bitch." He advanced towards her and held his fist back, ready to punch Zara in the face. As Zara closed her eyes and braced herself for the painful impact, nothing happened. She opened her eyes to see a thick length of rope around Greg's neck. Chris stood behind him.

"Go!" he told Zara. "Go now! Get out of here." Greg was choking, spluttering. Don lay on the mattress sobbing.

Zara stood and ran out of the motorhome, her naked body breaking out in goose bumps as it met the early morning air. She ran to Vanessa and Mike and shook them.

"Wake up. Wake up we've got to go."

They awoke and Mike hazily muttered, "Wh–Why, how come?"

Vanessa saw that Zara was naked and shrieked.

"Please, Vanessa," she said. "I just need to go right now. Please trust me on this but we've got to go now. Dad, promise me we can go now!" Zara shouted, panic and adrenaline screaming through her body, overtaking any sense of embarrassment at her nakedness.

Zara grabbed a coat and her bag and picked up her bike.

"No," Vanessa said and pointed to the car. "Let's take that."

Mike jumped in, his mind whirling from its rude awakening and the dawning horror of what may have happened to Zara. If they were in danger, if his daughter had been hurt, he wanted to do something. But Vanessa and Zara didn't give him time to speak, hurriedly throwing their bags in the back of the Kia and yelling at him to drive. Mike put the car in gear and pulled away.

Zara looked out the back window and saw Chris step out of the motorhome. He held a hand up to wave. Zara waved back. She turned to face Vanessa and Mike in the front seats and broke out into loud, uncontrollable sobs.

9

Mike followed the battered, rusty road signs to Canary Wharf. He felt powerless as his daughter wept and spluttered in the back seat, Vanessa rubbing her knee to give her comfort and helping her into a t-shirt and jeans in the confined space.

"They tried to rape me," she said.

Vanessa said nothing, just continued rubbing her stepdaughter's knee.

"Bastards. *Bastards!*" Mike said. He had half a mind to turn the car around and kill them.

"Did they hurt you?" Vanessa asked.

Zara shook her head. "It was partly my fault really. I suppose I was flirting a bit."

"No!" Vanessa said firmly, taking both Zara and Mike by surprise. "Never blame yourself. No man has a right to interfere with you like that."

"I wonder what Chris did to them," Zara said.

"I hope he finished them off," Mike said, to which Vanessa looked at him sharply.

"Maybe we should go back for him," Zara said.

"Maybe," Mike replied. "We'll see how it goes on the way back. He knows where our village is. If he wants to come up he'll find it. He helped you, but I'm not sure we can trust anyone at the moment, Zara."

Silence passed for a few minutes. "Are you okay, honey?" Vanessa asked.

"Yeah. Yeah, I think so," she replied. "Just a bit of a shock that's all."

Mike drove on eastwards. They passed Wembley Stadium, its huge arch jutting into the sky like some kind of alien spacecraft. Mike looked over and thought of all the sporting events that had taken place in his lifetime. The pitch was probably overgrown now, the grass around waist height and knotted with weeds. Zara and Vanessa looked out as the car rolled through Central London. Zara was amazed, she'd never seen such tall buildings. It was a world away from the lakes and mountains of where she'd grown up. She saw tall, silver buildings and noticed the River Thames, a murky grey color, cutting through the city, separating lines of skyscrapers on either side. The concrete sprouted large weeds between its yawning cracks and Zara saw several wild dogs roaming, scuttling between the abandoned cars and in and out of alleyways. Their ribs protruded jaggedly from their emaciated bodies, their faces drawn in single-minded, desperate focus to find any scraps of food. Several skeletons lined the roads, wearing ragged clothes but no flesh. Every ounce had either rotted away over the years or been picked clean by starving animals.

* * *

They didn't see a living human being in the entire journey. Zara put her head back on the seat. Did she expect any different? Did she really think that London would somehow be populated? She had met less than thirty living people in her entire life. What did this big, grey city have to offer her? More death and decay? More lawless behavior, people just taking what they want? The thoughts raced through her mind, causing some discomfort. She looked at the line of skyscrapers that towered over the city, their reflections in the soiled water making them appear elongated, even taller than they actually were.

"Dad?" It was the first time any of them had spoken for several minutes. "Has this city always looked like this? So dark and depressing?"

Mike laughed out loud. "You could say that," he said. "I grew up not far from here. I wouldn't say it's depressing, no. A lot of great things happened in this city. But compared to the Lakes?

Yep, I suppose it's a bit grim down here."

"It just looks imposing," Vanessa added. "So tall and busy. And that smell..."

Zara nodded. London smelled like death and decay. It was a city reliant on people to keep it alive. Without them, it had wilted and died. The tall buildings were empty, echoing with the sinister silence of death. Compared to the green and luscious environment of New Windermere, which would have survived and thrived for a thousand years without human touch, this was very much a city built by humans and one which would die a painful, ugly death without them.

A huge glass tower came into view, standing taller than all other buildings in the city. Zara gazed up in awe. The top was in the shape of a diamond, and it sparkled in the twilight. A huge red "R" twinkled in its center, looking over the city like a giant eye. Zara's jaw dropped open at the sight of the huge, monolithic structure.

"Is that...?"

"Yeah," Mike replied. "That's the tower. That's where we're going."

"RazorTower." Vanessa sighed. "I'd almost forgotten about that monstrosity of a building."

"I suppose I always quite liked it," Mike said. "The symbol of technology. A building that screams success and power."

The building did hold some bizarre beauty for Zara. It seemed alive somehow, looking down on all the other skyscrapers which were dead and dark in comparison. The red R was bright, reflecting the morning light, appearing a deep crimson color.

"So, what's the plan?" Vanessa asked. "We go over, give Razor a buzz? Knock on the door? Break in? Mike, if he's in there, he could be dangerous."

"I've not really planned it that far ahead," Mike replied, smiling without humor. "Let's park up nearby and assess the situation."

"Okay." Vanessa nodded.

Zara mirrored Vanessa's nod and looked up at the colossal tower. An overwhelming sense of fear crept across her skin, goose bumps appeared on her arms and she shivered with a feeling of foreboding terror.

10

They parked the car in a nearby street and approached RazorTower on foot. Zara couldn't help but gaze upwards towards the large diamond at the top of the building and the red "R". It looked even bigger from beneath and caused her to feel dizzy and look away to regain her bearings.

The building was made entirely out of glass and was wider at the bottom, giving it the impression of a giant bowling pin, although Mike had more salacious metaphors on his mind. "I wonder what Razor was trying to say when he built this?" he said, to which Vanessa hit him playfully. "You think he was compensating for something?"

The glass building caught the morning sun and reflected it across the city, casting a soft glow across the neighboring skyscrapers. Zara thought again that the building seemed alive in contrast to the dead and decaying buildings that surrounded it. The grey Thames flowed nearby, carrying the horrors of the new world with it; Zara looked down to see a dead dog floating downstream, along with bones and skulls bobbing in the murky water. Large grey rats scurried tirelessly across ledges above the river edge.

They approached a glass door at the foot of the tower. It contained a huge red "R", echoing the even bigger symbol at the tower's peak. Mike walked towards it first and Zara was amazed to see the door slide open before he even reached it.

"How did...?" She spoke without the ability or inclination to finish her question.

"I have no idea, but something is going on here," Mike replied. "We need to be careful."

They walked through the door to see a large foyer, sofas, chairs and desks. There were no skeletons in here, no rats sniffing the ground for signs of their next meal. The deathly smell that hung like a poisonous cloud over London was replaced with a clean, fresh aroma.

Mike led them to a set of glass doors labelled *lifts* and they all stood in front of seven, large-fronted elevators.

"Surely they can't work?" Vanessa asked, rhetorically. "I mean, would it be safe?"

"Not sure if it will be safe, but my legs are still pretty sore from that bike ride. I think we need to be at the top of the tower and see what's there. And I'm not too fussed about the hundreds of flights of stairs that will get me there," Mike replied. He was looking up, trying to see if there were any obstructions further up the lift shaft.

"Yeah," Zara said. "People are in this building. You can tell. How long will this take to get to the top?" she asked, pointing at the lifts.

"Not long at all," her father replied. "Shall we give it a go? We just need to be ready for what's up there. If Rick Razor is still alive and he doesn't want us here, we'll need to get out as fast as we can. Everyone stick closely to me."

Vanessa nodded. She stepped forward and pressed the button to call the lift. Zara was amazed to see the control panel light up and her amazement turned to shock when it spoke, a characterless female voice that said, "Lift called."

The lift came down smoothly and the glass doors opened. "Please select your floor," said the voice. Mike looked at the floor numbers. They were set up in the shape of the building. The number at the diamond at the top was in red and labelled 499. Red letters next to it read '*restricted: authorized personnel only.*' Mike pressed it and the numbers lit up. They began moving upwards smoothly, but quickly. The side of the lift opposite the door was also made of glass and looked out across the high cityscape, with the river at the bottom rapidly moving further away as they escalated towards the diamond-shaped top. The bottom of the lift was transparent, offering a view of the floor careering further away from under their feet. Zara looked in every direction and grasped the handrail, small beads of sweat forming on her temples. She had never experienced anything remotely like this in her life. Her entire body was overwhelmed by the alien feeling of being moved higher and higher at a speed she couldn't have believed was possible only minutes ago. She had heard about the technology of the Time Before but, like the holographic video of the US president, it was something she couldn't quite take in until it was in front of her or, in this case, propelling her high into the sky.

Zara looked at the tops of the other buildings and down onto the street. Soon, she could see nothing other than sky. This was the highest point in the city and nothing rivalled it in the London skyline. As her nerves settled and her body adjusted to the increasing altitude, Zara felt powerful, like a god looking over a shiny empire of glass and metal. It was the most exhilarating feeling of her life. She had climbed some of the peaks near Windermere before, but this was something else. The lift came to a smooth stop and Zara's stomach lurched, her head felt dizzy. She felt her ears pop and had to swallow hard to make them go back to normal.

"Floor 499 reached," said the synthetic voice. "Please be aware, you are entering a restricted area. Full scans will take place. Unauthorized personnel should descend to lower floors. Intruders will be prosecuted."

Mike shifted uncomfortably and looked at Vanessa. "Well I suppose this is it," he said. "You ready?" Vanessa took a deep breath. Zara looked down at her feet and felt unbalanced at the distance to the ground below. Looking out of the window behind her she saw only blue sky, the sun's morning rays dazzling her, causing her to squint.

"Yeah, I think so." She gulped and followed Mike and Vanessa out of the lift and into the 499th floor of RazorTower.

11

They walked out of the lift and were greeted by a huge expanse of glass and light. They could see up a few levels; the diamond was like a building itself, resting on the top of the tower. Zara inhaled and felt she could smell life. It wasn't unlike the air around the lake back home in New Windermere. A large spiral staircase made entirely of glass began in the middle of the floor and climbed to the levels above. Zara looked closer at the stairs and realized that she could see a figure descending them.

Zara noticed something startling as they approached the figure, now at the bottom of the stairs. She was naked other than a cloth wrapped around her hips and she was heavily pregnant, her swollen breasts resting atop her large belly.

"Good morning, Dr. Pilkington. Very nice to meet you. How was your journey today?"

Mike was lost for words. He attempted to speak but stuttered. This half-naked, pregnant woman knew who he was.

It was Vanessa who first managed to speak to her coherently. "How do you know who we are? Were you expecting us?"

"Oh no, don't be silly. Mr. Razor saw you on the cameras when you entered the building. We know about it when anyone comes through the doors. He sent me down here to greet you."

"So, Razor's alive? And he knows who I am? How is the power on?" Mike scratched his head in disbelief.

"All your questions will be answered in good time," the woman replied. "But look at me, how rude I've been. My name is Miranda. I'm Mr. Razor's wife."

Zara looked at her. Miranda couldn't have been any older than her late twenties, which would have made her no more than twelve years old when the world changed. She wondered how old this woman had been when Razor had married her.

"Did you travel all the way from the Lake District, Professor?"

Miranda asked.

"Er, well. Yes. But—"

Miranda smiled, but in an over-the-top false way. "Like I said, Professor. All in good time. Would you like to introduce me to your friends?"

"Yes. This is my wife, Vanessa."

Miranda kissed her on the cheek, her large belly brushing against Vanessa's hip.

"And this is my daughter, Zara." Miranda repeated the gesture with Zara and then looked at her, squinting.

"Wow, you were a baby when everything changed. I thought it might be you," Miranda said.

"Er, yes. I..."

"Follow me. You've come at a good time. Assembly is in fifteen minutes."

"Assembly?" Vanessa asked.

"Yes, Mr. Razor likes to get everyone together each day. You know, to raise morale, start the day as you mean to go on. We've got a brilliant community here, Vanessa. I think you'll like it."

"How many people live here?" Mike asked as they climbed the stairs behind Miranda, who was moving smoothly and nimbly for a woman so heavily pregnant.

"Last count was 96," she replied.

"Wow," Mike replied. "We have a community ourselves at Windermere but there are only eighteen of us."

"What a lovely place to start again," Miranda said. "I've heard all about the Lake District. One of our community used to live there. In the Old Way."

"The Old Way?" Vanessa asked.

"Yes, before, when the world was overpopulated. When there was a lack of common decency and the world was split into rich and poor. We're all lucky to be seeing the New Way."

"Not sure I felt so lucky when I saw my wife try to kill me and then die," Mike replied.

"Oh, I'm sorry to hear about that, Professor. Unfortunately, there was a lot of nastiness on the night that the Old Way ended. The world lost some good people. But I'm sure you'll agree the New Way will be better."

Mike, Vanessa and Zara remained silent as they climbed the last of the stairs. When they reached the first level, they were stunned into more silence. There was a giant floor space. People were milling around, all naked other than loincloths wrapped around their waists. Most were young. They were all drinking water, tea, milk and eating fruit. It reminded Zara of a textbook she had read in school about Roman times: the days of chariot racing and gladiatorial battles. In the center of the room was a large, enclosed bowl with a door which people were entering. It was an enormous egg-shape, almost following the contours of the diamond that they stood at the bottom of, and stretching up to sit in the middle of various levels above them. It was made of mirrored glass, giving an infinite impression of sky and sunlight. All around there were plants, green vines climbing the glass walls and potted flowers lining the walkways. The plants gave the atmosphere an easy, fresh feel, filling Zara's lungs as she inhaled.

When Zara looked back to the people, she noticed something even stranger. At least half of the women she could see were pregnant, their swollen stomachs and breasts exposed above their loincloths. Something about the sight made her uneasy and she thought back to her experience with Don and Greg; an encounter she couldn't shake out of her head and would struggle to forget for many years to come.

She looked at Miranda who was still smiling.

"Why are so many of the women pregnant?" she asked.

"Oh, yes. Of course. I'm so used to the New Way that I forget not everyone will know." She rubbed her stomach delicately. "They're the future. Within the bellies of these women lies the salvation of mankind. They will pioneer the New Way. But listen to me, I've already said too much. Mr. Razor will be so annoyed if I steal his thunder. He was so excited when he saw you walk through the door, Professor."

"How does he know who I am?" Mike asked.

"Like I said before, everything will become clear when Mr. Razor meets you. I don't want to spoil the surprise." Miranda looked at the trio's confused and agitated facial expressions. "I'm just as frustrated as you! I would love to tell you everything, it's so exciting. But I really don't want to make Mr. Razor angry."

Zara felt it strange that a wife would describe her husband in such a formal way, but there were so many things in this building, it was making her head spin to think of them all at once, not unlike the sensation of being on the lift, rising upwards at a fast rate.

"Come, he'll want you to be at the assembly. We'll have to stay at the back, otherwise you might cause a commotion with your different clothes."

They followed Miranda through the door into the egg-shaped building.

12

Miranda ushered them into a booth where they could sit at the back of the room, behind a barrier where only their heads were visible. Mike noticed they still received some strange looks from people who had seen them walk in and he felt a wave of self-consciousness engulf him. This community seemed bizarre in comparison to New Windermere.

The sky was an electric-blue color, lit up by the morning sun. To his right, he saw the enormous red "R" in reverse. As he looked to the top of the structure, he could see two men standing. They were at the tip of the diamond, and Mike thought it looked like they were outside. *Must be a hell of a view up there* he thought to himself. Were they lookouts? Mike wasn't sure, but Razor had known he was coming. *And he knew who Mike was.* In Mike's previous life he had been an expert in the field of Razor's work. It wasn't inconceivable that Razor would have at least heard of him, although flash entrepreneurs rarely took notice of academics who choose to analyze instead of do or create.

There was a collective murmuring as the egg-shaped auditorium filled up. Of the sixty or so women sitting in the seats around them, a good thirty were pregnant. And they were the only ones he could *tell* were carrying babies. Some of the others displayed sagging stomachs and stretch marks, suggesting they had given birth not long ago.

The murmuring stopped and silence fell. Mike looked down at the bottom of the auditorium to a raised area, like a stage. A man with long, grey hair, dressed like the others, in a loin cloth, walked into the center.

"Ladies and gentlemen. Welcome. Welcome one and all. Women, children, men and guests." A couple of people looked around to Mike, Zara and Vanessa. Miranda nudged Mike excitedly at their acknowledgement. Mike squinted to focus in on the man. The hair was different, the build was thinner but it was definitely him. The man stood addressing the crowd was an older Rick Razor. More feral somehow, but it was definitely him; the chiseled jaw, defined cheekbones and deep brown eyes were unmistakable.

The audience clapped. Razor continued. "It's a beautiful day out there today." His arm swept across to gesture at the blue sky outside the diamond's glass walls. "And a timely reminder of the beauty of life. The beauty of our new world. This beauty will only be kept by our way."

The audience all spoke at once, including Miranda, smiling as she joined the others in an almost hypnotic chant. "THE NEW WAY." Something about the uniformity of the answer gave Mike a chill that went right to his heart.

"Our New Way is about life over death. It's about family over adversity. Community over anonymity. We know the Old Way didn't work. And that is why I created the New Way." The crowd chanted back to him again. "THE NEW WAY." Mike glanced at Vanessa and she took his hand.

"To keep our community alive, we must purge what makes it bad. One rotten apple spoils the whole barrel."

There was a murmur in the crowd as the audience digested this wisdom from Razor. "We are building this community. And by the looks of a lot of you sitting before me, we've been very busy." The audience laughed. "To create life, we need a process. We have used science to plan our future. And we cannot tolerate any breach of this." He looked up to the top of the diamond. The audience followed his gaze and gasped collectively. Mike realized that they had not seen the men at the top of the roof; which meant that they weren't usually there.

"Peter Aspinall is up there. I trusted Peter, I took him into our community and welcomed him. I invited him to replace the Old Way with the New Way." The chant echoed back at him once more, although Mike thought he detected a new hint of sobriety and fear in its tone.

"And in the middle of this plan to rebuild our world, Peter Aspinall was caught in bed with Lisa Jane." There was another gasp from the audience. Miranda put her hand over her mouth, her eyes wide.

"As you know. This is a breach, punishable with banishment. The third breach of law since I began this community in 2038. Still people do not learn. People try to take it for granted. They try to sabotage my work in building this world. Nothing could be more threatening to the New Way." The chant echoed back at him once more.

"Lisa Jane is not pregnant with Peter Aspinall's baby." The audience all sighed with a few audible *phew* sounds coming from the crowd. "Nevertheless, she is in isolation for the next two months as punishment. Now, if you will look up, you will see my son Craig with Mr. Aspinall."

Razor put his hand in the air. Mike saw one of the men at the top of the diamond, presumably Razor's son, grab the other and hang him over the edge. The man doing the holding looked very strong. Razor kept his hand in the air and closed his eyes.

"We must purge ourselves of rot." The audience repeated his words. "We must embrace the New Way. We must cast aside the remnants of the Old Way. We cast out the darkness and welcome the light." Again, his words were repeated back to him. He opened his eyes.

"Farewell, Peter Aspinall. Hopefully we will meet in the next life and you will have atoned for your actions in this one." He brought his hand down and looked upwards.

Razor's son, seeing the signal, dropped the man over the edge. The audience shrieked as they saw the body fall the length of the diamond. Peter's face was a picture of fear, his mouth wide open and his hands flailing helplessly against the air as he dropped to his death. Vanessa squeezed Mike's hand so tight he felt one of his bones click.

Razor spoke again. "This is just a timely reminder for our community. Whether you have been here since birth, or only a matter of minutes..."

Mike was horrified to realize that Razor was looking up, straight at him.

"You must all follow the rules. No one man or woman is bigger than us. No man or woman will be allowed to stand in the way of our success. There will be zero tolerance for anyone who threatens our way." He raised his fist and yelled "The New Way!"

The crowd echoed back to him again, this time more vociferously and boldly than before. "THE NEW WAY!"

13

Miranda ushered them out of the auditorium and back to the outside level.

"Come. He'll see you in his quarters."

They followed her up a spiral set of stairs to another lift. The lift took them all the way to the top, with more astounding views over the dead city.

"Are you excited to meet him?" Miranda asked. She was grinning and could hardly contain her own excitement. "He's got a surprise for you!"

They reached the top of the diamond. It was a long, thin, triangular space with a mirrored room sectioned off in the corner. One small platform lift led to the top, where there was a balcony, on the outside. This was where Razor's son had thrown poor Peter Aspinall to his death.

Miranda pushed the door open to the room and knocked firmly. "Mr. Razor, are you ready for our guests," she said, her face a picture of glee, she bounced up and down as she spoke.

Mike heard a voice, muffled from behind the door. "Yes, of course, send them in."

They walked in and saw a large living space, completely made of glass. Rather than the lavish, comfortable place that Mike had expected, it was extremely basic. There was a blanket at one end, a pillow and a table with a paper and pen. Rick Razor stood at the center of the room. He was unshaven and close-up he looked old. His long, grey hair hung greasily past his ears and his bare torso was bony, his skin soft and sagging. Razor put his arm around Miranda, who giggled.

"Thanks, darling," he said and kissed her on the lips. The kiss lasted far too long, making Mike feel uncomfortable enough to look away. Razor then kneeled down and kissed Miranda's stomach. "Off you go now. Keep that baby warm and healthy!"

Miranda skipped out of the room. She stopped and hugged Mike, Zara and Vanessa on her way out. "It was so nice to meet you all." They all nodded and smiled nervously as she closed the door behind her.

Razor held out his hand. "Professor Pilkington! Very nice to meet you. I've heard so much about you."

"Ditto," Mike replied.

"Would you introduce me to your two lovely companions?" Razor asked.

"Yes," Mike answered, warily. "This is my wife, Vanessa, and this is my daughter, Zara."

"Ah," Razor said. "This is the baby that survived the great ordeal all those years ago."

"Yes. May I ask you something, Mr. Razor?"

"Please, call me Rick."

"How do you know so much about me? I asked your company several times if you would come to the university to speak and you never returned my communications. I asked several times if I could interview you for research purposes and each time I hit a brick wall. And now I finally meet you in this place and you seem to know everything about me. How did you know that I had survived?"

"So many questions, Professor! Of course, I had heard of you all those years ago. I even read your articles and watched a few of your videos. And I saw your image on a screen in the control room as you entered this building. I suppose I just had very little time back then. But now the world has changed I have a lot more time. And I am delighted to welcome you to join me in my new community."

"The New Way," Mike said.

Razor nodded, sensing Mike's skepticism.

"Mr. Razor. Rick. I have a lot of questions to ask you."

"I'm sure you do, Professor. Firstly, I'd like to invite you to join us in a celebration tonight. In honor of you coming along I would like to host a party. You'll experience our food, which is grown right here at the top of my tower, and our drink, which is also brewed here. We're completely self-sufficient in my community. The Old Way was not sustainable, Professor. We were living on borrowed time. Our reliance on technology had peaked and had passed the point of no return. Human life had been compromised, worsened. We had created something worse than any war, worse than any disease. A horrible indifference had fallen on civilization and it had been created by technology. *My* technology. Do you know how it feels, Professor, to be the man that created this new wave of insipid mankind, this detestable malaise? Seeing your creations being used to worsen the human race? It was unspeakable."

Mike raised a finger and pointed it at Razor, as if a sudden idea had come to him.

"You remind me of one of my students!" he said, thinking of Simon Churchill, his eminent PhD student who had begun to challenge the very core of Razor's ideas, purporting himself that Razor Technology was making the world a worse place.

Razor beamed. He closed his eyes and nodded his head. "Sorry, I was wanting to keep it longer but I really can't wait. I can't wait to see your face."

"What?" Mike asked. He looked back at Vanessa and Zara whose expressions mirrored his own confusion.

"The night before it happened, I received a call. Someone spoke to me and told me exactly what I was thinking. They made me realize that my plan, my New Way, was right. I let him in on my secret and he came along for the ride."

Mike's eyes sparkled with awareness. He opened his mouth to speak but his throat had dried up. Razor noticed this and nodded excitedly.

"Yes, yes, you've got it." He pressed a button on the glass wall, which lit up, and spoke into it. "You can come in now."

The glass door slid open and Simon Churchill walked into the room.

14

"What the hell?" Mike asked. "Simon!"

His face was older, crow's feet had developed at the corners of his eyes and his hair contained several coarse streaks of grey. But he still had the wise eyes and the inquisitive expression etched onto his features. It was unmistakably his former student.

"Hi, Mike."

"Simon. I haven't spoken to you since…"

"Yes. Since the night it all happened. I remember the call well. You were on your bike. We had an argument about this very man." He pointed at Razor, still smiling. "I told you I'd secured a phone call with him and I was going to give him a piece of my mind. Which I did, I might add."

Razor interrupted. "He certainly did. And I think Mr. Churchill was somewhat shocked to discover that I agreed with everything he said. His studies had been excellent. He correctly identified the part Razor Incorporated was playing in the widening gap between rich and poor. I'd dedicated a year of my life to see what could be done. But data had been compromised by several governments, including our own. We piloted free RazorVision in a small impoverished town in Africa, but the pilot went horribly wrong, causing a class war and each unit ended up being seized by the military. Elsewhere, terrorists were using RazorVision to co-ordinate atrocities. The genie was out of the bottle and no amount of strong arm tactics would force him back in there. The only option was to destroy the genie. A reboot, if you will."

"So your solution was mass murder!" Mike commented; a statement rather than a question.

"Mass murder?" Razor asked and looked at Simon. Both men sniggered. "Had I murdered people when a serial killer used RazorChat to meet their victims? I calculated that almost one thousand murders had been recorded with my technology used by the murderer to locate victims. There were probably thousands more. Every time a government extracted data from my system to imprison someone illicitly, was that on me? For every relationship that broke down because one person was having an affair, was that my fault? When a family went to the FA Cup final, and they all spent the full time interacting about the match on RazorVision instead of enjoying the guts and the glory of the football in front of them, did I spoil the culture of the sport?"

"No, of course not," Mike said.

"It fucking was! It was all my fault!" Razor was shouting. "I took it all on my shoulders. It was my fault. My issue. And I promised that I would fix it. If I left the world the way I had created it, it would have died. Something drastic was needed and I had to be strong to see it through. This was my responsibility, my time to step up to the mark. I had to fix my own mess."

"Oh, how very noble of you," Vanessa commented.

Razor ignored the sarcastic praise. "I needed to kill the genie and lift this malaise that was killing the world. When Simon phoned me, I realized we were on the same level, so I did something that I would never have dreamed of. I told him my plan. Luckily, he still had time to come down here. I sent my helicopter and he joined my select band of survivors, ready to see in the New Way."

"How long had you planned this?" Vanessa asked.

"A few months," Razor replied. "I only told select people who I trusted. My closest advisors. Some of them thought I was crazy, of course, but they didn't last to see the New Way."

"You killed them," said Vanessa.

"Yes. I put the world to sleep. An induced coma, if you will, to allow it to repair. When it's ready, it will wake up once more."

"And it was the video. Some kind of hypnosis that made people kill and then kill themselves?" Mike asked. He was furious that the men standing in front of him could be so matter-of-fact about a horrific act of genocidal proportions. He wanted answers.

"That's right," Razor said. "It was genius really. I myself had been having hypnosis for a year to aid confidence and decision making. My hypnotist was excellent, one of the most impressive men I've ever met. He *is* excellent, I should say. He lives in this commune with us. I shall introduce you tonight."

"Can't wait," Vanessa said.

Razor ignored her again. "He really is a talent. A few hundred years ago, he would have been burned at the stake. I sometimes think that what he does goes beyond any human ability. The man is capable of magic. Together, we realized that his talents, when mixed with the power of my technology network, could influence the majority of the world's population. Of course, the addition of suicide ensured that people weren't aimlessly wandering the earth like zombies. It meant it didn't drag on too long."

Mike grimaced, thinking of Henry West's wife and daughter, living out nearly two decades in their feral and miserable altered state.

"How many people died? How many survivors are there?" Mike asked.

Razor shrugged. "No idea. Simon tried doing some calculations before. We think around eighty percent of all people who saw the video will have been affected. Then we think that ninety-nine percent of survivors would have been killed by the affected people. So, you are the lucky few! Simon worked out the new population of the world to be around sixteen million. It sounds a lot, but the majority of these people will be situated in Africa, although we have not yet managed to make contact with anyone from outside the United Kingdom."

"Africa! Back to where we all began!" Simon added. "Of course, I was affected, along with a few of the survivors in the commune. But Mr. Razor had ensured that Karel, the hypnotist, was on hand, to bring us back round. I assume you were all immune to hypnosis and managed to hide or fight your way to safety?"

Mike, Vanessa and Zara all nodded in unison. "There's some poetry in the method though, don't you think? Razor Incorporated had ruined the world but it was through Razor Incorporated that we started again. We saved it."

"You can't really believe that!" Vanessa shouted. "You killed billions. You wiped out entire races. Generations won't live because of what you did."

"Charlie died, Simon," Mike added. "She tried to smother Zara's face with a pillow and then went for me. She broke her neck falling down the stairs." Mike looked at Zara and gulped. He was telling the story in all its stark horror, an account he had previously sugar coated for her ears or avoided telling altogether. Zara, though, appeared resolute at the description.

"I'm sorry to hear that, Mike," Simon replied. "But at least you know she, and others, died for the best possible reasons."

Mike screwed his face up. "What the fuck do you mean? Are you insane? You must be? Since when was mass murder a solution to any problem?"

"Mike, think back to the very formation of human culture. Even the stories they told back then. What was Noah doing with an ark? Why did he build it? What was the purpose?"

"God purged the world," Razor added. Mike thought that the two men had conducted this discussion between themselves many times and were glad to have an audience for their philosophies. "And that is what he is doing now, through me. My creations were being used for evil. Indifference had set upon the world. Beauty had disappeared. The world wasn't ready for my technology. Not the world as it was, anyway. I turned it all off. Other than the solar power which charges a few small things in this building, such as our lifts and some communications, there is no digital technology in the entire world today."

"You are not God!" shouted Vanessa. "This was not your world to create or fix."

"If not me then who?" he asked.

"There would have been other ways. Ways that would have been slow and taken time. But not ways that kill everyone. Your New Way sounds just like some kind of cult to me. Look at all of you. You even *look* like you're in a cult!"

Razor chuckled. "I like it, a cult. I suppose you have a point. Maybe it is. But you call it that because you don't understand."

"There are so many pregnant women here," Vanessa added. "Like you're re-populating the world. Right from here. Your big diamond-shaped ark in the sky."

"You are very perceptive, Vanessa," Razor said. "And again, you're not wrong. If I turn my technology back on, I want to make sure the future population that will rule over these ruins and grow it back to civility will make the world a better place. The best way to make that happen is to ensure the genes, the education and morals of these people are all under my control."

"You threw that man to his death for sleeping with someone! How is that fair?" she yelled.

"We need to enforce rules. We need to be strict. This is the New Way," Razor said. His face had turned from jovial to stern. "May I ask, what was your community like, where you have lived for all these years?"

"It was wonderful," Mike replied. "It *is* wonderful. We live off the land, we all look out for each other. There is no currency. We all work hard. And there is love amongst us. Real, family love."

"Excellent! Excellent," Razor repeated. "The very essence of the New Way is what you describe. When the world acts as your community does, it will be ready for technology."

"You talk about it as if you can just flick a switch and turn your machines back on," Zara said. "How could it be so simple."

"Oh, it is," Razor answered. "There is a locked vault in this very commune. All I need to open it is my iris recognition, the unique code held within my very eyes, and my passcode, which only me and my twin sons know. And it can pick up where it left off. Imagine, all that technology and power, in a world that is perfectly harmonious. With the right people, my technology could be used for amazing things. What about something right out of science fiction? Time travel, teleportation? Who knows? In this very building, we have been perfecting a 3D printer that can produce sheets of metal in seconds. It has been twenty years in the making, but when it's ready, I will be able to construct cities of titanium in a matter of weeks. The rebuilding of the world will be swift, once I can be sure that its citizens are worthy."

"I should cut out your eyeballs right now and throw them off the top of this tower. Your retina scan won't be much use then, will it? You're insane," Vanessa said.

"You talk about removing my eyeballs, and you call me insane?" Razor said, chuckling. "Look, we can pick up this discussion another time. You are welcome here. I think you'll find your community is not unlike my own. Miranda has selected some quarters for you a few levels below here. Tonight, we will throw a party to welcome you. You will see the New Way. You will come to understand."

15

So many questions were buzzing around Mike's head that he hadn't thought to ask when he had stood in front of Razor. How did he select the survivors that had lived at the top of his tower for almost twenty years? How did his plan not get leaked to anyone else? Surely, a hard-nosed journalist or a disgruntled employee or even a jealous friend could have found out. *But he controlled the flow of all the world's data*, Mike thought. *He would have sniffed out dissenters and killed them. He could have done that and wiped the evidence.* The breadth of Razor's power and influence began to dawn on Mike. Razor could have done anything he wanted. And he had.

But how could Simon be involved in this madness? How could murder and chaos sit so comfortably with this man, who used to be his best student? How could he not question these actions? Had Razor managed to hypnotize him somehow? Mike thought not; Simon seemed very clear in his own mind.

Miranda led them to their living quarters. They were basic. Three rugs lay on the floor, roughly half a meter apart. The floor was, like the rest of this building, glass, giving the impression of infinite light.

"Get yourselves settled in. There's some cloths there for you to wear so you can fit in with the community."

Vanessa was startled. "I'm not getting half naked!"

"Don't worry, you won't have to," Miranda interrupted. "The cloth should cover your top half too. We would prefer you to dress like we do but sometimes it takes a while to adjust. You'll get used to it," she said and looked down at her own bare, swollen breasts. "We're really not so bad up here, you know. And I can't wait for tonight. I hope you're all excited. I'll send the twins down in about half an hour. They'll give you the grand tour. I know the New Way takes a bit of time to get used to. But you're going to love it here. I promise."

She spun on her feet and skipped away with more grace than her heavily pregnant figure suggested she was capable of.

"The twins," Mike said, snorting, when she was gone. "One of whom just chucked some poor man off the top of this giant building."

"Dad," Zara said. "Whenever anyone talks to us they seem to assume we're staying. Why don't we just stay for tonight. We've found out. We know why. We could just sneak out tonight or tomorrow morning."

"Sounds good to me, Zara," he replied. "I think they're just pleased to see us. Most people who come here are probably looking for somewhere to stay. They probably don't realize how good we have it back home."

"Even though you told them," Vanessa said. "I don't like it here, Mike. It doesn't feel right at all. And I don't like Razor and I don't like Simon. Even Miranda seems false. And that assembly. The chanting. That man who died. All the pregnant women. It's like he's *growing* human beings for his own means. What you built in Windermere is utopia, Mike. This is dystopia."

Mike looked at Vanessa before moving toward her and grabbing her hand. They both looked at Zara.

"We're in this together," he continued. "We'll be on the road back to New Windermere in the morning. The car should have enough fuel in to get us to the Midlands at least. We'll bike the rest. We'll be home soon."

Zara nodded. "Yep, let's see what this party is all about. After Wycombe and the M25 I think we're due some luck."

"I think the world's luck ran out the day Rick Razor met that hypnotist," Vanessa said.

"I've got to say," Mike added, "the fact he could turn his technology back on whenever he takes the fancy. It doesn't sit too right with me."

"It's controlled with his eyes," Vanessa said. "I say we jab a fork into each one over the buffet tonight." They laughed awkwardly, all three of them sensing the half-truth in her suggestion.

There was a knock on the door. Two identical, dark-haired, handsome young men stood in the doorway.

"The Pilkingtons?" one of them said. "I hear you ordered the Razor tour. Craig and Scott at your service."

Zara straightened her loincloth and blushed.

16

The twins were charming and polite. Dazzling, Zara thought. They were the smoothest men she had ever met. She soon identified Scott from Craig. Craig had a more intense look about him while Scott had a softer appearance. Both were equally dashing, with their slick hair and their chiseled jaws and cheekbones. Even their loincloths seemed whiter, more stylish than everyone else's.

They showed Zara, Vanessa and Mike the nursery. It was a huge expanse, taking over two-thirds of the entire healthcare floor. Several doctors and nurses worked busily between patients.

"I understand you're a doctor yourself, Vanessa?" Craig asked.

"News travels fast in these parts," Vanessa replied. Her tone was jovial but her eyes were serious.

"We have a lot of healthcare professionals but we can always use more."

"These babies should be with their mothers, not cooped up in here like battery hens," Vanessa said.

"This is the way things are here," Scott said. "After birth, they are looked after in the system. Then they go through school and then work."

Zara looked at the twins, sizing them up. "Were you born in the old world or the new one?"

The twins both tried to talk at the same time, then looked at each other and laughed.

"We were born the day before. So, we are very much old world," Scott replied.

"That makes me the old one here then," Zara replied. "I was born in March 2038.

"So, soon we'll all be able to legally drink. Well, if old-world drinking rules still apply," Scott said, smiling.

They toured the sports level. The twins showed them several squash courts, a five-a-side football pitch, complete with real grass, and a gymnasium.

"This really is something," Mike said.

"Yep. This is our favorite level," Craig replied. "I'm the squash king around here."

Scott dug him in the ribs. "No. Not having that, sorry."

Zara giggled.

When they reached the livestock level, Zara was fascinated. A farm at the top of a skyscraper, it was an amazing sight. Cows grazed on the grass, *real grass*! Sheep wandered busily around a drinking trough. To the east side of the building, several square meters of vegetables grew, along with large, colorful flowers. This floor was alive with life. The smell reminded Zara of the rolling green of Windermere. The rich, earthy odor brought forward memories of the early mornings with the pigs, feeding the sheep and milking the cows. Rather than make her homesick, it gave Zara the feeling of contentment for the first time since she had stepped into Razor Tower a few hours before.

"This is my job," Scott said.

"You're a farmer too? And you feed everyone from this farm? Is that even possible up here?" Zara asked.

"We produce enough food to give everyone healthy diets. We ration, minimizing wastage. No beer bellies up here," he replied. "Big responsibility, feeding everyone in the tower. If I get something wrong, people could starve. Craig here operates as a law man and I look after animals. For identical twins we're not so similar, eh?"

They saved the most spectacular for last, going back to the top, past Rick Razor's private quarters and onto the platform that took them to the very peak of the diamond. Zara squinted from the blazing sun and looked down at the tiny scene below. The river, cutting through the city like a dirty, wet crack, looked minute, like a vein pulsating across a dying man's arm. The skyscrapers below looked like large stalagmites jutting up out of a cave floor. The breeze was bracing at the high altitude, making Zara's eyes water so much that tears fell onto her cheeks. Scott noticed this and wiped them away with his hand. Zara blushed once more.

"What a view," she said.

"Yes, a very romantic spot," Mike said, eyeing the twins suspiciously. "I seem to remember a chap falling down there a few hours ago."

The twins frowned. "Sometimes, things need to be done that aren't nice," Craig replied. "Sorry you had to see that. But we have rules here. My job here is enforcement."

Zara looked at Scott, the twin who had stayed silent during this exchange and she was sure she detected a hint of disagreement in his large brown eyes.

"What did he do exactly?" Zara asked.

Craig looked at her firmly. "He broke the rules. When you stay here for good, Dad will run through all the rules.

"What if we don't stay?" Vanessa asked.

"Ah, no one ever leaves here," Craig replied. "Well, that's not strictly true." He looked down the huge height to where Peter Aspinall met his death.

Zara looked around. The air was different up here. Sharper, somehow. She took a deep intake of breath and felt the alien cold air sting her lungs.

"I saw you coming from here," Scott said, looking at Zara. "Saw your car approaching along the river. Couldn't work out what it was at first, it'd been so long since I'd seen one. But I told my dad. Then we watched you all the way. Wasn't until you came closer to the entrance that Simon identified the Professor on the camera. You all caused a fair bit of excitement, I can tell you that."

He smiled coolly, and Zara returned the expression.

"I know it takes some getting used to, but you're going to like it here," Craig added.

"We're not staying," Mike said.

"We'll see about that," Craig replied. "My dad can be pretty persuasive."

Zara saw a large, wet heron coursing between the skyscrapers below. A cool breeze caught her bare shoulders, causing her to shudder.

Scott gently put his hand on her shoulder. "Come on, let's go down. The party will be starting soon."

They walked down to the dining level. Plates of lavish food were being distributed by bare-breasted women. Lamb burgers were served on fabulous, bouncy wedges of floury bread. Cheese and colorful vegetables were dished out to accompany the meat. Large carafes of wine, red and white, sat on each table. At the top of the room, a band set up, ready to sing.

"This is all for us?" Vanessa asked.

"Yes, we usually reserve this kind of thing for special occasions. New people coming in, Dad's birthday, Christmas," Craig said.

"It's very grand," Zara said. "The food is delicious."

"High praise coming from a fellow farmer!" Scott replied.

"Don't get used to it though," Craig said. "We still need to ration everything. Normally there's small portions and no alcohol. Especially for women of a baby-carrying age, if you know what I mean."

Vanessa looked shocked. "I really don't know what you mean. And remember, we're not staying long."

17

They sat and talked. As the music started, Zara's two glasses of wine had made her head buzz warmly. She felt great. She realized that she liked Scott much more than Craig, who had a steely intensity about him.

The band created pleasant music, but the songs were all about their situation. Zara picked out lines about *the great RazorTower, The New Way*, which was greeted noisily and enthusiastically by the crowd, and one song's chorus even highlighted the *Glorious Mr. Razor*. It was nothing like the majestic sounds she had heard from the CD player on the M25.

People kept coming up to the newcomers and nervously asking them their names, where they were from. Zara enjoyed the attention. She had heard stories from the Time Before about celebrities, people in films, people who played sport. They would sign shirts, sign photographs and they would be hounded everywhere they went. This was Zara's own taste of celebrity and, fueled by white wine and delicious food, she was beginning to like it.

Scott asked her to dance. Thankfully, the song was actually quite melodic and Zara didn't hear any propaganda in the lyrics.

As she went on the dance floor, Mike looked on, worriedly. Zara gave her father the thumbs up sign to reassure him. All the years that Nana Penny had told her about the discotheques of the 1980s, all the dancing practice that they giggled through in the old woman's quarters. She never thought she would get the opportunity to dance with a handsome boy, full of wine and listening to live music. The band began to play a slow number. Scott put his arms around Zara's shoulders.

"I really like you, Z," he said, drawing his mouth close to her ear to make himself heard over the music.

"Z? No one calls me that! But yes. I think you're okay, too!"

"You want to go somewhere private to talk?" he asked.

"Sure." After what happened on the M25, she had a glimmer of doubt, but there was something genuine and honest about Scott, something she trusted.

* * *

They stayed on the same level, on a viewing balcony at the west side of the diamond. Scott put his arm around Zara to protect her from the chill in the evening air. His torso was lean with thin, ropey muscles lining his arms. He had a beard but it wasn't as wild and untamed as his father's. His slick, black hair fell in front of his eyes, causing him to flick it back every few minutes. It was a little quirk that separated him from his twin, and Zara enjoyed the difference.

"Your brother. He's so different to you."

"Yes, he is. Zara, I'm going to tell you this right now. It's partly the reason I wanted to talk to you privately, with no one else around. My brother is a dangerous man."

Zara grimaced, thinking of the sight of Craig throwing a man off the top of the Tower just hours earlier. "That's your revelation? Scott, I think I worked that one out. He's awful."

"My brother is my father's son, Z. What do you think about what he did? About our *New Way*."

"It's difficult for me to judge. But it seems to be all about him."

Scott snapped his fingers and chuckled. "Yes, that's right. You have no idea, Zara. I can't compare it to anything as it's all I've ever known, but some of the stories of the old days, some of the things you say about your community. It just feels natural. Organic. This is all enforced and centered around my father. Don't get me wrong, he loves me and I love him. I even love my brother, even though he can be a shit."

"What did the man do who was thrown from the top today?"

"He slept with my father's wife."

"Miranda?"

Scott shook his head. "No, Lisa." He looked at Zara's face and read her confusion. "Zara, my father is married to nearly every female here. Every baby, every young person is his own."

Zara put her hand over her mouth, her eyes filling with tears.

Scott continued. "After everything went wrong before, he thinks the best way to make the world a better place is to have his own bloodline. He wants to rule the world again, but do it better than before. In a way, he feels responsible for the world's failings. He's desperate to start again."

"But he killed everyone! He killed my mother!"

Scott looked back at her, his eyes shadowed with sadness and guilt. "I know," he replied, nodding grimly. "I try not to think about it. I suppose I don't remember anything from back then, so it doesn't feel real to me."

"But it was real, Scott. Everything about this place is wrong. The songs the band are singing, the assembly, the punishments, even the clothes people wear. People have been living at the top of this tower for so long without leaving, without seeing any of the outside world. It just doesn't feel right, Scott. What would happen to me if I stayed?"

"I don't know, Z. I couldn't guarantee that my dad wouldn't see you as a baby-carrier. Maybe he would leave you for me."

Zara recoiled at his choice of words, memories of her experience on the M25 still painfully fresh.

"Sorry, that came out wrong. But you all keep talking about leaving. I'm not sure if you heard what Craig said. It's not really a choice."

"Why? How could we not just get the lift down and go back the way we came?"

Scott shrugged. "It's not as simple as that. A few people've escaped over the years. A couple of other people've gone the way Peter Aspinall went this morning." He pointed to the top of the tower and traced his finger towards the river below. "But no one's just left. It doesn't work like that here. It's in our laws. If you leave, it's on my dad's terms."

Zara looked down at her feet, and further, beyond the glass floor, to the tower below. "So, what can we do? I don't want to stay here, Scott. I don't want to be a part of your dad's world, with his baby factory and his crazy plans to rebuild with his new machines."

"I'm not sure there's anything we can do. Maybe we could think about an escape plan but it would take time. And the risks for both of us would be massive."

"Both of us? Would you come, too?"

"Yes. Even before you came along, I knew something wasn't right. That this New Way might not be the right way. But talking to you about your life made me realize how things could be different. Better."

"What do you think about the power going back on?" Zara asked.

"My dad seems sure that we can really create things. That cities will be rebuilt in steel overnight. But he also said it was the technology that was used for evil before. Who's to say it can't happen again? I think it will be a while before it happens, anyway. He wants to make sure his way is ingrained in everything first."

"I think his 'way' is probably as evil as anything that was happening before. Come on, Scott, we're talking about technology that makes it possible to read everyone's thoughts. That kind of thing can only lead to trouble."

"You might be right. I don't know. Maybe we have an opportunity to build things the right way. And maybe my dad's not the right man to do that. Maybe we shouldn't go back."

Zara's eyes widened. "Yes! That's what my nana meant. They were her last words, Scott. *Never go back.* She meant that our way was the right way. Your dad, he's like a dictator. We've got to stop him. If that power goes back on, the new world will be a terrible place."

"I'm starting to agree with you, Z. But how? How can we stop him?"

"We're going to have to kill him."

Scott exhaled loudly. "Zara, I'm not my brother. I've never killed a man in my life. Never mind my own father! I just can't do it. We're going to have to think of another way."

"Good luck with that!" Zara replied.

"Please. Give me a week and I'll work something out. You can join me managing the farm. I'll keep a close eye on you, make sure you're safe. We can get to know each other. And we'll look at getting out of here. My dad wants to see you all tonight. He'll read out the commune rules, the New Way. If any of you disagree" he inhaled sharply. "Just agree with it and give me time. I promise I'll sort something out."

"Promise?" she asked.

"Promise." He leaned in and pressed his lips to hers.

18

Zara and Scott re-joined the party. Mike was chatting to Simon at one of the tables while Vanessa was debating something with Craig. Both conversations looked heavy and in-depth. Zara and Scott sat on a nearby table and refilled their glasses.

"Simon, all I want to know is why? You were a good lad. A brilliant student. You cared about the world."

"And there you have answered your own question. I care about the world and this gave me the opportunity to play a part in its rebirth. What would you have done, Mike? If you had called up Rick Razor himself and he had told you his plan? Would you have hung up? Would you have tried to stop him? Or would you have taken advantage of the offer and jumped on his helicopter, coming down here to rebuild the world."

"No, Simon. You made the wrong choice, to be involved in this hideousness. All this about the rules. All the babies. All the children. They're all his, aren't they? Vanessa was right, Simon. It's like a cult here. A cult that worships him."

Simon nodded. "What is a cult, Mike? What exactly does that mean? Because where you see a cult, I see a group of people forming a community that will become the world's future. I see efficiency. I see birth. I see life continuing and developing."

"What about love? Do you see love? Do you see mutual respect? That's what we have at Windermere, Simon."

"Love is in the eye of the beholder, Mike. Surely an academic man knows that? I see love here. Our definitions and interpretations may be different but I don't think your community is so different from this."

Before Mike could respond, Craig came over to their table and slapped his hand firmly on Mike's bare shoulder.

"Dad wants to see you at the top."

"The top?" Mike gulped.

Craig grinned. "Don't worry. It's always where we read out the laws to our newcomers. Also, he wants you to meet Karel."

* * *

Razor and Karel stood on the platform at the top of the tower. Karel, a short, untidy man, with blotchy red cheeks and a slight sway to his gait, looked drunk.

Razor greeted them. "Our esteemed guests, welcome! First of all, before your initiation, I would like to introduce you to Karel van der Velden. Karel is the man behind that famous video. Or *infamous* video, if you would prefer."

"Nice to meet you," he said to Mike, Vanessa and Zara. Scott and Craig stood behind, listening.

Mike ignored Karel's outstretched hand. "So, this is all your doing?"

Karel smiled. He had been briefed. "Not all my doing. But my techniques are ground-breaking, I say without much modesty. You can see the results." He swept his hand around to the decaying City of London. "They speak for themselves."

"How did you do it?" Vanessa asked. "How did you know it would have that reaction?"

"Months of testing, of tweaking, refining. I had an office up here. There were many tests on people. Many deaths, unfortunately."

"You're a murderer!" Vanessa yelled. Her anger from the previous conversation with Razor had not abated.

Razor sighed impatiently. "I do believe we've been through this before. Look, it's almost midnight. It's time to go through our laws and officially swear you in."

"And what happens if we want to leave?" Vanessa asked. "I can't think of anything worse than your fucking cult."

Razor nodded at Craig, who stepped towards Vanessa. Craig's thick arms wrapped around Vanessa's body and he pushed her towards the edge of the balcony.

"There are two options in front of all of you," Razor said. "You either go through with the initiation and spend some time speaking to Karel here. Or, my son Craig frees you up, away from our "fucking cult" as you call it. Into the river below where you will spend an eternity rotting, being eaten by the local rats, along with our friend Peter Aspinall, and several others who refused to acknowledge the New Way. So, what do you say?"

Vanessa smashed her wine glass and threatened Craig with the sharp, broken edge. Craig easily batted it out of her hand. It spun away across the floor.

"I say fuck you!" she yelled. "I've come too far to spend the rest of my life here with you. I'd rather rot in the river than live in your commune. You're Hitler! You're a maniac! You're—"

Her words were cut short by the scene a few yards away. They all turned to look at Zara. Mike wailed in abject horror, the sound echoing across the darkness of the city.

His daughter was twitching, her head moving to the side with severe jerks.

* * *

Thick white drool poured from Zara's mouth and her eyes were bloodshot, bright red. Jerkily, but with speed, she picked up Vanessa's broken wine glass and plunged it deep into Simon Churchill's stomach. The sound was horrific, like ripping linen bedsheets.

Simon gulped loudly and thick bubbles of blood vomited from his gaping mouth. Still twitching, Zara twisted the glass and pulled it out of his body. Along with the glass came Simon's intestines, grey and slimy. They fell out of his stomach and hit the glass floor with a wet slap. Zara followed this up by stabbing Simon in the throat with the same glass. She pulled it out and Simon fell forward into his own messy intestines and a thick pool of blood, still spraying across the balcony. He was dead before he hit the ground.

Scott grabbed Zara from behind, causing her to drop the glass. He turned her round, grasping her wrists. Her gaping jaw drooled heavily and she snarled. Her eyes were vacant, but as they met Scott's they flickered with something. Recognition?

Mike screamed in anguish. "No! No!" His face drained of color and he started sobbing weakly. Jagged, painful thoughts flooded his mind, memories of his wife with the same affliction. He bustled forward towards Zara but Craig stopped him with a strong hand on Mike's shoulder.

Vanessa screamed, a high pitched, tearing sound that echoed darkly across the city rooftops.

"Karel, take Zara away and bring her back to normal!" shouted Razor. He pointed at Mike. "Craig, keep hold of him. We need him to stay here."

Craig grabbed Mike's arm, twisting it behind his back with a painful crunch as Mike sobbed uncontrollably. Karel went with Scott and Zara, back down into the building and into Razor's quarters.

"How the hell has that happened?" Razor asked, looking down at Simon's body. "I don't understand."

Mike, sweating despite the cool air at the top of the tower, looked at him, his voice breaking with panic. "Y–You can bring her back? Y–You can do that?"

Razor nodded briskly.

Mike composed himself and re-ordered his thoughts, breathing heavily. "A group of people showed her a clip of that video last night. Well, I suppose it was the early hours of this morning. It must have got to her."

"Jesus Christ," Razor said. "I thought we'd seen the last of that video. Craig, clear up this mess."

Craig let Mike's arm go, before effortlessly grabbing Simon Churchill's bloody corpse and throwing it over the edge of the balcony. After a period of around ten seconds, they heard a faint and distant splash as Simon's body entered the River Thames.

19

Scott held Zara's arms behind her back in Razor's office as Karel spoke softly to her.

The hypnotist sat on one side of a glass table with Zara opposite. He was staring into her eyes with both hands on her shoulders. Scott struggled, restraining her as she continued to twitch, her body convulsing rhythmically.

"You're back with me, you're back with me, you're back with me. You don't have this will anymore. You don't have this will anymore. You don't have this will anymore." His voice was soft and firm at the same time, focused and sharp while seeming distant and mild.

Zara felt her focus returning to normal. Her breathing increased and she locked eyes on Karel. She burst into tears. Scott hugged her, squeezing tight.

"And she's back," Karel said.

Zara looked up to Scott's handsome face. Her eyes were focused but a few specks of red remained. "I knew I was doing it. I could feel the glass in my hands but I just couldn't stop. It was like looking out from outside my body. It was horrible."

"You looked like you might have been coming round a bit," Scott replied, "when I looked into your eyes."

"I felt the same but I just couldn't fight it." She turned to Karel, her eyes narrowed and her cheeks flushed. "You did this! Billions of people went through what I just went through and you caused it all. All those poor people who killed others and then themselves, all the time knowing exactly what they were doing, totally helpless in their own body? You murdering bastard!"

Scott stopped her from lunging at Karel.

Then Karel said something that shocked both of them.

"Don't you think I know that?" Tears were forming in his eyes. "Don't you think I remember that, every waking minute of the day? Do you think I *like* what I contributed to?"

"Then why did you do it?" Scott asked.

"Your father is a very persuasive man. He told me his plans. Told me how important I was to their execution. Of course, I never really thought about killing people. It's indirect. I'm really not a bad man. I used to help people stop smoking, gain confidence, lose weight. Your father—"

"You're blaming other people!" Zara shouted. "You need to take this on your own shoulders. Both you and Razor are murderers! You killed the world. You killed my mother. *You* did that."

Karel began to cry.

Zara looked at him and realized how pathetic he was. She almost felt sorry for him. He was out of his depth, swept away with the ideologies of a maniacal billionaire without thinking of the consequences. Zara wondered if he had stored this guilt in some dark recess at the back of his mind and she was bringing it to the front for the very first time. She looked at Scott and he shrugged. Zara turned back to the weeping hypnotist.

"You want to make amends for what you've done?" she asked.

Karel nodded. "Yes. Anything!" he blurted out, accompanied by a considerable amount of spittle and tears.

"You need to kill Rick Razor."

Scott grimaced. Karel's head sank into his hands.

"I can't," he said, still crying. "I can't do it. I don't think I could kill a man."

"You killed billions of people!" Zara shouted. "You killed the entire world's population! How can you say that you can't kill a man? It's for the good of the world. He can't be allowed to continue."

Karel looked at Scott, to gather his stance on the matter.

Scott read the hypnotist's look and responded. "She's right. I know he's my dad but she's right. And you know it."

"Then why don't you do it?" Karel asked.

"I can't kill my own father. Sorry, I just can't. Killing my dad, I would probably have to kill my twin brother, too. I'm not sure I could put myself through that."

They both looked at Zara.

"Don't look at me like that. I just killed a man without even wanting to—" she stopped mid-sentence and put a finger in the air. "I've just had an idea. Karel, can you hypnotize someone to be affected as if they've seen that video?"

"Well, yes, I suppose I could."

"No, Zara," Scott said. "You can't do that again. It's too unpredictable. You can't get turned like that."

"Not me." She pointed at Karel. "He needs to atone for what he did to the world. He needs to kill your father. He needs to make up for all the lives lost, for all the death in the world. The skeletons that line the roads and the horrors that everyone I love has had to go through. He has a debt to pay to everyone and this is the only way to do it. Karel, could you hypnotize yourself? Or at least teach me to hypnotize you?"

"Well, I don't know, I'm not sure if— "

"Answer her question!" Scott shouted.

Karel gulped. "Yes, I can." Sweat was now rolling from Karel's thinning hairline and dripping onto the table.

"Well then," Zara said, smiling aggressively. "Let's get started."

20

Mike, Razor and Craig were arguing when Zara, Karel and Scott returned.

"That's how you say goodbye to people in your world?" Mike asked. A large vein on his forehead and a ruddy face highlighted his anger. "You throw them off the building? No ceremony, no words? He was my friend!"

Razor outstretched his hands, like a preacher delivering a sermon. "Dead bodies are empty shells, Mike. A man of your education should know that. What do you want us to do, hold hands and sing Kumbaya?"

"I expect you to show some respect to people. You manipulated him, brainwashed him. He was a good man and you swept him up with your evil plans."

"He *was* a good man. And he saw the sense in my plan. He saw the long-term future of the world. The world was sick, I just euthanized it. We've been over this, Mike. We can't go back."

"Leave it, Dad," Zara said.

Looking up and seeing his daughter had recovered from her affliction, he ran over and hugged her.

"Thank God!" he said, outstretching his arms to look her in the eyes. "Thank God. I thought you were... I thought..."

"I'm fine, Dad. I'm fine. I just want to get out of here."

"You're not going anywhere!" Razor boomed. He nodded to Craig, who grabbed Mike by the back of the neck. Mike swung for him and Craig easily brushed away his advances. He cracked Mike in the face with a right hook, bursting his lip and nose with a misty spray of blood and saliva. Mike sank to his knees and held his face. Razor nodded at Craig again. Craig struck a vicious kick into Mike's ribs.

"No! You're killing him!" Vanessa shouted.

Craig responded by slapping her hard in the face, causing

her to fall down and begin sobbing. Like with Mike, he followed it up with a swift kick, this time catching Vanessa square in the belly. She vomited immediately.

Zara gave Karel a hard push and he careered into Razor. The two men clashed and fell on the floor in a heap. Craig looked at Zara with utter fury and lunged at her. Scott stood in front of Zara and the twins came together, face-to-face.

"What the fuck are you doing?" Craig shouted.

"Stopping you for once. You and Dad, you're wrong. You've got to see that, Craig."

"All I'm seeing is you being a prick. You've thrown away your loyalty for a girl. I'm gonna batter you and then throw your whore over the edge."

Scott swung his fist and hit his brother square on the temple, throwing him to the floor. His head connected with the glass, knocking him unconscious.

Zara shouted, "AFFECT."

Razor turned to look at her. There had been much to process over the last few seconds and in his confused state, he didn't notice Karel begin to twitch and drool. "What the hell?" he uttered, as Karel grabbed him firmly by the throat and began pushing him towards the edge.

"Karel," Razor pleaded with a gurgling sound. He was coughing his words out with the pressure on his throat. They locked eyes. "Karel it's me. Stop. Karel, we're friends."

Karel's eyes unclouded and sparked with recognition and awareness. "Rick." He loosened his grip on Razor's throat.

"Yes. Yes, that's right. Thank God." Razor put his arms around Karel and hugged him warmly.

"No." Karel looked back at Razor, a severe focus brightened his bloodshot eyes and a shadow darkened his face. "What we did, Rick. What we caused. It was wrong." He put his hands back on Razor's throat and shifted his weight, lifting Razor on the balcony, using his legs to push both of them over the edge.

Razor screamed, an anguished and desperate sound that grew more distant as the two men plummeted hundreds of feet to the murky grey river below. A faint splash followed.

Scott took a heavy intake of breath and hugged Zara. "It's over," Scott said.

They went to Vanessa and Mike and helped them both up. They were in a bad way, both with bleeding faces. Mike had cracked the same ribs he had broken during that terrible night the world changed and held his side gingerly.

"He's gone. I saw him go over," Mike said. He looked at Scott and cowered. Zara realized that he couldn't tell which twin was which.

"It's okay, Dad, Scott's okay. He protected me against Craig."

Mike looked down and saw Craig unconscious on the floor.

"So," Vanessa said. "What do we do now?"

"I think we need to call an assembly," Mike answered. "Scott, please can you tie him up? Sorry to ask you to do that to your brother. But I've got a feeling that he's not going to be on board with what I'm going to say."

"And what will that be?" Zara asked.

Mike grimaced with pain as he spoke. A trickle of blood ran from his nose. "I'm going to see who wants to come back to Windermere and join us. We've got a second chance, an opportunity to start again. Now that Razor has gone, he can't turn the technology back on. The possibility of that happening has died with him. We need to make sure that our rebuilding is done with respect, with love. New Windermere is the perfect place to rebuild." He regarded the black skyline and inhaled the rancid smell of the city. "Not here. We need to help these people remember life's beauty. We need to remind them about love and community."

"Well, I'm in for a start," Scott replied. "I've seen too much of my dad's way. I think people need to see the truth of the New Way. We need to convince them that there's an alternative."

They nodded.

Zara sighed, a sound of pure relief. "Come on. Let's go home."

Epilogue

The red evening sun glistened across Lake Windermere, mixing with the dark blue water in a glorious sheen of color. Zara swam slowly, her breaststroke rhythmic and even in the deep water. She arced her body upwards and sank her head under the surface. She emerged after a few seconds and shook her head gracefully to remove the water from her face. She opened her eyes and smiled broadly, displaying her white teeth. Scott swam over to her from the edge of the lake. They kissed as Scott splashed Zara with water playfully. They swam over to the side of the lake and heaved themselves up to the bank on dry land. Their wet, naked bodies gleamed in the sunlight, the beads of water from the lake rolling down their skin. Scott kneeled to kiss Zara's swollen belly.

"I love you," he said.

"Which one of us?" Zara asked, smiling.

"Both of you, of course." He stood up and put his arms around her. "I'll always love you, Z. And little Z. I can't wait to meet him – or her."

"Little Z? I hope we can think of a better name than that."

"Oh, I'm sure we will. I love you so much."

"I love you, too."

They squeezed each other hard. Zara looked over to her mother's weeping willow by the lake, where her name was still carved into the light brown bark. "I love you, too," she repeated.

* * *

The red sun shone on Canary Wharf, causing a shadow to form underneath Razor Tower, enveloping the docks below in cold darkness. Craig swam in the brown, murky river, diving down every few seconds and searching in the depths. Several times he rubbed his eyes, stinging from the filth that floated in the river. He passed a rat, paddling busily, looking for a safe piece of dry land or a floating platform to escape the water. A skull floated by, which Craig grabbed to analyze and quickly threw back.

He saw what he was looking for and quickened his speed, breaking into a front crawl, his arms and legs displacing the acrid water in bursts of spray. He grabbed his father's rotting body. Several patches of skin had either fallen away or been eaten by a scavenger. Craig looked into his father's cold, dead eyes. He dug his thumbs into the sockets and yanked the eyeballs free of the dead nerves and veins, before kissing his forehead and pushing the body back down under the water. He held the pair of eyes in the palm of his wet hand and cackled, causing two herons to scatter over the grey, desolate city.

About the Author

As well as publishing *The Malaise,* David Turton has penned several short stories which have been published in magazines and anthologies.

David was born in Yorkshire and graduated with a degree in Journalism. He now lives by the sea in the North East of England.

For news on his future work, follow him on his website www.davidturtonauthor.wordpress.com, on Twitter @davidturton or search for *David Turton – Author* on Facebook.

COSMIC
EGG
BOOKS

Cosmic Egg Books

FANTASY, SCI-FI, HORROR & PARANORMAL

If you prefer to spend your nights with Vampires and Werewolves rather than the mundane then we publish the books for you. If your preference is for Dragons and Faeries or Angels and Demons – we should be your first stop. Perhaps your perfect partner has artificial skin or comes from another planet – step right this way. If your passion is Fantasy (including magical realism and spiritual fantasy), Metaphysical Cosmology, Horror or Science Fiction (including Steampunk), Cosmic Egg books will feed your hunger. Our curiosity shop contains treasures you will enjoy unearthing.

If you have enjoyed this book, why not tell other readers by posting a review on your preferred book site. Recent bestsellers from Cosmic Egg Books are:

The Zombie Rule Book
A Zombie Apocalypse Survival Guide
Tony Newton
The book the living-dead don't want you to have!
Paperback: 978-1-78279-334-2 ebook: 978-1-78279-333-5

Cryptogram
Because the Past is Never Past
Michael Tobert
Welcome to the dystopian world of 2050, where three lovers are haunted by echoes from eight-hundred years ago.
Paperback: 978-1-78279-681-7 ebook: 978-1-78279-680-0

Purefinder
Ben Gwalchmai
London, 1858. A child is dead; a man is blamed and dragged through hell in this Dantean tale of loss, mystery and fraternity.
Paperback: 978-1-78279-098-3 ebook: 978-1-78279-097-6

600ppm
A Novel of Climate Change
Clarke W. Owens
Nature is collapsing. The government doesn't want you to know why. Welcome to 2051 and 600ppm.
Paperback: 978-1-78279-992-4 ebook: 978-1-78279-993-1

Creations
William Mitchell
Earth 2040 is on the brink of disaster. Can Max Lowrie stop the self-replicating machines before it's too late?
Paperback: 978-1-78279-186-7 ebook: 978-1-78279-161-4

The Gawain Legacy
Jon Mackley

If you try to control every secret, secrets may end up controlling you.

Paperback: 978-1-78279-485-1 ebook: 978-1-78279-484-4

Mirror Image
Beth Murray

When Detective Jack Daniels discovers the journal of female serial killer Sarah he is dragged into a supernatural world, where people's dark sides are not always hidden.

Paperback: 978-1-78279-482-0 ebook: 978-1-78279-481-3

Moon Song
Elen Sentier

Tristan died too soon, Isoldé must bring him back to finish his job… to write the Moon Song.

Paperback: 978-1-78279-807-1 ebook: 978-1-78279-806-4

Perception
Alaric Albertsson

The first ship was sighted over St. Louis...and then St. Louis was gone.

Paperback: 978-1-78279-261-1 ebook: 978-1-78279-262-8

Readers of ebooks can buy or view any of these bestsellers by clicking on the live link in the title. Most titles are published in paperback and as an ebook. Paperbacks are available in traditional bookshops. Both print and ebook formats are available online.

Find more titles and sign up to our readers' newsletter at
http://www.johnhuntpublishing.com/fiction
Follow us on Facebook at https://www.facebook.com/JHPfiction
and Twitter at https://twitter.com/JHPFiction